SHAKK ATTACK

The SHAKK (Seeking Hypersonic Ammunition Kinetik Kill) is my favorite future weaponry. The ammo, a translucent bead about half the size of a BB, finds whatever was in the sights when you pulled the trigger, out to about six miles, at Mach 10.

I took the shot at his wrist. I saw the hand jerk as the shot entered his arm, and steered up through it, the shock wave making his arm first bulge and then collapse. Blood sprayed from the shattered wrist, burst from the shoulder as the shot crossed to his head, sprayed once more as the shot went in through his eye; then used up its remaining energy spiralling around inside his head, turning everything inside it into runny jelly.

I enjoyed it. If that sounds horrible, well, Closers are horrible and I like to see bad things happen to them.

Books by John Barnes

The Man Who Pulled Down the Sky
Sin of Origin
Orbital Resonance
A Million Open Doors
Mother of Storms
Kaleidoscope Century
One for the Morning Glory

The Timeline Wars series:
Patton's Spaceship*
Washington's Dirigible*
Caesar's Bicycle**

By Buzz Aldrin and John Barnes

Encounter with Tiber

*Published by HarperPrism
**coming soon

Washington's Dirigible

TIMELINE WARS #2

JOHN BARNES

HarperPrism
An Imprint of HarperPaperbacks

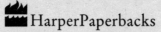
HarperPaperbacks

A Division of HarperCollins*Publishers*
10 East 53rd Street, New York, N.Y. 10022-5299

Copyright © 1997 by John Barnes

ISBN 0-06-105660-X

HarperPrism is an imprint of HarperPaperbacks.

HarperCollins®, ®, HarperPaperbacks™, and
HarperPrism® are trademarks of HarperCollins*Publishers* Inc.

Cover illustration by Vincent DiFate

First printing: May 1997

Printed in the United States of America

Visit HarperPaperbacks on the World Wide Web at
http://www.harpercollins.com/paperbacks

❖ 10 9 8 7 6 5 4 3 2 1

*This one's for Nathan Hurwitz and
for Ron Richards.
God, won't they be embarrassed.*

1

Chrysamen ja N'wook has big, dark eyes it's real easy to get lost in, cheekbones high enough for an elf, wavy hair black as coal, and skin the color of fresh coffee with a lot of cream. At the moment she was looking into my eyes and smiling, and what she was saying was, "Remember how happy we were when we got this assignment?"

I did my best to grin back at her. "Remember who said she'd rather ski than swim?"

We shook hands and got into the doors of our separate dropwings. Back where I come from there would have been hundreds of technicians clicking around behind us, reading boards and checking lights, and somebody called Mission Control would be drawling instructions to us. Here, at ATN Crux Operations Training Area (COTA, or at least that's how most of us pronounced it), shots into orbit were so routine that they were handled automatically, like getting a Coke from a machine. They figured, I suppose, that if you were dumb enough to get into a spacecraft unprepared, you were probably too dumb to be a Crux Op anyway.

My gear was already in my pack, strapped to my chest, balancing my parachute; between all that and the winter-weather coverall, I had about fifty pounds of gear on me. It's a good thing that the little throwaway ships are so reliable that you don't bother with a space suit. The only special requirement is that, since a dropwing's boost is in the direction of your feet, if you're male you'd better be wearing a jockstrap. (I didn't know what special equipment Chrys might have to wear under her coverall, but even now, with a lot on my mind, I would have been happy to investigate.)

I stretched out in the coffinlike slot in the dropwing, facedown, so that my chest pack fit into the depression. There was a window in front of me but right now all I could see through it was the side of the booster, a scant couple of inches away, and dark because the lander was tied on with a fairing to prevent the wind from shearing it off. I grasped the overhead handles and pulled the trigger to close and seal the bubble doors above me.

Chrys's voice came over the speakers. "So, ready to zoombang?"

The autotranslators embedded as chips in our heads were a constant source of amusement; they allowed her to speak her native Arabo-Polynesian, and me to speak English, and us to understand each other—but words and expressions that didn't exist in the other's language tended to come through in a very strange fashion. From talking with her before, I knew what she had said was the equivalent of "Ready to party?" so I said, "Let's blow this Popsicle stand, dudette." From the shriek of laughter I figured her translator had come up with something interesting.

"All right, enough silliness, we have the Dalai Lama to rescue," she said. "Cuing to go . . . *now.*"

Acceleration slammed into me as if the floor had leaped up to hit me in the soles of the feet. It yanked my guts downward and seemed to press the air in my lungs against my diaphragm; I felt for an instant as if my face would run down the front of my skull like molten wax. Then it steadied down to about two and a half g's, and I became aware of sounds again—mostly the thunder of the engines, mixed with Chrys going "Whoooo!" through the speakers. All right, she wasn't *quite* perfect. She wasn't decently scared out of her mind like I was. I'd taken four dropwing flights in training and never gotten to like it one bit.

A long three minutes clocked by as we shot on up and out of the atmosphere, and then finally the booster stage blew clear, as the explosive bolts in the fairing kicked it away. I blinked hard, saw Chris's dropwing fall off to the side and roll away, and looked at the display projected on my window. Beyond the display, the Earth rolled by, as it did in billions of other timelines.

This was an Earth without human beings—I had seen the herds of woolly mammoth in Kansas and the blue whales in the Gulf of California to prove it—and thus a perfect training ground. For two years, we and the rest of our class of cadet Crux Ops had climbed untamed mountains, sailed empty seas, trekked across empty deserts—and practiced with every weapon invented in a million timelines, from the SHAKK of the High Athenians, to the boomerang and atl-atl; driven and flown everything from Piper Cubs and Stanley Steamers to spaceships and chariots; ridden on horses, camels, elephants, killer whales, and moas. It had been a little like military basic (or so the vets in the group assured me), a little like fraternity hazing, and a lot like every kid's fantasy of the perfect summer camp.

Now we were two weeks from graduation, and I was looking down on that empty world, where no lines of highways showed and no cities burned like jewels in the darkness, and found myself thinking a just slightly sentimental good-bye at it.

For that matter, it was also the world on which I had met Chrys, and she was the first woman I'd cared about at all since my wife had been murdered, back in my home timeline.

I suppose I could have gotten much more choked up if I hadn't had that terrifying feeling you get, of falling forever, in orbit. I've heard all the old lines, and I don't care. I know that in orbit you're falling *around* the planet, and not into it, and that after all the fall doesn't hurt, the landing does, and all that. I'm scared of the falling, thank you very much, and that's that.

But being scared doesn't mean you get out of doing your job. I watched the green vector line till it hit the target point, then triggered the burn. At once I felt more comfortable—I had half a g pushing me—and in parallel with Chrys, off to my port side and below me, I rose into a higher and more inclined orbit. We were to come in from the southwest, which meant getting an inclination of almost fifty degrees; there were to be two more burns after this.

Cutoff—the engine shut down—and I was falling again, frightened again, and my eyes were locked on that green line. The green line entered the circle, and I pulled the trigger again—once again there was gravity, once again I could enjoy the spectacular view as we swung up over empty Europe, looking down across the forests of Italy to those of Lebanon and Syria—man had indeed left no mark here.

There was one more heart-stopping lurch of weightlessness, a short one this time, and then our engines blazed briefly as we got into the right relative positions, about 140 miles above the North Pole, and swung around to face backward. Now it was just twenty minutes till we started the retroburn.

Twenty minutes of falling without end, but scared as I was I did my best to enjoy the view of the Americas and the Antarctic ice cap.

Then the engines roared to life one more time, and there was weight under my feet as we slowed, slowed, started to plunge . . .

Our dropwings rotated, using their positioning jets, and now we were nose-down into our descents. One each side of me, through my window on the underside, I could see the long white wings curving down under the ship, the steep curve of the Earth beneath us, the Cape and Madagascar spread out before us, with India smeared out near the horizon and the great bumps of the Himalayas—where we were going.

There was the tiniest tug of "gravity," and I knew the wings were beginning to bite air, and that I was decelerating toward the target. From here on out I would have to trust the machine, until very late in the flight—at these speeds no human pilot could cope with the job.

Abruptly my view of the Indian Ocean was closed off by a bright orange curtain, and I felt a throb in my body. A shock wave—a sort of captured sonic boom—had formed in the enclosure under the dropwing, and the blazing heat of reentry would be directed against that wave, not against the surface of the dropwing. The drag became stronger and stronger, the deceleration greater, and the plasma before me glowed a painful white before the window automatically darkened.

This went on for quite a while—seventeen and a half minutes by the clock, to be exact.

It was our final field problem, and the fact that *we* had had to propose it had not made it any easier. The final exercise before you graduated was to construct a plausible mission that Crux Ops might have to accomplish, carry it out in mock-up, and then write a lengthy critique all about how you could have handled it better, what else might have gone wrong, and what you would have done then. You proposed them in teams of two, and I had been flattered beyond words when Chrys had asked me to partner with her. I didn't think it was anything romantic . . . but I wasn't dead certain it wasn't, either, and I had looked forward to it because of that.

It was all a daydream, anyway—it would be years, normally, before two Crux Ops would have any say in who they partnered with on missions. Besides that, most missions were solo. And on top of everything, normally they posted us back to our home timelines, and ours diverged somewhere around 500 A.D. I guess we could be pen pals or something.

I realized that I was letting myself get into a mental loop here, and I should know better. Besides, I could also look forward to seeing my father, my sister Carrie, and my ward Porter in just a short while . . . no, that led to other trains of thought that would take me far away from the mission again . . .

Repeat to self. Practice drill. Chrys is just my partner for a practice drill. We are going to land at the site of Lhasa, walk northward into China for a pickup, while carrying weapons enough to take on a light division back home. This is to simulate a mission in which we rescue the Dalai Lama and an ATN advisor from a world with a technological level about that of 1890 A.D. That's all I need to think about. Land, ski, climb, ski some more, climb some more. Nice to have Chrys along for a partner because . . . because she's very good at this, of course. Especially she climbs a lot better than I do, and I ski better than she does, so it's a good combination.

At eighty thousand feet, the plasma in front of my face went from white back to orange, and then disappeared, leaving me with a literally breathtaking view—I had to remind myself to take a breath some seconds later—of the peaks of the Himalayas below and ahead of us. It was a full moonlit night as we plunged over into Tibet.

The high peaks all around reflected so much light that only the ground below us seemed dark. The sky was full of light and stars. I saw Chrys make her eject at seven thousand meters, then ejected myself a moment later; the ice-cold sky leaped into my face, my harness yanked me straight back and up, and I was lost in the job of steering the parawing. The thing are like big awkward kites, and it swayed from side to side ominously.

At least it usually swayed side to side for me; there were people at COTA for whom they worked a lot better, and some, including Chrys, who even claimed they liked them. For me, the best part of the thing was that I had so much trouble steering and holding on to lunch that I didn't look down very often, and therefore wasn't quite as scared by the ground rushing up.

Meanwhile, of course, Chrys was going "Whoooo!" and zooming all over around me for fun. I did kind of hope she wouldn't do that on a real mission.

The peaks were getting closer, but the sky was still light. The snowy mountains were like high islands around us, as if we sailed just above a great sea of darkness that sank away from our boots as we descended.

The parawings worked more efficiently close to a flat surface, and we leveled off as we approached our drop zone. Finally we came gliding in like immense owls about twenty feet over a wide, flat field of snow. That is, if you can imagine a gorgeous Arabo-Polynesian owl gliding in gracefully going "Whooooo! Come on, Mark, lighten up, this is fun!" and a square-built muscular owl flailing around, swinging from side to side, going "Ooops, oops, oops," under his breath, just before doing a face-plant into a snowdrift.

By the time I had backed out, wiped the snow from my face, and begun to wrestle my parawing into behaving, Chrys had hers furled and was stand-ing by. I gulped hard at my pride, and said, "Er, I could use some help."

She didn't even smile, just moved in close, pulled on a line here and a flexrib there, and presto—my parawing was furled neatly. In another minute, I had earned my keep by digging a stash-hole on the windy side of the drift. Our parawings went into the hole, along with a bacteria mix that would destroy them within hours, leaving only a thin water solu-tion of fertilizer.

"The Sierra Club would love this gear," I mum-bled.

"You have a political party devoted to moun-tains?" Chrys asked. "For or against?"

"Translation problem," I said. "It used to be a hik-ing club. Now it puts people out of work."

The translator chips, as I said, are great, but they're not perfect. I mentioned a "Baptist Ice Cream Social" once and everyone wondered how you baptize people with ice and what that has to do with public ownership of the dairy industry. It's a good thing Crux Ops normally only have to say things like "Watch out!" "Behind you!" and "Cover me!"

Not that good a thing. It would have been nice to have a reliable language in common with Chrys . . .

I told myself to forget those thoughts again, but I took it as a sign of health—I'd been widowed for some years, back in my own timeline, and any interest at all was probably healthy.

Anyway, now that we were down on the ground with our kits intact, the job was to walk from here, about where Lhasa was in many timelines, to a point 160 kilometers away for pickup three days later.

In most ways it was really just an orienteering problem. Crux Ops normally operate alone or with just one partner, and we do our own planning (something like packing your own chute). Most of us are crazy enough to win the fights we get into, but nothing is as likely to cause a mission failure as trying to carry too much or do too much, and nobody is more likely to plan too much than a bunch of overachievers like typical Crux Ops. Thus our final exercise—work out a plan and see if the one you had worked out was one you could do.

With everything under wraps, Chrys and I started the long trip. We unrolled skis and sprayed them with the stuff to make them rigid, then extended the poles, swung our chest packs around into the backpack position, and glided out into the emptiness of Tibet.

An hour later, Chrys said, "It's very beautiful in the moonlight."

I agreed, and asked, "What's Tibet like where you come from?"

She made a face. "Completely overrun with tourists; Lhasa is where everyone goes on their honeymoon. How about yours?"

"A little underpopulated country occupied by a big power," I said. "Not a good place."

We skied on in silence, and I had a lot of time to wonder just how different our worlds were. I knew that in hers, Islam had overrun Europe in the 700s A.D., conquered all of Eurasia before 1000 A.D., and then turned Sufi and pacifist; she was from about 2400 A.D. in her timeline, so presumably she was a long way past war (except, of course, the war against the Closers). Had I shocked her with mentioning things like that? Would she hold it against me?

It was like being back in junior high. I desperately wished we had more to do.

It was getting near daylight and time to stop when our earphones crackled. "Provisional agents Strang and ja N'wook—attention. First added problem."

We rolled our eyes at each other; they were going to complicate it for us, to teach us something about unpredictability, I guess. Considering I had gotten into this line of work, once, by getting into a shoot-out in a parking garage, and later by diving into what looked like a hole in a void, it didn't seem to me I needed such training, but that wasn't mine to decide.

"We're going to simulate two complications in your mission: the Dalai Lama was wounded severely during the escape, and the Special Agent you were rescuing was killed. To simulate this, please dig a shallow grave and refill it; then fill a GP bag with rocks and snow to simulate the weight of the Dalai Lama, take it with you, and continue."

They clicked off. We groaned, but it was their game and their rules. We dug that hole and filled it in, there in the dark, in frozen ground. "At least they said a *shallow* grave," I said. "Couldn't we just agree that the Special Agent was a midget?"

Chrys laughed, but we kept digging. Then when we got all done we filled the hole in.

"I don't suppose any rule requires us to fill the bag with more dirt than we've broken out of the frozen ground," I pointed out. "Let's make our Lama out of dirt from the grave."

"Good idea."

In short order we had laid out a sled and sprayed it rigid, dropped the Dalai Lama (a very unconvincing sack of rocks) onto it, and started on our way. As the stronger skier, I got to pull it over the level ground until we got to the first bout of climbing, where Chrys was to take over.

The sun was coming up now, the pale sky suddenly turning blue, light blazing off the mountains around us. "Come on, Lama," I muttered, as we skied the last two hundred meters to the first cliff we would have to climb down.

"Not much of a talker, is he?" Chrys commented. "We'll need to take a rest break up here, because it's going to take some time to get the climbing gear in order for this job. So you'll at least get a breather then."

"Good," I said. "Are we running far behind?"

"We already made up most of the time we'd lost—you ski about as fast towing that sled as I do with just my pack, Mark. We might as well stick to the original plan. It's just not as likely that we'll get in early, is all. I'll let you have the honor of dumping out the Lama when we get there—bet you're looking forward to it."

"Yep. Hope we don't have to be politically sensitive to his feelings."

"Obviously he fainted from wounds. Is there anything we should do differently for the next stretch on the sled, right now while your muscles are telling you about it?"

"Not a thing. The harness works fine. It's just that between the bag and the sled, I feel like a reindeer."

That got us into a half hour conversation about Santa Claus, Christmas trees, hanging stockings, and mistletoe, none of which her home timeline had. We talked about a lot of things like family traditions and holidays and so forth while I got the ski stuff stowed and she got the climbing stuff out. Apparently in her timeline Ramadan was a fast, just as it was in ours, but it was followed by a feast that commemorated a bunch of miracles that had something to do with world peace.

"How did your people ever beat back the Closers and join ATN?" I asked. "It sounds like you were pacifists by the time you were invaded."

She nodded. "We had been for fifteen hundred years. We'd already settled large parts of the solar system and had probes on their way to the stars. Then the Closers crashed in. We call it the Bloody Generation—the thirty years before ATN found us. Fortunately we at least had a long tradition of nonviolent action."

"How can you passively resist an army that never takes prisoners and kills for fun?"

"Mostly we just died. There were only about a third as many of us by the time ATN agents showed up. By that time tradition had weakened, a lot. The rebellion was pretty ugly, and my grandfather, who fought in it, still won't talk about it. The Closers, the collaborators, all the people who had gone over to them in the slightest way . . . well, it was gruesome. How about your timeline?"

"The Closers just started infiltrating about twenty years before I got into it, and ATN was maybe ten years behind the Closers," I said. "But we're still very divided politically—there are about 180 countries, most of them armed to the teeth. And the operation in which I was recruited destroyed the timeline the Closers were planning to stage their invasion from— or destroyed it for them, anyway—I expect they'll eventually join ATN. So my guess is they're going to be looking for a softer target . . . besides, Closers don't want timelines with nuclear energy, they're phobic about it. My timeline has more than a thousand reactors running worldwide, and what with all the testing, several hundred nuclear bombs have been exploded in my timeline." I figured I'd better not tell her about Hiroshima and Nagasaki . . . it seemed like bad publicity somehow. "From the Closer standpoint we all glow in the dark."

"I'd have said 'spoiled meat,' but it's the same idea. The signal to start our rebellion was nuking a big Closer holiday celebration on the Riviera."

"Nice job," I said.

She grinned. "Thank you. Perhaps we can do a

massacre together someday. Okay, if you've got all the ski stuff packed away, I'm all set to rig us—and the Lama, here—for climbing. I suppose we should get on with it before they think of something else for us to do."

"You're the captain, Captain," I said. "I'd a lot rather climb with what you rig than with what I come up with." Supposedly all of us can do whatever is needed, but reality is a bit different. Most of us have seen most things done and are willing to try, all of us have several things we are experts at, and a very few of us—those with twenty years in, those teaching at COTA—really can do anything.

Vertical face climbing was in my "seen it and willing to try" category, but it was one of Chrys's strongest points, so as far as I was concerned, she was in charge for this next leg of the trip. (She had a bunch of other strong points, too—notably parawing. In our line you'd better not be a narrow specialist!)

Thus the job of getting us and the Lama down was all hers, and she went about it a lot more quickly and efficiently than I could even understand what she was doing. ATN climbing harnesses are made out of some miracle stuff that hangs on to you wherever it can get a grip and knows how not to hurt you, so you put them on by stuffing them down the neck of your clothing and pressing a button. An instant later you feel exactly like a marionette on a string. The little "walker" that comes down the cliff face above you steers itself and the climbers it's belaying according to the captain's orders; the whole thing looked like two toy soldiers and a bag of garbage hanging from one of the Willie the Wall Walker toys I had as a kid.

The first thing for which I was really useful was hefting up the Dalai Lama and pushing him over the side after Chrys had tied him off to the walker. "Oooogh," I gasped, "couldn't we just decide he'd lost, oh, say, thirty pounds of blood, and pull out the rocks?"

"People don't have thirty pounds of blood."

"Okay, we had to amputate his legs."

Her eyebrow was up, and I could tell she was teasing, but all the same she seemed a little irritated. "Does your culture have the concept of 'sportsmanship'?"

"Uh, yeah, but we also have a concept called 'Nice guys finish last.'"

She looked startled, then thoughtful. "I just heard you say something like 'Decent people are there to be eaten,' which is a pretty strange translator error."

"I'm afraid that all that got lost in the translation was the politeness," I said.

"Hmm." She seemed thoughtful, and I was afraid I had offended her, but whether I had or not, her attention was now all on the steep descent in front of us. It was a series of cliffs and ledges, like a steep staircase, with the ledges cutting deep into the face, so that we were actually shooting for only very small patches of accessible, level ground, and there was a great risk of fouling a line from the walker. I suppose she must have wanted all her concentration for the job at hand.

Then she reached over to my harness and said, "If you'll excuse me, I do want to check you out as well.

Partners falling to their deaths is just the kind of thing that could get me a bad grade." She ran her hands over the harness, and then said, "Now, what could this huge thing be? Could it be the thing Mark Strang is most known for at COTA?"

I snorted. "You can make fun of it all you want, but it makes me feel secure just to be able to get my hand on it when I need to."

We were talking about my Colt Model 1911A1, the .45 automatic I carry with me everywhere. I had carried it in my job as a bodyguard in my home timeline, carried it through three years of being accidentally stranded in another timeline, and I had lost count of the number of times that this little habit had saved my life.

"I wouldn't dream of depriving you of it," she said, "but you know the harness only accommodates itself to your living body, and it doesn't realize that it can't attach to your shoulder holster. I've got it pulled away now, but if it slips back, it may bind and cause trouble. Are you sure you wouldn't rather just put it in your pack with your SHAKK and NIF?"

"Call me superstitious, but no. I know perfectly well that there's nothing dangerous anywhere around and that we're the only people for a thousand miles in any direction. And I don't care. I'd rather have it at hand." I was doing my best to smile as I said all that—while, of course, carefully not relaxing on the basic point: I wanted the Colt to stay where I could grab it.

She sighed. "I'll just have to think of it as a religious object. All right, let's go."

We didn't talk at all as we started the descent.

With the ATN belay, you really just climb downward as if it were a free climb, but taking more chances because your belay is perfect and has electronic-speed reflexes. If you hit a stretch where you need to descend on the line, you just speak to the walker via your mouthpiece, show it where you're trying to go with your optical designator, and it will pay out for you as you push out, keeping your speed reasonable and helping you steer to your target.

I had asked once what we would do if the climbing equipment failed us, and they explained that it failed safe—if anything went wrong, it just worked like regular climbing gear. The next day we started a week of practice with plain old "dumb" climbing gear. All of the other trainees blamed me for that. I decided that after that experience, I wasn't going to ask any questions unless I was fairly sure the answers did not require demonstration.

It was actually a good season for climbing—late summer, with most of the stuff, snow and loose rock, that was going to fall, already fallen. We made quick progress despite our lack of sleep.

By around 8 A.M. local solar time, we were most of the way down, just about twenty meters above the level area on which we planned to camp before resuming our skiing the next night. We were most of the way down to the next ledge, and I was already trying to think of something clever to amuse Chrys, when the walker blew to pieces.

The bag of rocks that represented the Dalai Lama plunged past me and dropped onto the rocks below; it was only then that I realized that when the walker dropped my line, my line promptly snagged the rocks and shortened up enough to catch me before I fell far. I now had a belay line twenty feet over my head with about fifteen more feet to go. I hit the emergency reel—I didn't understand how that worked, either, there was no actual spool, but it seemed to take up or pay out a few meters of line as needed into a small black box—and sank rapidly to the ledge below, Chrys running out her line beside me less than a meter away.

As our boots touched the narrow, boulder-choked ledge, and we found our balance, the thought finally formed. "I think they blew up the walker as part of the test," I said, looking out at the vast empty plain in front of our cliff. "I guess we're supposed to—"

There was a slim dart of silver in the morning sun, high above us in the blue vault of the sky. It was falling, and though it wasn't big, it was coming very fast. I hadn't yet thought about it in words when I dove on Chrys and pressed both of us back behind a large boulder, against the rock face behind us.

A great shock leaped through the stone to our bodies. A huge clatter of stones, some bigger than our bodies, fell past our opening in the cliff and into the empty space beyond. "Missile," I shouted in Chrys's ear.

"Closers!" she responded, and I realized she was right. The stuff that had been thrown at us had not been the kind of thing they do in training, at all. This had been stuff that could easily have killed us, even just by accident . . . and that meant hostiles. Which meant Closers.

They had found the timeline of ATN's secret

training base, and they were after us. For all we knew everyone at COTA was dead. If we were going to get out of this, it would have to be just the two of us.

I pulled my .45 from its shoulder holster and started looking for a target, or at least for whatever had shot at us. Out beyond the rim of boulders, the sky and land were empty.

2

I didn't have to wait long. There was a strange low-pitched thrum in the air, and then I spotted the small aircraft coming in low. I said "helicopter" and Chrysamen said "ornithopter"—what it would have been in our home timelines—but it wasn't either of those.

It flew on four spinning plates that pumped up and down on their axles beneath it, and the axles came out of four long spidery arms that extended out at right angles from the cab. The cab itself was a windowed box of what looked like yellow plastic, and inside it, three guys, with firearms (or at least it looked like they had a stock and a barrel) slung on their shoulders, held on to straps like the ones on a city bus or subway. A fourth guy standing at the back was hanging on to a horizontal bar, pulling it back and forth and twisting it.

Since then, for the heck of it, I've asked six engineers in a few timelines how such a thing could fly. I've gotten three different explanations, plus three other explanations of why it couldn't possibly have worked and how I could not have seen what I did.

As the gadget swept in toward us, I leaned forward across a boulder, braced the Colt in both hands, made the guess that the guy holding the horizontal stick at the back was the pilot, and put four rounds in the direction of his chest, hoping one of them would connect.

I don't know if I got him or just scared him into letting go of the tiller. The little flying machine veered sideways in a spin, then abruptly flipped over and plunged cab-first onto the frozen ground below.

I braced for an explosion. There was none. Maybe it didn't have fuel tanks, or maybe it just happened that nothing caught fire. Anyway, nothing came out of it alive, and the cab seemed to have smashed like an egg.

That was comforting but no help. I had gotten myself behind a rock as soon as I'd fired my last shot—if you're fighting anyone with homing AP ammo, you never get exposed at all if you can help it.

If they'd been on the ball, the two seconds it took me to use the automatic would have been my last. But the good thing about fighting Closers—maybe the only good thing—is that they have very little initiative and little ability to get off the plan.

The plan must have been that the missiles—the one that got the walker and the one that followed it—would kill or disable us, and the guys in the bizarre flying machine would then land and confirm we were dead, or make sure of it, or maybe take any survivor prisoner. The others out there in the plain were just there as backup or to do scut work afterward, and no one had told them to provide any covering fire or retaliation. By now, of course, some Closer officer was screaming orders at them, but it was too late.

The Closers teach their slaves, even their very highly trusted ones in their armies, not to make decisions without checking first, and always to do exactly what they're told. It makes for great slaves, but lousy improvisers. And in combat, there's a lot more call for improvisers.

The delay not only gave me time to get back under cover after having gotten a good look at the landscape; it also gave Chrysamen enough time to get into the packs and get out the SHAKKs and NIFs.

The SHAKK is my favorite gadget in all of future technology. When I had gotten stranded in another timeline, I practically won World War II all by myself with a SHAKK. The initials stand for Seeking Hypersonic Ammunition Kinetic Kill, and the weapon itself looks a bit like one of the super squirt guns painted silver—but there the resemblance ends. Point it, squeeze the trigger, and the ammo—a spherical translucent bead about half the size of a BB shot—finds and hits whatever was in the sights at the time you pulled the trigger, out to about six miles, at Mach 10. You have two thousand rounds in the magazine, and on full auto it fires four hundred of those per minute.

I unclipped the remote sight from underneath my

SHAKK and cautiously crawled over, staying under cover, to set it on a boulder a few steps away. Now I could look through the little screen in the recess the remote sight had left, move a cursor, squeeze the trigger, and as long as I had left a meter cubic space for the shot to turn around in, let the shot find its way to the target.

How does it work? You got me. I just use it. My sister Carrie, the physics prof, says she can see nine ways it might work, all of them impossible. But then she also thinks she can prove that time travel and multiple timelines are impossible.

Possible or not, I love the SHAKK. I didn't expect to see anything at first—they'd probably all been told to stay under cover, and they were probably more afraid of their officers than they were of us. Sure enough, nothing moved for a while.

The remote sight scanned back and forth over the broken country below, all rock, snow, and hillocks, much too high up to have trees. There were no signs of life for two long breaths, so I flicked to infrared. Another three long breaths went by.

A hand glowed for a moment as it set a remote sight up on a rock. I moved the cursor with the tiny slides until it overlapped his hand—indeed, thumbing the enlargement upward, I took the shot specifically at his wrist. When I squeezed the trigger there was a sound like a whip cracking, another like a furious hornet, and then a high-pitched scream, all in less time than it takes to blink twice.

The sound the SHAKK makes is not from the pressure released from the muzzle as the projectile is expelled, like the guns of our timeline—what you're hearing is the sonic boom as the tiny engines on the shot propel it up to Mach 10 within less than a meter. The high-pitched scream, a little like a ricochet from an old movie played on a sped-up turntable, came from the engines braking and curving the shot almost 180 degrees within that short distance, then reaccelerating it.

Sis assures me that that can't be done either, and that the reason they told me that the shot doesn't leave a glowing tail like a meteor—that it recovers and reuses most of the energy from atmospheric heating of its surface—is even more impossible. I fall back on the position of flying-saucer nuts and miracle-cure enthusiasts: but it *did*.

The scream of the departing shot had not yet faded out when I saw the hand in the sight fly up into the air, jerking as the round entered his arm, and steered up through it (the shock wave making the arm first bulge and then collapse, like a toy balloon hooked to a compressed-air line).

Too fast to see that it happened at different times, blood sprayed from the shattered wrist, burst from his shoulder as the shot crossed to his head, sprayed once more as the shot went in through the eye. Then, in less than a hundredth of a second, it used up its remaining energy spiraling around inside his head. The shock wave in that confined space turned everything from his spine up into runny jelly.

I had to imagine that last part, but I enjoyed imagining it—if that sounds too horrible, well, Closers are horrible, and I like to see bad things happen to them. I knew that the watery goo that had been flesh, bone, blood, and brains would spray in a fine mist out through his nose, mouth, ears, and eye sockets, leaving his head to collapse into a bag of skin.

First time I saw that I upchucked. After I got to know Closers ... I could do it over dinner and still order dessert.

My remote sight vaporized in a bright flash-and-bang.

An instant later Chrysamen's NIF was spraying fléchettes in a black streak like a swarm of wasps into the open space before us. It occurred to me I was a bit of an idiot—the NIF was a much better weapon for this situation because the fléchettes home on human bodies within the target area and thus can find their targets without being aimed.

Maybe I'm just a caveman—the SHAKK is a much higher-powered weapon, so I prefer it. But by using the NIF in this situation, Chrys was probably taking out 90 percent of the enemy.

NIF stands for Neural Induction Fléchette. The gadget itself looks a lot like a cordless electric drill, and makes a squealing noise that's downright unpleasant when fired. The fléchettes—tiny needles no bigger than pencil points—fly for about three miles in about half a minute. But those three miles are only rarely in a straight line—normally the fléchettes circle the target area till they find the target people. When they do, they hit, burrow into the skin till they find a nerve—and then they take control. That is, they induce signals that make the nervous system do funny things—knock you out; give you terrible pain all over your body; turn your heart off; or temporarily blind you and make you vomit, lose bowel and bladder control, and itch all over (no kidding—that particular setting is very useful in riot work!).

So by setting her NIF to spray the area, Chrys had probably gotten the great majority of them—which unfortunately left a minority that was sighted in on us. The Closers don't seem to have NIF, but their homing gear, if anything, is a little better than ours (somehow they seem to be able to detect any sight we aim through, which was how they got my remote so quickly). Moreover, they like brute force. I was expecting them to blow the whole mountainside apart any second.

I carefully slid to the side, then tossed out my second (and last) remote sight. I wasn't eager to fire again, but I wanted to know what was going on.

Long seconds went by without motion. The thing about these future weapons that was really eerie was that since they only hit what you aimed at, even though a battle had just flared across the lumpy, snowy plain in front of us, even though somewhere out there a dozen Closer troops might still be sitting with fingers on triggers, or getting ready for an assault—the rocks and little hills looked just as they had before. No shell craters, no ripped lines from machine-gun fire, just one splash of blood, bright red in the morning sun, from the man I had hit. If not for that, the frozen waste in front of us could have been empty.

After more time, Chrys breathed, "I couldn't have gotten all of them. They must want us alive for some reason."

"Except they could easily have killed us with those first missiles. I think they're trying for definitely dead, so they want to have our bodies in hand for sure, which is why they can't use anything that won't leave them enough to prove they got us. Did you set off a help beacon?"

"First thing. I bet you forgot again."

"Sure did," I admitted. "Reckon it'll come out of my grade?"

I had only the corner of my eye to enjoy Chrys's grin with; most of my attention had to be on the remote sight. "You're incorrigible," she whispered. After a long pause, she added, "How long do you expect we'll have to wait for help?"

"Well, we've been fighting . . ." I checked a time on my SHAKK. "I shot that man twelve minutes ago. Figure we started five before that. So I'd say there's three possibilities . . . One, this is part of the exercise, those are androids and not real Closers out there, and we're supposed to improvise our way out of this. Two, those are Closers, COTA Main Base is already halfway down to hell, and we're stuck here. In which case, we have to improvise our way out of this."

She nodded. "And three is, 'something you haven't thought of'?"

"Bingo. You know my methods . . . but anyway, the point is, if this isn't part of the exercise—and I don't think it is, because it's way too realistic and expensive to waste on our field problem—then it's a real Closer attack, and what are the odds they'll attack two trainees out in the middle of a field exercise, and *not* go after any of the larger bases? My guess is they hit Main Base and everything else that shows from orbit five or ten minutes after the last time we talked to COTA, right after we got told to fill that silly bag with rocks and pretend it was the Dalai Lama. So if I had to bet, I'd bet we're the last two ATN agents alive and at large on Earth in this timeline. The ATN will be back but it could be days, weeks, or years."

She nodded solemnly, then suddenly heaved a baseball-sized rock up against the ledge above us, so that it bounced down onto the steep cliffside in front of us. On its third bounce it was blasted into gravel, stone chips flying all over. I got the position of two weapons from that and squeezed off ten NIF rounds, set to kill, toward each hiding place, but I wasn't optimistic. After all, those guys were in holes that had evaded Chrys's earlier shots, so chances were they were in pretty good cover.

"I don't think it's a training exercise," Chrys said. "That was less than two seconds to track on the object and blow it apart. And moving as eccentrically as it was, that's about the time you'd expect a machine already sighted in to take."

"Yeah." Another reason my shots had probably had no effect . . . most likely I was shooting at a weapon that was running on automatic control, and the soldier was somewhere else by then.

"I wouldn't bet on it either," I said. "Chrys, it really doesn't look like we're getting out alive; what's the most effective thing we can do before they get us?"

"Record what we've got, but our recorders have been running right along. Maybe get a couple more of them. Damn, Mark, I had a grudge against these people, and it looks like we'll never get a real shot at them."

"I had one real shot at them before I was recruited," I said, "and the revenge was just as good as you're imagining."

"What'd they do to you?"

"Killed most of my family. My mother and wife among them. Listen, I've got a ward—"

"A what? Translator problem—"

"I've got a kind of adopted daughter, back in my timeline. If you get out, and I don't, nag ATN about seeing that she gets taken care of. Poor kid lost her mother to a Closer operation."

"Sure," Chrysamen nodded emphatically. "And there's a guy I want you to look up for me, if you get out and I don't."

How is it possible at a time like that to feel your heart sink as if you were in eighth grade? But that's exactly what I felt, there, wedged into those cold rocks in Tibet, eyeing the remote sight and waiting for the final attack.

"He's my brother," she added. "He's quadriplegic . . . he was a Special Agent until the Closers did that to him."

Despite the fact that probably we would be dead before the hour was out, the world suddenly looked a lot better. "Of course I will, if the need comes up," I said. I chucked another rock, this time sideways down the slope, and they blew it apart again, from the same two positions. Whatever was down there, the NIF wasn't working on it.

"Note for whoever reads the recording," I said,

"unless you're a Closer, in which case let me say I'm sorry I didn't get a chance to stake your mother out on an anthill. It would be very nice if in the next version of the SHAKK there were a way of recording a target position, then turning off the remote sight, and then firing, so that we didn't have to give away the remote's position when we shot. Right now I can see them, and if I wasn't going to lose the sight as soon as I tried it, I'd be firing hex bursts from the SHAKK to get them out of their holes."

Chrys nodded, and added, "Mark's teammate enthusiastically agrees." Then she thought for a moment and said, "What would happen if you shot those hex bursts and then I knocked the sight off its rock? It seemed to take them a couple of seconds to hit it the last time; maybe they'd hit where it was, rather than where it had been knocked to."

"You're not going to try to move sight? They'd sight in on your hand."

"I just planned to hit it with a rock. If it doesn't bounce anywhere where we can get it, we still have another SHAKK left with two remote sights. We'll just have to be careful in setting it up."

"Unh-hunh. Well, it's a lot nicer than sitting here and waiting for them to bring in more forces. Okay, let's try it. I know which two rocks they're behind; I'll sight in, squeeze off, oh, say, four hex bursts, do it again. At the end of my second group of four, you chuck a rock at the sight."

Chrys nodded, and said, "Probably it won't work, but it's better than sitting on our butts. But before we do that, let me see if I can get the other remote set up, so we can see what happens." She detached a remote sight from the other SHAKK, crawled down the ledge, then carefully took the bowl from her mess kit, balanced the sight on top of it, balanced that on top of a tent pole, and raised the whole thing to the top of a pile of scree. The sight fell off the bowl, but it landed facing outward, and when we checked we found we had a decent view of the country in front of us.

"Okay," she said. "You'll fire four bursts, reaim, fire four more. On the fourth, I knock over your remote with this." The rock in her hand was the size of a tennis ball. "Then we see what happens. Just to liven it up I'm going to spray the target spots with the NIF right after all that, in case you've flushed anything human from cover."

"Deal," I said. "Let's see how this one goes."

I sighted carefully on the better of the two targets, a narrow cleft between a couple of boulders; I figured there was some kind of microcave there, probably our boy was lying in under a slab of rock held up by two boulders, and that the NIF fléchettes just hadn't been able to see him in there. "Ready?" I asked.

"Ready," Chrys responded.

I squeezed the trigger four times, as fast as I could. There were four deep roars. A hex burst is the middle setting on the SHAKK; it fires a group of six rounds that fly in formation to the target, then strike in a hexagon pattern about a meter across. There's about as much kinetic energy in a SHAKK round as there is energy in one of our hand grenades, and so the effect is pretty spectacular.

I wasn't watching; I twiggled the cursor over to

the other target. This one was a crevice under a large boulder; I wasn't at all sure how he was managing to fire from under there. Maybe he was sitting behind the boulder, sighting with a remote sight that I hadn't spotted, and then firing through a hole that led under the boulder and connected to the crevice I could see. Anyway, I moved the cursor to the crevice and squeezed the trigger as hard as I could four times.

Beside me, Chrys's wrist and elbow snapped in a hard sidearm throw. The rock flew straight and true and knocked over the remote sight—which promptly fell forward and rolled down the cliffside.

There was a hail of shots as the remote sight was chewed to bits by Closer fire, but as we watched on the other remote sight, we saw it was coming from other locations. "Great," Chrys said. "We got two, and three more are revealed. At this rate we only need about a dozen remote sights to be sure we get them all."

I nodded. "Pity we only have two left. Did you see what happened to the targets?"

"The little cave collapsed when the boulders in front of it blew apart. You probably buried that guy under a twenty-ton slab."

"Good," I said. "I hope he's still alive under there."

"Mark, sometimes you turn my stomach. I don't like them either, and I'm glad to do them harm, but spare me your bloodthirstiness, please . . . I don't see any reason to rejoice in pain and suffering." She sighed. "Anyway, I saw the other one take a NIF hit—he was trying to crawl out from the rubble where his hiding place got torn up."

"So . . . want to hit those three hiding places and then see where matters stand?"

"Sounds good. Let me find the right-sized rock. We cut that one pretty close last time—if you're going to do three, I think you'd probably better keep it to three bursts each."

"Sounds right to me. My turn to set the remote sight." I crawled forward and to the side with it, then very gently pushed it over the side of a boulder so that it fell onto a lower one, facing outward. "You want to do the honors with the SHAKK, or shall I?"

"You go ahead. Let's not break up a winning pattern."

This time it went a little better, at least at first. The nine hex bursts whizzed out toward the little cracks and crevices where the Closers had dug in, and Chrys said that the ground exploded nicely around every one of them. She NIFfed at least one more of them, and another hidey-hole sprayed blood, indicating that probably a round had found its way to the warm human body concealed within.

This time she got the remote sight with the rock so that it fell into a concealed place, a little spot behind a rock, but to get to it we would have had to climb down through two whole meters of open ground, and it was pointed facedown into the ground, so it might as well have been on the Moon for all the good it did us. I was just about to say something when it suddenly blew to pieces; that better Closer homing ammo had done its trick.

"Just one place shot—but that might only mean

there was just one target," Chrysamen said, looking through the screen of her SHAKK. "Maybe we should—"

With a flash and bang, the last remaining remote sight blew up. Now we couldn't look at them without being shot—I remembered how easily I had hit the hand of the Closer setting his sight, and what had happened to him, and shuddered a little. To shoot a SHAKK at them now with any chance of success, I would have to poke my head out. It would be only an instant until it was blown apart; it didn't give me any additional sympathy for the Closers, but I couldn't help wondering what one of those slugs spiraling around in the brain pan at hypersonic speeds would feel like. Probably like nothing at all . . . it would happen too fast. I hoped.

"Got any ideas for last-ditch procedures?" Chrys asked.

"Move back as far as we can into the best cover we can find, spray with NIFs at intervals to slow them down, and SHAKK anything that pops its head up at us." *And try to look brave while they kill us,* I added mentally.

"That's what I thought of," she said. "And we'll have to not talk, since we'll need our ears."

"Far back" wasn't much—the hole in the cliff we were in wasn't more than twenty-five feet deep, and so all we could really do was move from our position behind the boulders covering the ledge in front of us, into the rubble at the back. It gave us maybe fifteen feet, which was nothing at all. I crouched behind one boulder, watching the line of rocks in front of us with my SHAKK in hand and Chrys's beside me; a scant six feet to my right, Chrys squatted behind rubble, her NIF and mine ready to hand, watching her watch. When she judged enough time had gone by, she sprayed the NIF once, in a short burst, out over the outer rim of the boulders; this far back in the shallow cave, the squealing echoed weirdly, like a flock of rabid bats bursting from the bowels of the Earth.

We held our breaths, listening for anything—and then suddenly there was a wailing, ululating, sobbing sound far out beyond us, followed by the booming report of a SHAKK-type weapon.

I glanced at her curiously; she let loose another squealing flock of fléchettes, and then we waited a long time, but there was no further sound.

"I set it to start at high pain and keep adding pain till blackout, then kill," Chrys said. "Hoping it would give us some idea how many of them were moving around out there."

"At least two, before," I said, "and now probably still at least one."

We couldn't talk any longer—we had to keep our ears open for the danger approaching us. The cave was amazingly cold, and my position was getting cramped and uncomfortable; I realized the sun probably never penetrated this far, and these rocks hadn't been warmed since they'd cooled from their making. It was still midmorning, less than an hour after our battle had started.

I crouched, looked through the sight of my SHAKK, and waited.

Chrys counted off another time interval—I knew without checking that she was smart enough to vary them—and sprayed again. This time there were no screams, and we sat still. More minutes ticked by, and again she sent a flight of fléchettes squealing into the space in front of us. This time there were screams, probably from two or three people; they went on for quite a while, and no shot ended them, but one screamer stopped abruptly, and then the other. She sprayed again, and no sound came.

I glanced sideways at her. She was listening with all her attention for the sounds that did not come. Her coverall was grimy from climbing, and under her hard hat her soft black curls were beginning to escape in little, untidy ringlets. Her breath hissed out in a white cloud, and finally she said, "That might have been it. Now we wait and stay on the drill for a while."

I nodded. "How's the supply of fléchettes?"

"One NIF is almost empty. I've given it a load of dirt, two candy bars, and an earring I didn't want anymore, and I'm using the other."

Because Crux Ops often operate in primitive conditions, far from supply bases, our weapons are always capable of manufacturing their own ammunition—but the worse the raw materials you start with, the longer it takes and the more waste it produces. "Is it giving you any numbers?"

"Looks like I'm short on copper and iron."

Keeping my eyes forward through the SHAKK, I pulled a spare clip of .45 ammo out, emptied it into my hand, and edged sideways to her, exposing myself for a brief instant as I did so. "Here, add these."

She did, and the NIF reported it had everything it

needed to reload itself completely. Meanwhile, she had the other one with a full charge. Since it had been a few minutes, she sprayed again; I was beginning to find the squeal of the NIF more than a little unnerving. But then I can't imagine that anyone alive out there liked it much, either.

I waited in the silence. My shoulder was within an inch of Chrys's; now that we were physically close together, given just how bad the situation was, it seemed too comforting to move away from her, and she seemed in no hurry to move away from me, either. At best our "cross fire" would be no more than ten feet of separation, anyway.

Time rattled on, marked only by our steady breathing. She checked her watch, fired the NIF again. No sound came from the slopes below, but that might mean only that they were under cover.

She kept firing at irregular intervals, but the intervals grew longer. Just before one, she explained, "I'm spacing them wider to give the enemy a chance to get overconfident and stick their heads up. Of course, if they're smart—or all dead—they won't take the bait." She fired the squealing burst. There was no response after a full minute.

"You know," I said, "we can't stay here. If they're still out there, they called for help, and it will get here sooner or later. And even if they didn't, someone will come looking for them. The longer we stay here making sure there's no one to shoot us, the less time we have to escape and get a long way from here."

She nodded. "Yeah. Well, are you ready to try?"

I checked my watch. "Since the last time anyone

screamed, they've had three hours to get up here, and it shouldn't have taken them twenty minutes, even in a very careful buddy rush. Hell, if I were as ruthless as they are, I'd have let the screaming cover my advance and gotten here sooner. Even assuming they're out there and really taking their time, there shouldn't be more than three or so of them left, anyway. Why don't we at least move back to our old front line?"

We did. Nothing happened.

Chrys wanted to flip a coin, but I insisted that since she was the one who was any good with the NIF, I be the one to peek out and see what happened. I crept a little distance from her, took my SHAKK in hand, and peeked. I took a couple of long swallows to count the six visible corpses out there—against the dingy gray-white background they were not hard to spot. I pulled my head in, counted off a full minute.

My head did not explode in a nasty pink mist, and my body did not suddenly leap and jump with pain. I took a deep breath and did part two of the plan—I stood straight up.

It had been so long since I had done that, that I felt light-headed, and my legs ached. I took a long deep breath; took two more; and let myself relax a bit. Chrys, still from cover, sprayed the landscape thoroughly. After the long shriek of the NIF died out, I stood and watched for some minutes; out there, I knew, the neural induction fléchettes were seeking, cross-cutting, patrolling a few inches off the snow for anything at human body temperature. In a few minutes they would begin to run out of whatever their fuel was (nobody ever seemed to be able to explain that to me, and I couldn't understand even whether they were telling me that the information was classified or that I didn't know enough physics to understand it). Then they'd glide down into the snow, bury themselves, switch off permanently (unless Chrys was setting them to function as mines, and she hadn't been), and start the chemical process that would, within a day at most, turn all the tiny darts into indistinguishable little lumps of organic matter that would fade into the soil without much trace.

As I watched, hundreds of little puffs of snow popped up in the sunlit field; the fléchettes were gone.

Tentatively, Chrys stood. She, too, needed to stretch out a little. We reloaded our packs, made sure our weapons were ready to hand, stuck a line to the cave wall, and did a fast rappel down the face to get to the bottom as soon as possible. Nothing moved except tiny puffs of wind-driven snow; there was no sound but our breathing and the wind itself.

At the bottom we hurriedly stowed the climbing gear, unshipped the skis, and got ready for an afternoon of fast, hard skiing. With little hope that our pickup would be there for us, we were going to head off at almost a right angle to our original direction, both to put them off our track if possible, and to take advantage of the direction in which we could move farthest fastest.

"Well," I said, as we strapped up, "here we go. With two days' rations we ought to be able to make it to somewhere where we can start living off the land. I suppose eventually—"

"Eventually we'll be dead," Chrys said. "But maybe we can delay it a long time."

I grinned; she was right. "Okay, let's go."

At least I wasn't pulling a bag of rocks behind me, and we were moving in a direction that the ground favored. In a short time we had logged a couple of miles, and the future was beginning to feel just a little brighter. Chrys was puffing a bit, so I slowed the pace, figuring in a while she'd want to talk. After another mile, as we wound through a narrow defile, I ventured to say, "We seem to be doing all right. Want to get a few more miles?"

Before she could answer, a male voice behind us said, "Keep your hands away from your weapons. Now raise your hands. Now turn around slowly."

3

They had us perfectly; we couldn't do anything except what we were told, at least not if we wanted to stay alive.

We turned to find six men facing us in the snow—all of them in COTA coveralls and holding NIFs on us. There was a startled instant of realization—and then we recognized several of the instructors from COTA.

"You can put your hands down now, ja N'wook and Strang, if you've recognized us," Captain Malecela said, grinning at us. "We don't want to end up like all those Closers you dealt with back there."

I wasn't sure which was more remarkable—that Malecela was here or that he was smiling. He was commander of combat training at COTA, and most of us were more afraid of him than of anything the enemy could throw at us.

Physically a remarkably strong man, he would

have turned a lot of heads on any beach in any timeline if it weren't for the faint lines of scars that stretched across his face. I'd heard a lot of stories about where he got those, and I believed all of them. He was black, and from some timeline where Zanzibar was the capital of the Earth; it was said he was some relation to the Emperor there and had given up titles and wealth to enlist.

I had seen him do a number of things, physically, that I would have reckoned impossible. Malecela had caught two students trying to steal a bronze bust of the founder of COTA, as a prank, to move it onto the ad building roof. He had shown them "how to do it right"—tucked it under one arm and took it up the four stories one-handed, then brought it back down the same way, and then demanded that they either do the same, or give him a thousand sit-ups. They did all thousand, then and there.

He had a standing offer that if there was any weapon of your home timeline and you gave him one day to practice, he could do better than you with it. It had only taken him half a day to shoot a better round than I did with the Model 1911A1, three hours to throw the razor-edged boomerang better than Simil Patapahani, and about a day to get better with the *linea mortifera*—kind of a cross between a lariat, fly rod, and garotte—than Marcellus Guttierez-Jenkins.

Of course we were relieved to see him there—but if it was going to be anyone from our side, it would be him.

"There are some minor details to discuss," he said, "but you two did pretty well. It wasn't the field problem we set you, but we think you improvised pretty well. I'll give you a passing score, anyway."

"The Main Base—" I asked.

"Completely untouched, so far. We're getting an evacuation under way. But you two were the only ones actually attacked by Closers."

Chrysamen looked as startled as I did, I'm sure, but Malecela just grinned some more—maybe he was just getting it out of his system before he'd have to be in front of other candidates again. "All right, the way for you two to look at this right now is that you're going to get hot showers, real food, and comfortable beds a couple of days early, and that you're about as safe as anyone else is right now. Let's get you home."

The liftwing turned out to be waiting less than a mile away, and in less than an hour we were flying back to COTA Main Base itself, not far from where Perth is in Australia in our timeline.

"We got the help beacon, and then no words, so we shot up a reconnaissance satellite, and it dropped a ground-observer package," Malecela was explaining to us. "You can imagine our surprise. That was excellent shooting for nonhoming ammunition, by the way, Strang, and it's good that you had the foresight to use nonlethal instructions in the NIF, ja N'wook, because the med teams tell me we might very well get ten or more for interrogation."

"You did what?" I asked her.

"I wish I could take credit for brains," Chrysamen said, looking down at her hands, "but it really doesn't come easy for me to set a weapon to 'kill' unless I know I have to. It was just what I did naturally."

Malecela shrugged. "Part of the secret of success is learning to take credit for your lucky guesses. And anyway, it probably didn't occur to you, but once you won the fight and started to run, anyone you were leaving knocked out was going to be frozen solid by nightfall anyway."

She shuddered. "No, I didn't think of that."

"Anyway, I would bet neither of you will ever let your more modern weapons get out of your reach again, if you can help it," Malecela said, going on without acknowledging her reaction. "And thanks, by the way, Strang, for pushing to make the SHAKK more programmable when it's being used on remote sight. Clearly the Closers have figured out some way to home on its wireless communication. If they can hit the remote sight today, figure in two weeks they'll have a way to hit the SHAKK itself—which is going to be damned unpleasant if you're holding it. I've been telling them about all that for years, and it's good to be able to show them that any old candidate can see the same thing."

He leaned back in his seat. "We have a big job ahead of us. Construction battalions by the dozen will be coming in to get COTA moved across to another timeline, and to convert this facility to a surprise for the Closers in case they turn up in force. But the situation is different for you two . . . you're going direct to Hyper Athens, to the Crux Ops center there. We'll be putting you two into the transmitter about an hour after we land. Orders of the high command."

For the rest of the liftwing ride, we didn't say much. After the ship had risen vertically, like an elevator, until the sky was black in the daytime, the stars were out, and the Earth's curve showed below us, it began to accelerate at about a g; somewhere over Sumatra it whirled around and fired its engines to decelerate, then smoothly spun again to ride down like the space shuttle. It was one terrific ride, and since we had nothing to do but enjoy it, we did.

In this timeline, Australia had an inner sea, probably because the sea level was a lot higher, and there were thick forests around it, so the view down below us was pretty wonderful, and I was kind of lost in it when Chrys abruptly said, "If we're supposed to go to Hyper Athens, why the delay here? You could have packed us and just thrown us in after our stuff."

Malecela grinned again. "You'll see."

All right, so I'm sentimental. I still get a little choked up when I think about it. They held a special graduation for us, right there at the airfield, with all our classmates there, and gave us a little time to shake hands and accept congratulations.

But it was only brief. They had other things to get done, too, and in almost no time we were standing in the now-familiar booth of the transmitter.

Malecela nodded one more time, and said, "That was excellent work, both of you."

"All we did," I pointed out, for some perverse reason, "was save our own lives."

"You're valuable ATN assets," Malecela said. "So you prevented valuable assets from falling into Closer hands. I think that's pretty respectable."

Then he stepped back, and we got into the booth.

Then there was no light. The world fell away, as if

we had dropped back into the weightlessness of space, and our surroundings were silent as vacuum. I had no sensation of being in my body for a long instant that might have been half a second or a thousand years for all the difference it made. Then I was facing an even, dim gray light in all directions, which got brighter, began to differentiate like a photograph developing, and abruptly burst through into color. As this happened there was a low humming that was about an octave lower than the sixty-cycle hum you sometimes hear on stereo systems.

The world started to take shape again.

We were at Crux Ops Central, on the giant space station of Hyper Athens, in the thirty-second century since Perikles founded the Federated Democratic Poleis; or if you want, what would have been in the twenty-seventh century A.D. if there had been a Christ in this timeline, or the twenty-first century since the *hegira*, if there had been a Mohammed. I had been here three times before, and though nothing quite equaled the experience of being dumped here unexpectedly after a firefight, as I had the first time, it still impressed me.

The platform we arrived on was open to the "sky," the miles-wide space inside the great wheel that was Hyper Athens. From where we stood, we were on the roof of a low building, between what at first glance looked like great rows of mile-high skyscrapers, but were actually the working and living areas that formed the sidewalls of the huge structure. Far above us, we could see through the glass centers of the sidewalls, and watched as first the Moon, and then the Earth, rolled into our view.

Hyper Athens rotated about every ten minutes, to supply a gravity of about one g at its edges; at that speed, you could see a lot of sunrises.

"Friend-daughter ja N'wook?" a familiar voice asked, "and I do believe Mister Strang, as well."

I turned and smiled. "Citizen Lao. It's good to see you again."

"And you, Mister Strang. Someone had to meet you here, and since I was in the base, it seemed reasonable."

Ariadne Lao is something over six feet tall and built like a serious triathlete. Her features are Eurasian and heavy-boned, extremely well formed but not at all the delicate kind of thing that's in fashion in our timeline. Hollywood would cast her as a prison matron or the bad guy's assistant, but they'd be wrong; she's startlingly attractive with her ice-blue eyes and black hair, even if she does look like she could deck a bear.

"It's a pleasure," I said.

She nodded to Chrysamen, including her in the conversation. "It happened I was the Crux Op on duty when Mister Strang first got involved in crosstime affairs, and later in recruiting him into the service." And turning back to me, she added, "I was absolutely delighted to hear that you had decided to join and that you were doing well in training. But this latest set of events absolutely justifies my faith in you."

She might have said more except that at that moment the sky darkened above us; a passenger dirigible was coming in. I wondered how Chrys was reacting to all this; I knew her home civilization was spacefaring, but after some roaming around in the timelines you realize that's a bit like knowing that a civilization uses counterpoint in music or the arch a lot in architecture—it isn't the fact that they use it, but what they do with it, that really matters. Some civilizations—like the one I come from—just do engineering and stop there, so that our space facilities all look like industrial plants, with a lot of machinery slapped together any old way that fits. I've seen pictures from many that seem to do everything in very simple geometries—all spheres, lines, annuli, pyramids, triangles, and cylinders. And then there are the ones like this one, the headquarters of ATN, the place where the battle against the Closers began . . . where if something is worth doing, it is worth doing beautifully and gracefully.

The timeline was currently going through an artistic period that was a bit like our Art Deco, and so the inside of the dirigible, like the shapes of the "skyscrapers" surrounding us, was made up of Z- and S-curves, with a lot of rounding and simplifying, elegance for no other reason than that it was elegant. As Chrysamen and I sat over juice, and Ariadne Lao gave us the quick tour of the station, I noted once again what a spectacular place Hyper Athens really is.

Traffic was heavy that day through the center of the great wheel-shaped space station, so we went around the rim, between the walls of mile-high buildings. Hyper Athens is sixty miles around the outside edge, and our destination was about a third of the way around from the transmission station, so it would take us a little time.

Above the tops of the buildings, and well down into the space between them, I could see a dozen dirigibles and perhaps twice as many little silver airplanes. In a space station that uses centrifugal force for gravity, the gravity falls off rapidly as you move toward the center. Thus very little energy is required to fly, even though gravity in the "street" is Earth-normal.

Beyond the building tops I could see the great clear space of the windows, and through it, when the angle was right, the Earth on one side, covering almost a fifth of the sky, and the Sun and a crescent Moon close to each other on the other side. It's a pity that kids have ruined the use of the word "awesome" to mean nothing more than "good" or "impressive," because this view was really awesome.

As we watched, a big space freighter, delicately woven of ellipsoidal capsules joined by curved and recurved girders, came into the transparent airlock that sat like a bubble on the Earth side of the station, and space-suited workers moored it with cables.

Chrysamen seemed oddly quiet, and there wasn't actually much catching up to do with Citizen Lao, so conversation lapsed until the dirigible dropped us off on top of one of the skyscrapers.

We were to meet with some higher-ups the next day. The building we had been taken to was the equivalent of a hotel—actually a wealthy person's house with a group of guest rooms, because the Athenians think of having guests as an honor. Since, Hyper Athens time, it was about time for supper, as soon as we were shown to our rooms we were given

passes to a local restaurant and told to make ourselves comfortable until the next morning, when we
would have some sort of meeting over breakfast.

In the Athenian timeline nobody ever invented
the menu; you eat what the restaurant has. This
time it was something that looked and tasted a little
like sweet-and-sour pork with a lot of pepper poured
over spaghetti, and a side dish of apples and cucum-
bers chopped into yogurt. It was good enough to
keep us both from talking much during the meal.

Afterward, as we sat over coffee, Chrysamen said,
"Citizen Lao seems to like you."

I nodded. "She recruited me; I suppose I'm sort of
her protégé, and when I do well it reflects on her."

Chrysamen nodded, and asked, "How did you
end up getting recruited? You said you went
crosstime accidentally . . . ?"

"It's a very long story," I said. "I can abbreviate.
Back in my own timeline, I had been an art historian. It happened my father was a Middle East affairs
specialist. He was investigating a new terrorist group
. . . which we didn't know was a front for the
Closers."

"What's a terrorist?" Chrysamen asked.

God, there were times I wished that I, too, had
grown up in a pacifist timeline. "Uh, military forces
or guerillas that attack civilians. In order to scare the
hell out of people, which gets them attention and
also pressures the authorities."

"Doesn't it also make them angry?"

"Well, yeah. That's certainly how it worked out
for my family." I took a long, slow drink of my coffee, reached for the pot, and poured myself more.

"Anyway, they set off a bomb that killed my mother, brother, and wife and left my sister with just her right arm. Happened right in front of my father and me, at a family celebration."

"Oh, god, Mark—" Those huge dark eyes looked a little damp, and she reached out and took my hand.

The trouble with sympathy is that if you're not careful you get to enjoy it, and before you know it you spend all your time getting it, so I said, "It was nine years ago, at least as I've experienced the time. You never get over it, but you do go on. And anyway, if we're going to be . . . uh, friends, then you had to know sometime."

She started a little at "friends." I mentally marked that for future reference, and went on, "So, anyway, I sort of found something else I could do for a while that made me feel better—I became a licensed private bodyguard."

Chrys sat back a moment. "Your timeline must be terribly violent if people can make a living at that."

"I'm a rich kid—I could run the business as a hobby. But yeah, it's a terribly violent timeline. If you're good at hurting people and not letting them hurt you, you can always make a living." I had some more coffee; this was probably shocking her, and I already had a feeling she thought I was a barbarian. "Well, to make it really short . . . I had two cases that turned out to be related. One was a little girl I was guarding for another reason, who turned out to be important in . . . well, at the time they said fifty timelines, now they say more than two hundred. I don't know much about all that, by choice, because I don't want to put any load of pressure on her, and from my viewpoint she's just a nice kid. She's my ward, back in my own timeline."

"You miss her?"

"Oh, yeah. When I return she'll be about fifteen, which is kind of a difficult age, or so I'm told. Fortunately she's got my father and sister on one side of things—and two of the best bodyguards in the business as well, my assistants Robbie and Paula. So no doubt she's just fine, but I really miss her anyway.

"Well, the other case turned out to be a Special Agent who was supposed to be keeping an eye on me and on that girl, and who got into a messy situation with the Closers. There was a lot of shooting, and a lot of people died, including the Special Agent, and I sort of kept falling through things. Finally I ended up—just improvising, mind you, because ATN barely knew I existed and had no idea where I was—stowing away through a Closer gate into a world where the Nazis won World War II. Since you didn't have either Nazis or World War II in your timeline, that probably doesn't mean much to you . . . "

"Not a lot. The Nazis sound a lot like what the followers of Suleiman the Butcher could have turned into, if he hadn't dropped dead of a stroke in a very embarrassing situation. One of those timelines where there's a tiny little group of masters and everyone else is a different degree of slave?"

"Right. Anyway, I was there for two and a half years till they found me again, and I just kind of improvised, and, uh, things broke right. That whole timeline was turned to ATN—and now it's an important new ally, I understand.

"But I have to admit all that does something to you. I'm afraid I'm pretty cold-blooded . . . well. No, not really. Actually, I *enjoy* killing Closers. I got to see enough of them and their stand-ins to feel about the same way I would killing a nest of copperheads under my house."

She nodded. "I can see how you could get to be that way. Er . . . there's something, too, that I want you to know. You know that I'd never killed anyone before, uh—"

"You didn't kill very many," I pointed out. "You set it for stun. Just the few who died of cold and the ones we got with the SHAKK died."

"Um, yes . . ." She was quiet for a long time, looking into her coffee and stirring it slowly. "Anyway, what I was going to say . . . well. I had kind of thought that tonight we might . . . uh, that is, I might drop by your room and we could be . . . "

The word didn't translate. Damn this not knowing each other's language.

"Uh, maybe the closest thing would be 'bed-friends'? It's not like it's marriage or anything but . . . "

"I'd be honored," I said.

"The problem is, religiously, I can't do that unless I er, well, I guess purify myself. I've taken human life. The prayer and ritual take about an hour or so. If that's, um, getting too late—"

"I can wait," I said. "Do I need to be purified as well?"

"No, it's just for . . . people of the Faith. Or at least for our version of the Faith. Er, maybe I should . . . go get started with it? We want some time to sleep tonight, too."

"That sounds reasonable," I said, and we headed back to our rooms, enjoying the walk through one of the many little parks in the Hyper Athens station. Chrys went off to her room to meditate and pray and do whatever else was involved in getting purified, and I stretched out for a quick catnap. I was excited about the fact that a beautiful girl was coming to share the bed with me, but I'd learned from bitter experience never to pass up a chance to sleep. Or to eat or take a leak for that matter.

As I drifted off, the one other thought that occurred to me was that this was would be the first time I'd made love—as opposed to getting laid—since my wife Marie had been killed. It seemed like it was about time. I curled up on the bed and let myself relax into a warm, happy state—

I woke abruptly when I heard a SHAKK being fired two doors away. I had left the lights on, and I rolled sideways; it was only a heartbeat before I held my own weapon and was standing upright.

I'd have had to get up anyway, because at that moment the door blew in with a roar and landed all over the bed. The light in the room went out. Something moved in the doorway, and I popped it with a SHAKK shot; I heard the body hit the floor.

I heard another SHAKK burst; it had to be Chrysamen, and thinking of her reminded me to pop the help button, the little tag we have that calls for a backup. Then I crept closer to the door, SHAKK at ready.

The next guy cleverly tried to just stick a gun in and squeeze off a homing round that would find me; but that meant exposing the muzzle, and a SHAKK round, pointed at any tube weapon, is smart enough to go in the open end and look for the round and firing mechanism. It blew apart in his hands, he screamed and fell forward, and a second shot converted his head to an empty bag. I flopped down on the floor and watched for feet; of course, sooner or later one of them would think of firing through the wall—unless the ATN had armored these against—

There was a clatter of bangs and pings and the wall beside me shook, but it held. Apparently I was in an armored box—

Something hit the floor and bounced, and I sprayed it with SHAKK fire, hoping it was not—

It was. There was a boom and flash, and I was temporarily blind and deaf; they'd tossed a PRAMIAC, a sort of smart grenade, into the room. The high-tech gadgets, if you get SHAKK rounds into them fast enough, will sometimes just fizzle—they don't work like old-fashioned high explosives. I'd been fast enough, I judged, since if I hadn't, that wing of the house would likely have been blown right out through the floor into space. In the dark I couldn't tell if it was an ATN or a Closer model

I couldn't see or hear well at the moment, but something was moving, so I fired. An instant later there was a painful jolt in my left hand; someone had gotten a homing round down the muzzle of my SHAKK and it had blown to pieces. I couldn't seem to get my left hand to do anything, but I groped for my shoulder holster with my right, drew out the Colt, swung my head from side to side, and perceived something in my peripheral vision near the door—

It was fine shot if I say so myself; I knew where I was, where the door was, and sort of where he was relative to the doorway. I pointed the .45, squeezed the trigger gently, and put a round up into his chest. I later found out it went right through his lungs, cut his pulmonary artery, and blew out through the back of his neck, shattering his spine and brain stem. He was dead before he slammed against the doorframe.

Something shoved in front of him, and I squeezed the trigger again; the Colt roared.

When the flash, bang, and acrid smoke cleared from my perception, someone was screaming. At least it wasn't me. I saw no more motion, but that might only mean they were being cautious; then I glanced down at the pistol and gulped.

Smokestack jam.

Every so often a spent casing doesn't clear, but ends up jammed by the slide, sticking out of the top of the weapon like a smokestack. When that happens, you've got to pull it back to clear it, which normally takes a second.

If you don't have that second, you're in a bad way. If you don't have that second, *and* you don't have your left hand in working order to do the job, you're dead.

I was trying to work it with my teeth—and noticing how badly my left hand hurt where it was getting squashed under me—when hands came down on my shoulder, something stung my thigh, and I slipped into unconsciousness.

A moment later the world was turning gray around me, and then shapes were forming. My left hand hurt like it was on fire, and my head seemed to have the Mother of All Hangovers, whereas my stomach wanted to eat without stopping for a week. I was in a set of restraints; had I been taken prisoner or—

"Some men will do anything to find a polite way out of a social engagement," Chrysamen said, standing over me. I looked up and saw that she had a bandage over one eye, her hair looked strangely mauled to one side, and there were several plasters and bandages visible on her bare arms. She was wearing a hospital gown. "Here, drink this," she added, bringing a glass to my lips.

It was strong, sweet, orange-and-strawberry, and I gulped it down. That told me once and for all that I was still in the ATN timeline and hadn't been taken prisoner; it's one of the favorite flavors there. Closers would never stoop to doing anything decent for a prisoner.

I finished the drink, and said, "You can release the restraints now—I know where I am and I won't come up swinging."

"Good," she said, letting me loose. "I'm afraid they put these on you because of what I did."

"What did you do?"

"Punched out the doctor when I woke up. It was their silly fault anyway; they knocked me out right at the end of a fight and then expected me to wake up realizing I was among friends."

I sat up and looked at my left arm. It was practically all pink, and when I touched it gingerly I found the skin was still a bit sensitive. "That must have been almost gone. My SHAKK blew up in my left hand," I said. "No wonder I'm starving. The nanos must be running on overdrive. How long have I been under?"

Chrys nodded sympathetically. "They said it was pretty bad; I know they had to give you a lot of IV to keep the nanos supplied. It's been about two days since the attack. They say we each have about a day to go. In another few hours I get to try out my new eye."

"Just so it matches your old one," I said. Nanos are tiny machines—small enough to pass through your capillaries—that work like little robots. They put a few million into you, the little rascals read your genetic code, and they start fixing things to fit the code, kind of like building supers for the body, except I've never seen a building supervisor get anything up to code. It has its weird effects; typically they get rid of scars, tattoos, trick hips and shoulders, old injuries of any kind. The first time I got treated at Hyper Athens they not only repaired bullet holes, and got rid of an old football injury, they also gave me my appendix and my tonsils back. "Were you hit badly?" I asked Chrys.

"Oh, if we hadn't been at Hyper Athens, we would probably both have died," she said, and sat down in a chair close to the bed. "They were wearing our uniforms and carrying SHAKKs, so the rounds homed on my weapon, not my head, and I got these holes in me from when my SHAKK blew up. I lost the eye to shrapnel. But my score was pretty good, too—I had to do another purification—I got six of them."

"Ahead of me," I said. "I only recall getting four."

"They told me five—you must have been too busy to count accurately," she said. "Malecela seems to be very pleased, to judge by the letter he sent. Eleven of them dead and both of us alive, or at least salvageable. Not bad for a couple of trainees, especially since this was one of their assassination squads."

"What the hell were Closers doing at Hyper Athens, anyway?" I asked. "And those assassination squads are supposed to be suicide missions, and eleven is a lot—that's *two* assassination squads."

"Exactly what we're trying to figure out," Ariadne Lao said, coming in through a door that had just formed in the wall. "We wish we knew why they're so determined to kill both of you, but now at least we can be pretty sure it's both of you." She nodded at Chrysamen, and said, "Friend-daughter ja N'wook, clearly you're feeling better."

"Still itches a little around the eye, Citizen," Chrys said.

"And you look like you're able to be up and around, Mister Strang?"

"I think so."

"Good then. To tell you both the absolute truth, we don't have much of any idea what's going on; Closers trying to assassinate trainees like this is way outside of normal behavior. So we're going to sit down with the intelligence analysts and do our best to figure out just what exactly is going on—as soon as we get enough food poured into you two."

Nanos run on your blood sugar, the same as you do, so when you have them in there you're generally eating for ten million or so; I've long figured if I knew enough to know how to make them and patent them in our timeline, I'd sell them as a weight-loss system. It takes a lot of energy to rebuild an arm out of hamburger.

The meeting room was a short walk away, and when we got there, there was an enormous supply of noodles, bread, rice, and chapatis, and a huge array of sauces to put on them. We didn't say much as we ate until we were stuffed; as I was having the last of a whole pastry that sort of resembled a football-sized éclair with pumpkin-pie filling, and Chrys was having a last bowl of clear noodles in sweetened cream, the ATN people came in, nodding polite greetings and talking among themselves. With a sigh, Chrys and I poured ourselves huge mugs of the thick coffee, added condensed milk to it, and joined them at the table. After a short spell of everyone telling us how glad they were that we were still alive, we got down to business.

4

The discussions went on all afternoon, which is what you expect of a committee no matter what timeline you are in. Finally it all boiled down to three facts: One, the Closers knew something or other that made them consider it worthwhile to eliminate Chris and me no matter what the cost. Two, I had already been assigned a first mission, so it seemed likely that if the Closers were trying now, something about that first mission was more important than anyone on our side had guessed. And finally, we had no idea what was so important.

The puzzling thing, too, was that Chrys had not yet been assigned a first mission, so whatever important thing she was going to do was much more up in the air than it was for me.

One puzzle for them was what to do now. Mission assignments certainly were not random—they were made carefully and systematically—and now that it was known that Chrys's mission was important, it was simply not possible to make the decision in the same way it would have been made before. In that sense the Closers had already scored some points—knowing we would do something to damage them, they had forced us to change that decision. That didn't mean we wouldn't come up with something else to hurt them, merely that whatever it was we had had before was now lost to us.

Weighed against that, though, was the fact that Chrysamen and I were still alive; the Closers must be worried pretty badly back at their headquarters, on whatever Earth that might be. Moreover, we had at least the start of a plan—do whatever we had been planning to do before.

The drawback to that, of course, was that if we stuck with it, clearly they would know what our next move was.

And yet they might not, for the one thing they could not know was whether we would stay on our original plan or not . . . .

The arguments went on and on. They kept circling back—if you ever try to think about time travel for any length of time, you'll notice that's what your thoughts do, keep returning to their original point—and finally they settled on the fact that they had a mission already planned for me which they knew was at least potentially going to hurt the Closers, and with a bit of luck what use they were to make of Chrys would soon turn up as well.

So, finally, after all the discussion, it boiled down to their doing exactly what they would have done anyway—sending me home for some leave, prepping me for the same first mission they'd have sent me on anyway, and putting Chrys into the pool of agents waiting to be assigned missions. It seemed like a lot of discussion to get to that point, but then I'm either a professional esthete or a professional thug, depending on which job you count as primary, not a politician, and maybe a politician would see matters differently.

One thing I'll say for ATN, when they make a decision they make it, and they put it into practice, and there's very little nonsense in between. Of course, from the standpoint of Chrys and me getting some hours together, this was no advantage at all. We had about fifteen minutes to say that we liked each other, we didn't think we'd see each other again for years, and it sure would have been nice but we'd write when we could. Then Chrysamen ja N'wook was headed to the new ATN training base (in a timeline the Closers hadn't found yet), and they were getting me dressed in the clothes for my home timeline, handing me all the materials I was supposed to have, and briefing me as quickly as possible about everything that had happened that I needed to know.

The big surprise was that another governor nobody had ever heard of was president, and again, after electing him, people mostly didn't like him. Porter had turned out to be unusually talented musically so she was getting a lot of private piano and violin lessons. My sister Carrie was apparently continuing her career in physics and getting some kind of acclaim for it, my father was on some consulting gig in the Middle East, and everyone was pretty much fine.

Oh, and with accumulated pay converted first to gold, then to marks, and finally to dollars, I was now a millionaire twenty times over, after taxes. Not a bad thing to know . . .

The transfer was simple. An ATN courier who looked something like me got onto an airliner headed into Pittsburgh, with a ticket in my name, checking all the bags I had taken with me to the alternate timelines. The courier went into the bathroom, locked the door, and signaled; then the ATN crew opened a portal between the two timelines, right into the airliner bathroom. He stepped out and handed me the ticket; I got in, they closed the portal, and I walked back to my seat.

I noticed one bored-looking man, balding with a bushy beard and huge black eyebrows, a typical college-prof type, who looked up from his book and watched me closely, as if he didn't quite recognize me. He shrugged, as anyone would; after all, there's no way for one guy to go into an airliner bathroom and another to come out, right? Still, the fact that he had noticed at all would have to go into my report. No point getting sloppy—the Closers know where our timeline is and there's always a risk of reinvasion.

If you like giant shopping malls with high prices and a lot of very upset children, the Pittsburgh air terminal is terrific. Otherwise, it's a place to hurry through. I got off the plane, not really expecting there to be anyone to meet me, and to my surprise Robbie and Porter were waiting for me. Robbie Wilmadottir looked her usual self—small, lean, dark-haired, with a crew cut, eyes darting around all the time. She was in skirt, flat shoes, and sweater, dressed more like a woman than usual, though I noted that the jacket she was wearing over the sweater was the usual heavy-grade polyester thing that hides (not well) a thin sheet of Kevlar and provides enough space to make a shoulder holster less conspicuous. Go to any rock concert, any place where a prominent politician is speaking, or any time a big movie star has a press conference, hang around looking crazy and talking to yourself, and you get to meet people who wear jackets just like that.

Porter Brunreich, my ward, seemed to be three inches taller. She was wearing ripped jeans, a sweatshirt for Oxford University (I wondered for a moment if Oxford actually *had* sweatshirts), a backward tractor cap, and a pretty amazing number of earrings in each ear; it occurred to me that after all the trouble I'd gone to keeping her from getting holes in her body, she'd probably put more holes in her ears than the Closers would have in the rest of her. I told them they both looked terrific, and I meant it about Robbie.

"Nice to have you back, boss. Do I have to stop embezzling from the till?" Robbie asked.

"Hi, Mark," Porter said. "You look pretty good yourself. Who picked out your suit?"

I grinned at her. "I don't suppose the court would look on it kindly if I locked you in your room for the next five years, but think of the studying you could get done for college." I draped an arm around her shoulders, and we went off to catch the silly little train that takes you to baggage claim.

Robbie had the Mercedes convertible waiting for me in short-term parking; knowing she likes to drive it a lot, I suggested she drive us home. Porter got into the backseat, we rolled the top down, and we were off.

It was a bright, clear, not-cold October afternoon, the kind that makes you think about football and hayrides and all that other Americana, when you know it will get cold that night but right now the air just has a pleasant bite to it. Porter leaned forward to get her head between me and Robbie, and we conversed in occasional shouts.

"I'm legally required," I bellowed, "to ask you how school is going."

"*Ça va,*" Porter shouted.

"You're taking French?"

"No, but all my friends are. I'm taking Latin."

It was a typical Pittsburgh fall day, all right; people were lurching onto the Parkway like maniacs, and Robbie was veering around all those pop-up roadblocks gracefully. I saw a couple of surprised old codgers suddenly realizing we had been there as we roared past. Public conveyances eight hundred years in a more advanced future may actually move faster and be safer, but there's a lot more romance in a plain old piece of German iron with a ragtop.

A lot of Porter's blond hair had escaped from the back of her cap and was whipping around in the wind; it occurred to me that uncool as it might be to be seen with adults, when I was her age I'd certainly have been delighted to be seen in a car like this.

"Okay, so school's okay. Now I'm supposed to tell you that you can bring all your problems to me."

"Sure, if anyone's trying to shoot me!" she said. "Violence to you; math, science, and love life to Carrie; Latin and history to the Prof [that's what she calls my father]; and athletic coaching to Robbie and Paula."

"I wasn't aware you had a love life!" I kept my tone light, but I have to admit that the idea made me a little nervous; first of all, it's bad enough to be the de facto father of a teenager, but when she's a target for an organization which could, if it wanted, infiltrate an assassin who looked for all the world like a ninth-grade boy . . . well, let's say it doesn't really add to the normal Dad-paranoia, but it sure gives you a great excuse for it.

"Not yet!" Porter said. "But with Carrie's advice, there's always hope."

Well, Sis wouldn't steer Porter too far wrong, anyway. Not necessarily in the direction I'd pick, but not *wrong*. Always assuming you could steer Porter at all. I tried not to assume that.

"What's this I hear about you and music?"

"Well, they say I have talent," she said.

"Hah!" Robbie said.

"'Hah' she has talent, or 'Hah!' they say that?" I asked.

"'Hah!' Porter has talent like water is wet and the sky is up." Robbie downshifted, shot us around a truck through a hole that I wouldn't have said was there, whipped us back into the right-hand lane, and added, "Let me steal her thunder. She's performing with the symphony tomorrow night. One piece each, piano, violin, cello, and flute. The critics are calling her the phenomenon of the century, and they're right, whatever you might think of them."

"You don't even like classical music much," Porter pointed out. "And, okay, yeah, I'm pretty good, but I know I could be a lot better; I've got a lot of work to do."

By now I was gaping. "You learned all four instruments in the two years since I saw you last?"

"No, I started Suzuki violin when I was three and did it for five years. But I didn't have much idea what music was all about when I was eight, and my hands wouldn't do what I wanted them to, so I got bored." That last sentence came out as a shriek; Robbie, who always drove with the radio on, had heard that the Fort Pitt tunnel was closed, and made an across-four-lanes last-minute diversion to 51 South, to take us through the Liberty Tubes and into the city that way. "Yeah, I know I'm supposed to be good and all that," she added as we began to rocket down the highway again. Fifty-one winds a lot, working its way along the back side of the ridge that separates it from the Allegheny, and it's in comparatively lousy shape; Robbie was being held down to not more than twenty over the speed limit. A lot of cops knew me, knew her, and knew the car, and it was a good thing most of them liked us.

"It sounds more like you're a genius," I said, and from the face she made at me I knew she'd heard that particular word too often.

"Yeah, right," she said. "You know what a genius is?"

"A chick who stays home on prom night," Robbie volunteered.

"No kidding," Porter said. "And not only that, it's also somebody that teachers and everyone act completely weird around. I mean, I love you and your family, Mark, and Robbie and Paula are great, but . . . you know, I want some friends who are . . . uh . . . "

"Your own age," I finished for her. "Understood. I hope I've at least got a ticket to see you play. I promise I'll wear a suit and behave myself at the performance."

"Of course you have a ticket!" she said. "Um, um . . . there's this one other thing, too."

"I'll be sitting next to a boy, and you don't want me to act like a geek in front of him."

"Don't I wish! No, it's just something else . . . Carrie said I could ask you after the concert but I thought if maybe you got a chance to think about it first. . . . Well, anyway, I just don't want to sneak around and surprise you or anything, I wanted to ask permission . . . "

"If it's marriage, heroin, or enlisting, the answer is no; otherwise, we can discuss it," I said.

"I want to have my nose pierced."

"Then again, if it's marriage, heroin, enlisting, or getting your nose pierced . . . " I tried to keep the tone light because I really didn't want to have an argument with her about it. It also occurred to me that I'd better see what Sis had come up with in the way of answers to that one; Porter was a good kid, but any kid will try to play both ends against the middle.

"Aw, Mark . . . "

"I didn't actually say 'no,'" I pointed out. "I was teasing you till I get used to the idea. I know a lot of

women younger than me—a lot younger than me—
do that. It looks horrible to me, and I hate like hell
to imagine having a cold with one of those. But I
also know that if you change your mind later the
hole will heal up pretty fast, so it's not like a tattoo;
I figure chances are that there aren't many infec-
tions or I wouldn't see so many girls doing it; and
besides, you aren't interested, really, in how your
guardian reacts to it, but in how kids your age do. So
I'm going to wait and think a little, okay?"

"Okay. I knew you'd be reasonable."

"If I'm being reasonable, it's only with an effort.
Bear in mind that your guardian also thinks of it as
'mutilating your nose,' okay?"

"'Kay. I won't bring it up for . . . oh, a week?"

"Deal," I said. "By that time I'll try to have an
opinion instead of a reaction."

I'm not parent material, and getting stuck being
one was not the best of things that could have happened to me. Still, if you have to do it, I recommend
the way I got into it—Porter already knew me and
trusted me long before her dad died and left me as
her guardian, and she didn't move in with my family until she was thirteen. That meant nobody had a
habit of thinking of her as a little girl to overcome,
and moreover she didn't have any past memories of
thinking of us as omnipotent.

She thought of *Robbie* as omnipotent . . .

It left me smiling a little to think that. From the
first day we'd been guarding that kid, Robbie had
been her hero.

"What?" Porter demanded.

"What what?"

"You were smiling."

"Well, I'll never do that again, then."

"Mark!"

"You're a terrific kid, Porter, I'm very proud of you, and I love you very much."

"Oh, sure. Pull out your sneakiest tricks," she said, but she was smiling, and she didn't hassle me again about my mystery smile.

Robbie took a second to wink at me—I'm never sure how I feel about her taking her eyes off the road—zipped around to the left, and took us into the Liberty Tubes.

Say what you like about Pittsburgh, coming into it from any direction, the view is amazing. From either of the tunnels, you come bursting out of the dark and there's the whole mighty array of skyscrapers in the Golden Triangle right in front of you across the Monongahela. From there it was only a few minutes home to Frick Park.

Dad came bustling out, a big healthy guy with a mane of white hair, and a moment later Paula (Robbie's partner and the other reason my agency keeps functioning in my absence) came around the corner pushing Carrie's wheelchair. The gathering was complete.

There was a certain awkwardness, glad as I was to see Robbie and Paula, for they always had the impression that I was doing secret work for a federal agency that couldn't be named, and thus I couldn't exactly talk about where I'd been or what I'd been doing. Dad had set up sort of a small party that afternoon, and we all sat around and talked about nothing and laughed.

Finally, at dinner, after Robbie and Paula had gone—and for Porter's safety, I had made sure the .45 was ready for action and that the SHAKK was in easy reach—we all sat down around the table, and I told them about what I'd been up to. I wasn't sure whether I should be pleased or embarrassed at the interest that Porter and Carrie took in Chrysamen. I explained again that I wasn't likely to see her for a long time, that we were actually from centuries apart, and that anyway Crux Ops age at different rates from each other because we get different durations and schedules for missions. "Chrys and I could end up thirty years apart in age or more, within just a few years," I explained. "And it's just . . . well, it's a very close friendship," I said, "but it's not exactly a romance, yet, and we're going to write, but it's important not to have too much hope about that."

They both nodded solemnly, which immediately told me that they didn't believe a word of it. It figured. Carrie had been twenty-three when the bomb went off, which made it a lot tougher for her to have a love life. Porter was still too young to have any idea. That is, they were both naive enough to believe that love conquered all.

After Porter went off to do some homework, and Carrie was enlisted to help her through it, I was left alone with Dad. Now that there were just the two of us, he said, "Welcome home again, son. Sounds like you've given a good account of yourself."

"Fair, I'd say," I said. "Dad, what the hell do you suppose all this means? I know I'm smarter than most people, and I'm good in a fight, but why, out of all the tens of thousands of Crux Ops scattered across a couple of million timelines, would the Closers dedicate themselves to killing just one rookie?"

"Well," Dad said, "my first thought is that the Closers who have attacked you are from somewhere in the future of the timelines you were in. There's something they know will happen because of you and this Chrysamen ja N'wook. That's about all I can say."

"But what am I going to do?" I asked.

"You may not even know when you do it," Dad pointed out. "Suppose you were a machine gunner for the Brits in World War I. One day things went just a little differently, and you bagged Adolf Hitler; a month later you were with an antiaircraft battery and you got Goering with a lucky shot. World War II would be a pretty different affair, and all because of you, but how would you ever know that? Even if you knew about the existence of other timelines—how would you know which, of the thousands of things you had done, had made the difference? Grant, Sherman, Lee, and Stonewall Jackson all served near each other in the Mexican War. Get them all into one bar and give them bad liquor, and what would have happened to the Civil War? And would the guy who distilled the liquor, or the unimportant lieutenant who invited all of them to come along, have ever known what he'd done?"

I sighed. "Yeah, I know. Still, it's a pretty oppressive thing to have hanging over your head. I'd a lot rather have been insignificant."

"Wouldn't we all. Nobody gets that choice, Mark, nobody. If you're a king or president, it might be very obvious that you're significant, but think about what I just said. You never know. The guy that washes a windshield doesn't do his job right, a smear on the windshield picks up the glare, a car goes off the road, and the girl who would have been mother of a Nobel Prize winner dies at age ten. That windshield washer doesn't know.

"You don't even get to pick which way things go, or whether doing your job well is the best thing you can do. Suppose you're a bus driver and you're careful to be on schedule. A guy running late for the bus doesn't get on yours—and he never meets the people who would have given him his start in business, and a whole giant corporation doesn't happen. You can only see a short way into the future, and absolutely not reliably. You don't have to have traveled across twenty timelines to know that."

I leaned back and thought for a long moment. Dad had sort of a sardonic grin under his halo of white hair. Sourly, I said, "That's not fair, all the same."

"Unh-hunh. If we had any choice, none of us would go to the future without a firm contract."

I had to grin at that. *If we had the choice . . .*

Anyway, I quit worrying and let myself relax into my old life. At the bodyguard agency, I answered the phone, talked to people, set them up with guards, and did no work myself. I spent a fair amount of time walking in the park with Porter, talked with Dad about various alternate worlds I'd visited or heard about, tried to get Carrie to explain a few things to me about what she was doing— apparently what I had told her was possible was having some kind of influence on her work, and she was trying to figure out how a projectile could draw on the heat of its passage for propulsion—and, in general, spent two glorious months of working out to stay in shape, shooting a lot to stay sharp, and unwinding till I was comfortable, healthy, and bored out of my mind.

Porter played her date with the symphony, and offers started to come in from everywhere. There was a brief period of reporters tromping through the house, because besides Porter's status as a prodigy, they connected her with me, and me with my father's long battle with Blade of the Most Merciful, the Closer front group in our timeline, and with the "heroic recovery" stories they used to do about Sis. They dredged up the fact that Blade terrorists had killed Porter's mother before her eyes (in fact, Closer agents had been trying to kill Porter, but her mother had switched passports) and that her father had died in prison. There was even a little bit in there about me; just who I worked for that caused me to be absent for so much of the time (and made me so well-off) was a regular matter for speculation.

I didn't worry about that. Nobody in my timeline was going to figure it out, and the Closers already knew who I worked for and where I was. If they wanted to try to come and get me, well, they'd had a shot or two at me before, and it hadn't gotten them very far.

There was a letter from Chrysamen every day, and I wrote back every day, too. The letters appeared and disappeared from the small safe in my office;

sometime during the night a tiny crosstime port would automatically open. Outgoing mail would leave and incoming mail would arrive. For weeks there was just Chrysamen's letter, and every other week a large paycheck in dollars (which I deposited locally) and an obscenely large paycheck in Swiss francs (which I mailed to a bank in Zurich, via a drop service in Amsterdam that looked like an art history journal).

We talked about a lot—family and friends, how bored she was waiting in Hawaii to get her assignment, how we never quite had enough time to get to know each other. At least we were still in sync, one of her days corresponding to one of mine.

One day Porter and I were coming back from the airport after a trip out of town. She had gone to St. Louis for a concert with the symphony there—and to demonstrate the three new instruments she had also acquired in less than a month's time. Thanksgiving had been a few days before, and mostly we were talking about Christmas plans.

"They won't call you up just before the holiday, will they?" she asked.

"They try not to do that to anyone. But I'm expecting to have to go in the first week of January or so."

She nodded. "There's something I was going to talk to you about. I've been thinking I want to cut back on the concerts . . . there's something I'd like to work on."

I nodded, being careful not to apply too much pressure, in case this was a momentary whim. "It's very much your choice, Porter."

"I know. But I'm a little nervous, and I'd like to make the change while you're here."

"Make what change?" I asked.

"I'd like to work more on composition. Now that I understand so many instruments . . . well, I'm realizing part of the problem I'm having with not always liking what I play is that there isn't much music written that's really what I want to hear." She turned a little sideways in the car seat, to face me more. "Do you think that will be okay? Are people going to get mad if I cut back on public appearances? And will it make the reporters come back?"

"No way of telling, but I don't think it will be a problem. Especially if you don't cut it back to zero." I shrugged. "You're the one who knows anything about this, Porter. If you say you want to do, say, just a few concerts a year, and put more of your time into composition, I think mostly you'll just get a very attentive hearing."

"Good." She took a long pause. "And can I get my nose pierced?"

"It's your nose, kid."

I never did get used to that little lump of gold on the side of her nose, but I was as good a sport as I could manage. I even got her a tiny gold hoop for it for Christmas.

Letters kept getting longer between Chrys and me. She finally got notified that she was being put in command of a standby combat team—ten people that would come in shooting when a big situation demanded major action. If you figured how many targets they could actually *hit* per minute, those ten people had greater firepower than one of our infantry divisions. But since it cost a lot, even by ATN standards, to move much mass back in time, they would probably not go at all during the year she would be assigned to the team. It was fundamentally a training command—the officer was at the top of her class, but the other fighters were at the bottom, people who were good enough to pull a trigger but had to be watched. She was bitterly disappointed.

On January 3, I got my orders. I had two days for good-byes, and then I was off to the crosstime port in Manhattan; in the timeline where the mission was, I would be landing in colonial Boston, 1775.

At least I figured I knew the basics of what would be going on.

5

"Excuse my asking, but what language is that?" The woman in the aisle seat looked kind and grand-motherly, but she was leaning way over the middle seat to look at the Crux Operations briefing I was reading. The flight to La Guardia is short, but some flights aren't short enough.

"I am your pardon please?" I replied.

"What-a language-o is that?" she asked, very broadly and loudly. Some people believe that any foreigner will understand them if they just talk slowly and loudly enough.

"Tilde umlaut?" I said brightly.

She peered at me closely and then, with a slight click of the tongue, went back to her airline maga-zine. I got back into my briefing.

I'd read it before, but you never know which little fact is going to turn out to be important, so you try to get as much of it into memory as you possibly can.

The timeline I was going to was one deliberately created by ATN, one that would eventually (it was hoped) become a powerful and well-armed ally. Though crosstime travel was fairly cheap, if you went forward or backward in time, the cost went up enormously, so that when either the Closers or ATN started most new timelines, they usually did it by sending a single agent back in time to a crux, a period when things could have gone very differently.

Even then, the agent had to work pretty hard. Timelines like to remerge with each other, so it's generally only possible at a crux to get a new timeline started fast enough, and make it diverge far enough from its "parent" line, and at the crux you still have to do everything you can to make matters different. History can stay perfectly on track with slight discrepancies. (Ever find yourself arguing with someone about something you remember perfectly? A little micro-crux may have opened in your life at that point—and closed up afterward, leaving two people with slightly different memories.) Thus the new timeline not only has to be made different, it has to be made *drastically* different, or the timelines will reconverge, leaving nothing but puzzles for historians. Ever wonder about Pope Joan, Prester John, Atlantis, the Seven Cities of Cibola? Or why it's so difficult to find cities like Camelot and Tarshish archaeologically? All of those, I suspect, were failed crux changes, either from ATN or Closer operations, or just maybe from other organizations or individuals that we don't know about.

Rey Luc, the Special Agent on the job, had really

taken that lesson to heart. He had arrived in London, in the same timeline our history comes from, in 1738, as a man in his mid-twenties, and set up shop as a doctor, investor, and eccentric scientist. With some judicious use of antibiotics and nanos, he had achieved a reputation for miracle cures.

In 1751, in our timeline, Frederick, the Prince of Wales, son of George II and father of George III, died after a brief illness caused by an abscessed injury. George II lasted till 1760, and was replaced by George III—the "Fat George" that the American colonies were to rebel against, "Mad George" who was to pose such a problem to British politicians during the Napoleonic age.

Now, George III wasn't a particularly stupid man; he was headstrong and had bad advice, and once he formed an opinion he tended to stay with it. He'd have fit in perfectly in the Johnson or Nixon White Houses as a staffer in charge of Vietnam policy. But he was generous and loyal to his friends, perhaps a bit too easily led in his younger years, maybe a little too easily manipulated—none of these needed to be fatal character flaws. His real tragedy was probably only that he came to the throne at the age of twenty-one, when he had many of the common failings of young men, and because there were few to tell him no, he never really outgrew them.

Still, his record as king was mixed, not atrocious; Britain had worse monarchs as well as better ones, and there were many places where he showed some real talent for government.

If his father had just lasted a few years longer—and his grandfather had lasted not quite so long—

George III could have come to the throne as a mature, self-confident man. If he could have gotten a better education, instead of being spoiled by the tutors his mother found for him (mostly for political reasons rather than their knowledge or wisdom), he might also have been a capable and effective person.

So that was the first thing Rey Luc set out to change. He cured Frederick in 1751—probably just some penicillin would have done it, but it sounded as if he'd used the nanos to really fix the old guy up. He managed things one way or another (that's a part of the job I'll never get to like) so that within a year of that, George II died nine years early.

(I've known many Special Agents, and that's a part of the job they just won't talk about. Usually it's done with tailored viruses aimed at one particular individual to produce a sudden, painless death in sleep—their heart just shuts down. And of course when a historical figure is "erased"—the euphemism most of them use—he or she is still alive in the main time frame, so in a sense they are just killing one of the alternatives. But killing is killing, and most of them always feel a little sick about having to do it.)

Frederick was a smart man, and an efficient king. He saw to the education of his son—and Rey Luc saw to it that it was a different education. Most fundamentally, Luc arranged to get a special tutor hired for the future George III, a man who would have been a good influence on anyone: Benjamin Franklin.

When I hit that part I nearly choked with laughter. Franklin, of course, was already known in Europe by the time, and had made a good name for himself in a dozen ways; he was an obvious choice, and one could hardly imagine a better teacher for the young prince.

Meanwhile, Rey Luc had not been idle in other areas, either. Britain and her American colonies in the 1700s were among the most progressive, forward-thinking, and innovative societies on Earth, but that was still only by eighteenth-century standards. Ideas developed very slowly by the standards of even 1850, and it wasn't even very clearly understood that technological changes could make big differences in life.

Through a dozen fronts and hidden organizations, Rey Luc set out to give technology a big push. Better steels were introduced, and cheaper ways of making them; the steam engine came along quickly. The Minié ball made breech-loading rifles possible and was an idea that could have been invented any time from the mid-1500s onward; in our timeline it took till almost the American Civil War, but Rey Luc had the British army equipped with breech-loading rifles at the beginning of the Seven Years' War in 1754. By 1760, there were electric motors and generators (though they were crude), and by 1765 the first dirigibles were flying regular service in the Thirteen Colonies and around Britain.

The Seven Years' War wasn't called that, because it had lasted just two; the better ships and cannon of the British Navy had swept the French from the seas, frontiersmen equipped with bolt-action rifles had chased the French and Indian forces back to Canada and taken every chunk of French land on the mainland, and on Christmas Day 1755, Paris had surrendered to British invaders. Thus instead of the Seven Years' War (as Europeans call it in our timeline) or the French and Indian War (as we call it), it was known simply as the Conquest War. After some strategic purchases, it left Britain in possession of North America from the Nueces River and the Columbia River north, all of India, and great parts of France itself.

In the aftermath of the war, the young George, as Prince of Wales, had taken an extended tour of the American colonies. He had visited Boston, Charleston, New York, and Baltimore. With Colonel George Washington as his guide, he had gone up the frontier road through Ticonderoga and Saratoga to Canada, come back via a ship across Lake Erie and through Fort Pitt, met town merchants, farmers, frontiersmen, and ordinary people, and been cheered wherever he went. In one of Luc's reports he had noted, with justifiable pride, that in *this* timeline, George III was the most passionately pro-American person in Britain.

Luc had been a busy little devil—all Special Agents starting timelines are—and he'd also managed to introduce the ideas of Adam Smith, David Ricardo, and the other early free-market economists more than a generation early; not that they were the last word, or that their solutions would work for all purposes, but by tying the British Empire together into a vast free-trade area, he had managed to create fast economic growth and the basic conditions for peace—merchants are not big fans of war, France was disarmed, Russia not yet a serious foe, Spain and Holland too weak to challenge Britain, and thus the whole world had a very small number of men at arms, and trade rather than war was the major activity.

Last and not at all least, he was encouraging George to have a lot of kids, and maneuvering those kids onto every throne he could find—a step not unlike the one that Queen Victoria took naturally, a century later, in our timeline.

The plan was that by 1800, there would be railways from Savannah to Quebec City and all over Britain, dirigible service across the Atlantic, and a British-controlled telegraph net from Rangoon to the American Pacific Northwest. By 1850, there would be airplanes, telephones, and a world federation of peoples built around the British royal family; and by 1900, human beings would be settling the Moon and Mars, ocean farming would abolish hunger, and the ATN would have a new powerful and prosperous ally.

The one catch in all of those splendid plans was a great big one.

After a routine report in 1771, detailing the first actions of King George since Frederick had died the year before, and explaining that he himself was going to go to Boston to move along the dawning railroad industry and push the movement to change the Empire into a Federation, Rey Luc had disappeared. There were no further reports and no word of any kind. Moreover, thus far ATN's Time Scouts had been unable to find any of the descendants of the new timeline, which meant that it was still in a state of "chronflux"—whichever way it was going to go had not settled out, and there were at least some high probabilities that it wouldn't go in the direction ATN had been aiming for.

Time for a Crux Op, then. Chances were that Rey Luc had died, been taken sick, or otherwise gone off the case, and things had slipped in his absence. Another possibility was that matters had simply turned out to be very delicate indeed, and his communications were being lost in the chronflux—in which case the attempt to transmit me would get nowhere, and I'd be on vacation for another month.

There was also, always, the possibility that the Closers had intervened, but normally that was a low probability—even though the two sides were at bitter war, time, with all its parallel tracks, is *big*. Agents only rarely ran into each other—most of the time ATN and Closers developed their own set of timelines without the other side even being aware of it. Of our million and a half timelines, the Closers knew about perhaps six thousand; of their two or three million, we knew of only ten thousand or so.

This was a different case, though, because the Closers had taken such an interest in me. It was quite possible that they had found and invaded this time track, and they might well be there waiting for me in force.

I sighed and put the briefings back in my case. The pilot was just announcing the approach to La Guardia; I had flown into it in another timeline where it was called Jimmy Walker, and in one where it was called Charles de Gaulle, but given the size of the flat patch in Queens, and the rarity of such in the city, if they had airplanes, there was usually an airport there. Moreover, it was usually a boring, routine place, and all the ones I had been to had been old and beat-up.

The cab ride was dull, the city seemed drab in the gray January midafternoon, and nobody was around on the quiet floor of the midtown office building that was my destination. I used my key, walked in, checked my watch—half an hour to go—and went to the can, sitting down to read the briefings again. By now I figured I could even spot Rey in any wig, which was going to be important—his introduction of rayon had led to the spread of wigs down the social ladder (when they didn't have to be made of human hair, and would stay white without powdering, they could be a lot cheaper). Rey would probably be wearing one, and there was no telling what the fashionable shape for them would be by the time I got there, so I needed to know his face in any hair.

When the portal opened, I was ready. I stepped through into a prep room—there was nothing to indicate the century or the timeline, it was just a white room with nothing in it except a table with the things I needed arranged on it. I picked up a backpack that held more supplies, a freshly charged and loaded NIF and SHAKK, and a large array of technical information in very small electronic storage (not just the *Encyclopedia Britannica* on a pinhead, but several of the great libraries of a variety of timelines in a container the size of a matchbox). I set my old SHAKK down on the table for the routine maintenance guys to pick up, changed quickly into a period outfit, and glanced through my trunk to make sure I had decent clothing for where I was going, indicated I was ready by saying so, and felt the world go abruptly dark, darker than it ever is except in a deep cave.

Sound and weight disappeared together, and then the sense of having a body. A pale gray halftone light, even in all directions, swelled up around me, and the low rumble that always came at this point, and then the world began to swim into existence around me, first shapes and vague sounds, then colors and tones, and finally with detail and precision.

I was in the upstairs room of the Quiet Woman tavern, on Arch Street, in Boston, April 1775. At least that part had gone right—by dropping a note with a couple of gold pieces into the local postal service, Crux Operations had set up the room for me. Well, it was the right place, there was no one here, and a note on the pillow of the small bed said that the owner hoped it was all in accord with my wishes. Thus far thus good.

I moved my trunk to a better location and began to get things into some kind of order. It was midafternoon when I arrived, and I figured the first day would be a matter of looking for anything big and obviously wrong, but I wasn't expecting to find anything like that. Usually, at least according to the training, it took a while to see what wasn't the way it should be.

Of course in my own experience, I had just lunged out into Nazi-occupied San Francisco, and been attacked by crazed Boy Scouts, but then what did I know? The odds of anything big happening the first time I walked out the door were practically zero.

I made sure everything was in good order, and all the stuff that was supposed to be concealed was well concealed. Then I sat down on the bed to think for a moment.

There was a knock at the door. "Come in," I said.

The woman who came in looked strangely like a high-school pageant version of a colonial woman, because though the clothing style was not much different in general line from what I remembered of fashion history, some of the materials were obviously synthetic, and the dress itself hung a little strangely—I suspected that undergarments had changed and perhaps were not as voluminous.

"Oh, hello, Mr. Strang, I didn't see you come in," she said. "I was coming up to ask if you'd be with us long?"

"Well, I have business in the city," I said, "and so I might be here some months."

She giggled; now that I looked more closely I saw that she was about seventeen or eighteen at oldest. "Business in the city? And so you do. I was wondering, sir, if perhaps your quarters at Province House were in need of repair or some such, and as I'd heard nothing from tradesmen about that, I thought perhaps you might know how long you'd need this room."

"Oh," I said, completely baffled. There had been a message to Rey Luc but he hadn't acknowledged it; had he perhaps set me up with a room elsewhere in the city and then for some reason not told anyone else? But then why would anyone else know I might have been there? And anyway, the translator chip behind my right ear had just supplied the information that Province House, in Marlborough Street, was where the Royal Governor's residence was.

It was a bit like checking into a Motel Six in Washington, D.C., and having them assume you normally stayed at the White House.

All that took just a moment to think. "I suppose then that you hadn't heard. Well, I was hoping to keep the matter quiet—a little disagreement, you know, one of those things where it just seemed best—"

"You can count on me," she said, and winked broadly. She set down a large pitcher of water, which the thing in my ear told me was for washing and drinking, and then went out. From the way she had smiled and the interest she took in my business, I concluded that whatever it was that she thought was going on would be all over town before I ever got downstairs onto the street.

Well, there was clearly no reason to delay and a lot of reasons to get moving. I tucked my .45 into my shoulder holster, concealed the SHAKK in a special pocket inside the coat between my shoulder blades, and tucked the NIF into a special slot in my left boot. I was ready for a lot.

Then I pulled out my transponder tracker. All Special Agents, Time Scouts, and Crux Ops have a surgically implanted radio transmitter that charges up off your body heat and runs for ten years after you're dead. It's a low-powered weak affair, and it only transmits in the event of a coded signal, to prevent the enemy getting any use out of it, but if you're within about two miles, you're wearing a transponder, and a tracker switches on, it should be able to get at least a direction and an estimate of distance on you.

There was nothing. This didn't necessarily mean anything—he could be back in London, or over in New York, or anywhere else. His last three messages had said he was making Boston his headquarters, but that had been four years ago. For all I knew he'd decided to take some time off and go find himself with a guru in Tibet.

There were voices on the stairs. "Well, gentlemen, if you have business with him, you can ask him yourself." It was the voice of the girl who had come in to check the room.

A soft voice said something I couldn't hear, and then a louder one added, "How the deuce did he get all the way here so quickly anyway? Unless perhaps his engagement up in the Mill Pond went faster than he imagined it would. And thank God we ran into your father, Sally, or we'd have gone over to Province House instead—"

Three possibilities. Mark Strang is a common name; maybe they just had the wrong one. Rey Luc was doing fine but for some reason couldn't even manage to leave a note in an emergency drop box; thus these were men to take me to him.

Or they were Closer agents, and I was totally blown—my mission and I were hopelessly un-secret to the enemy.

If there was another Mark Strang, and he was an important guy in the town, the odds that nobody had talked to him about this room reservation were zip. And I could think of no way that a man could pick up signals from base, arrange meetings and deliveries, and yet be unable to put a note inside any of a dozen locking boxes, for ATN to retrieve.

So it was probably Possibility Three: the Closers were here already.

All that I had in that room was a change of clothes, all the weapons were already on me, so I checked the view out the window. By now their footsteps were reaching the top of the stairs.

There was a large overhang under my window, and it seemed to reach a third of the way into the street. I rolled out my window, slid down the roof of the overhang, clutched the wooden-trough rain gutter, let myself drop into the street, and walked away in a hurry. Whenever you do something weird, get away from the witnesses as fast as you can.

People seemed very surprised, but I avoided making eye contact and hurried through an alley that wound about as it led away.

The alley made two more bends and came into a small dark courtyard. It was what you expect in a preindustrial, or just barely industrial, city—a muddy, filthy space ringed by two- and three-story buildings in bad repair, in which wash was hung out to dry and into which garbage pails and chamber pots were emptied. Fortunately someone had laid a board sidewalk around it to where another alley led away.

As I went around on the boards, which rolled and bounced beneath my feet, I heard odd scurrying noises. It did seem strange that there were no children watching me, or at least none I could see; normally a place like this is full of kids, housewives, goats, and chickens . . .

No one spoke to me, but now that I looked

around I could see a ball, a hoop, and stick, and something that probably was a hobbyhorse on a stick, much handed down. Moreover, I had to step over smeared areas where a goat had probably been tied. It was as if everyone had left just seconds before I came.

The next alley wound to the north, and I figured I was probably making toward what's now Franklin Place. I had been there a few times in my own timeline, but this was going to be different—so much land had been filled in, especially around the Neck, that the peninsula was a completely different shape.

Sure enough, there was a bigger street there; there were no street signs to identify it, but I doubt that any eighteenth-century cities had street signs anyway. I slipped quietly out of the alley and merged as inconspicuously as possible into the foot traffic.

Or I tried to, anyway. As I passed two distinguished-looking gentlemen, they tipped their hats and greeted me by name. A woman nodded and wished me, "Good day, Mr. Strang."

"Thursday at one o' the clock, Mr. Strang," another called out, tapping his forehead with the palm of his hand, clearly reminding himself of an appointment he believed that we had.

I nodded and waved back; no one seemed to find these things unusual. I let myself slow a bit, took a coin from my pocket, and turned to buy an apple from a street vendor. The apples were small and scrawny by the standards of a twentieth-century supermarket, and had probably spent the winter in a cellar, but good "keeping apples" are usually sweet.

"Oh, no, Mr. Strang, just take one if you like," the vendor said. "Gift for His Majesty's servant. Always glad to be of help."

It was on the tip of my tongue to just ask him outright what I was doing for His Majesty these days, but I nodded, took the apple, and thanked him warmly.

The apple was what I expected—mealy but sweet and with a strong flavor. If someone could persuade this timeline to hang on to its genetic stocks for a century or two, they'd have at least one terrific export ready to go.

Another advantage of eating an apple: you can keep your hand over your face. Fewer people seemed to recognize me.

Now to do some thinking. Clearly not only did everyone here think they'd seen Mark Strang before, but they thought they knew Mark Strang well, and they knew him by sight. A common name is one thing, but an identical twin in another timeline . . . wouldn't be odd at all. But not in this century, surely?

All right. Facts I knew. Something was seriously wrong in this timeline. Somebody who was apparently me was already here. He lived at Province House, which was the governor's mansion.

That was where I needed to go, then; for what it was worth, I wouldn't be conspicuous there, or at least not until my doppelgänger turned up. Whatever the answers were, they were more likely to be there than anywhere else.

I was on the brink of asking someone for directions when I realized that *that* would really be the height of conspicuousness—a prominent citizen, probably a government official, asking where the governor's house was? No way.

It wasn't as bad as I thought it might be. After a while I noticed that a few buildings every so often would have a street number plus a street name on their placards, and by dint of a lot of wandering around, and keeping in mind that Marlborough Street was one of the largest in town (it was part of the old High Street that was now known successively as Orange Street along the Neck, Newbury Street as it neared South End, then Marlborough and finally Cornhill), I eventually found, after walking nearly to the Long Wharf, what I hoped was the right direction. It was a good long walk, and my shoes were unfortunately much too authentic—this was a long time before the development of the concept of right and left shoes, and my feet were beginning to kill me.

I could see, ahead of me, one of the few buildings that the little interpreter in the back corner of my head seemed to recognize. The gadget told me it was the State House, and I realized that, with a modification or two, I was looking at something I had seen in my own time.

A light went on in my head; Cornhill, Marlborough, and the rest were actually Washington Street. Now that I knew where I was, I could just go there, and I began to walk quickly, even though my feet hurt, and I had been walking for a couple of hours.

I had expected Boston to look Georgian—it was the Georgian era, and had been for decades, so I was expecting a lot of red brick and tall white columns.

Instead it was more like what you would see in a movie set for something in Shakespearean times, lots of lumpy buildings with rough plastering on the outside, mixed with unpainted clapboard. It was one of the biggest English-speaking cities in the 1770s of our timeline, and it was three times bigger here—but it still looked poor, dumpy, and squalid.

I had just come into Marlborough Street proper when I noticed graffiti on a building—something you didn't see in Boston at that time. It was just three words: SONS OF LIBERTY.

There shouldn't have been any such movement in this timeline. I stood and stared at it. One of the most radical patriot groups from my timeline, a driving force for the revolution . . . what was it doing here? The British regime was benign and pro-colonial; there wasn't supposed to be any Revolution at all.

I was just considering that question when a pistol shot buzzed by my head and sent a shower of brick chips spraying outward, stinging my face. I spun around to find I faced four hooded men, all with muskets.

6

Only one musket was leveled, and it had just fired. The others waited at ready. One of them started to say "You had better come with—"

Adrenaline and training cut through the situation. The .45 popped out of my shoulder holster and I braced and fired four times before I drew a breath, some of the fastest shooting I'd ever done. At the range—less than fifteen yards—you'd have to be a lot worse shot than I was to miss. The man who had fired, and had nothing to shoot with, was my fourth target, and he didn't quite have time to turn around before my shot flung him, turned half-around, facedown onto the muddy brick street.

There were screams and people running everywhere. I looked at the crowd running toward me from both sides and vaulted the wall.

"Mr. Strang, I *beg* your pardon!" a young woman

said. I had just managed to miss her as I came down into a secluded back garden.

I jammed the Colt back into my shoulder holster and did my best to manage a bow. "I hope you'll forgive me, but I've been attacked," I said, "and forced to defend myself. We'd best get away from here before—"

On the other side of the wall there were screams, groans, and moaning, shouts of "Help! Murder!" and what sounded like fistfights and screaming matches breaking out. It was going to be a full-fledged riot soon, and one concept that the eighteenth-century English-speaking world didn't have was a police force. I remembered someone, Orwell I think, said there was no level of force possible between closing the shutters and volleys of musket fire.

Obviously some thought like that had crossed her mind, too, for she hurried up the garden path as I followed. "It was the Sons of Liberty, wasn't it?" she said. "Of course it was. Papa had just sent for men to scour the brickwork—we'd only just found out that was on our wall—"

Behind us there was more shouting, the sounds of breaking glass, and cries of "Fire! Fire!" and "The Redcoats!"

This house obviously belonged to somebody with money, and I was just as obviously known here. I just hoped it wasn't my brother-in-law or something.

Even in our hurry, I managed to notice that the small garden was formal in a very English way, that there was glass in the windows, and that the combination of red brick and white woodwork and columns was what I'd have called Georgian. Clearly this was someone who paid attention to English fashions.

It was just as clear from the look of his daughter; if I remembered right, bustles and low necklines were just coming into fashion in Europe, and she was definitely wearing both.

We hurried into a high-ceilinged room, and she told a black servant, "Fetch my father at once." He bowed and hurried away.

With a loud pop, she shot out a fan and began waving it in front of her face. "Entirely too much excitement," she said. "The doctor will be very unhappy with me."

She looked to be about twenty-two or twenty-three, dark-haired, moon-faced, with a pouty red mouth and not much of a chin, pretty but not exceptional. A quick estimate was that she was probably brainier than she was given credit for, almost certainly didn't have enough to do, and, if I were any judge, was her father's pet even though he never listened to her.

The man who came down the stairs wore a large, old-fashioned full-bottomed wig that made him look more like a British judge than anything else. He was fat by our standards, or healthy-looking by theirs, and his red face looked like it got that way from beer and wine rather than the sun.

"Mr. Strang leaped our garden wall, Papa, to get away from a mob," the girl explained.

"Well . . . hmmph. It's certainly better than getting murdered, now isn't it?" the old guy said. "You honor me with your visit, sir, even if it was no choice of your own. I trust you are aware that the sentiments upon my wall are not my own. Now I suppose I shall have to have a man or two stand with a gun to protect the workmen erasing that mess from my wall. The Sons of Liberty, faugh and damn 'em, are inclined to think every wall is their own."

"I shot four of them," I said, "and I'm not sure what the results were. At least two of them were still making noise as we ran to the house."

"Quite good shooting, that, and lucky you had a second brace about you."

Single shot pistols normally come in braces of three, the translator in my head supplied. "Er, yes," I said. "I'm not sure how much effect I really had on them all—it's just as likely as not that they're all alive but frightened."

"I should hope so, Mr. Strang" the girl said. "It would be such an inconvenience to you and to the whole colony if you should have to stand trial."

"Hah," her father said. "Inconvenient indeed, sir, but not at all a bad thing. We might establish a precedent that permits the shooting of vermin, and there's something to be said for that. And I should think, speaking as a judge, that any reasonable judge would see matters the way I do, and if any damned jury doesn't, well, we'll see how they like the pillory and the stocks. Now, tell me, were they—"

There was a crash of breaking glass. Shutters began to slam all over the house, and I heard the servants running frantically; a moment later the butler burst in to announce, "A mob, sir, they say they want—"

"Me," I said. "I'd better get out of here and let you show them that I'm not here."

"What, and invite a rabble into my house to inspect it? Thank you, sir, but no thank you, I like my silverware where it is, in my possession. My servants are tolerable marksmen, and I think we might have some good shooting from the roof if you like— see if any of those hooded rapscallions has escaped you, eh?"

"Papa, they might all rush at once. They might set fire to the house."

"Honoria, they might also all decorate the end of a rope. I daresay you've been right all along, Strang, for all our arguing in the past."

"Uh, right about what?" I asked, as I looked around for an escape. Apparently this old judge intended to put up a fight here, and I hadn't seen any evidence that the house could stand the fight. It seemed a poor way to pay him and his daughter back for taking me in. Presumably if the mob wanted me, they would follow me when I left—

"Why, right, sir, in what you've always argued before me and my daughter, at many an evening of whist."

Oh, hell, I have no idea how to play whist, was my first thought, but then he went on:

"The natural arrangement of mankind is masters and their servants, and this country should have been settled by a few wealthy men and their trusted overseers, plus all the niggers we needed from Africa. It was allowing free white paupers into this country that has made all the trouble, for you can't shoot 'em when they're wrong, you're at the expense of a trial every time one needs hanging, and most of all the filthy bastards *will* go thinking themselves your equals. That's what you've said and by god the events of the last year have convinced me."

I was spared from hearing any more of my opinions—just who the hell was I in this timeline, anyway?—by a rattle of gunfire from the upper floors. There were wild yells up there, so either they'd hit something or they thought they had.

"Just the same," I said, "if you'll hold them briefly, I'll be over your garden wall again, dash around, get the crowd's attention, and get them away from your valuable property. I can get away quite safely, I assure you; it'll only take a little nerve and luck."

"Oh, godspeed, sir," Honoria said, and extended her hand to be kissed. As an art historian, I knew she was premature—the Romantic Era wasn't due to start for another half generation—but still, if you grew up on movies, how could you resist a moment like that? I kissed her hand, smiled at her, and said, "All right, then, over the wall and I shall see you sometime later."

It was just a quick dash back to the brick wall, and it was a lot easier to make the jump from this side, since there was a bench in the right place. I bounded over, dropped into an empty street—the whole mob must have been around the front—and raced around the block, yanking the NIF from my boot.

There's a setting on there for "temporary hallucinatory panic," a fancy way of saying the dart gives you six hours of nightmares in broad daylight. I figured in an age like this one, when every kind of raving lunatic was let loose to wander in the streets, it might pass unnoticed, with a little luck.

They actually weren't much of a mob, and I saw why Honoria and the judge hadn't been very frightened. When I rounded the corner and crouched behind a wooden horse trough, I saw that there were really only about seventy of them, and almost all of them were hanging back and shouting, trying to egg on the few who were considering throwing rocks. Not one even had a firearm in hand.

None of them were on the ground, so I figured that the volley of fire from the house had frightened them but not hit them; the translator in my head explained quickly that though the Minié ball had made firearms more accurate in this timeline, and with cartridges they loaded faster, they were still no great shakes as weapons, and a few of them going off was frightening but not a reason to turn and run. Better machining, and thus more efficient human slaughter, wasn't due to be introduced for another generation in the master plan—they wanted to get a couple of wars over with first, apparently.

At least it was nice to know that the shot that went by my head had probably been aimed at it. I'd been thinking that if it was a warning shot, perhaps shooting at and hitting all four of them had been an overreaction.

I set the NIF for temporary hallucinatory panic and squeezed ten shots into the mob.

There was an instant change; a few fell to the ground and others began to shout. When you give someone hallucinations, he sees things that are part of his culture, things his culture thinks about a lot. A man who knows nothing of elephants doesn't hallucinate pink elephants no matter what he drinks; a Muslim doesn't see Jesus.

These people were definitely not Muslims.

I should have figured that in a Puritan city—especially since in most places the poor are more religious than the rich—what I'd touch off was a whole series of religious revelations. And sure enough, that's exactly what happened. One old codger with a lot of stains on his trousers, and a pale thin young girl with a big basket of buns, began to talk loudly to Jesus, who seemed to be very angry with both of them, to judge from just the side of the conversation I could see. A younger man, who looked like he'd been spending time at the tavern drinking on someone else's tab before he joined the crowd, thought that Catholics were sending devils to torture him. A plump, dowdy woman began to scream that Quakers and Anabaptists were coming out of the sky to roast and eat her children.

Moreover, they all sort of fed ideas back to each other, so that in short order they were all having the same vision, and then a bunch of people who hadn't been hit got the idea, too. There's a certain prestige, in certain circles, about having been god-attacked, and, besides, some people are naturally prone to it, so that although I'd only fired ten fléchettes, it was only half a minute before there were twenty people having visions.

The idea was screamed by a red-haired freckled boy, everyone else took it up, and then they were all running down to the harbor to try to walk to Charles Town, across the water (and *not* via the bridge) for some reason or other. I stood and watched them go; none of the crowd seemed to remember me.

They had gotten almost out of sight when I heard the gunshots. I ran to see what was going on, and there in the street was—

Me.

He wasn't dressed exactly like I was, or like I would have been if I still had my trunk, and his wig had fallen to the side, but he looked like me, he had several braces of pistols slung over his shoulders like an overgarlanded Christmas tree, and he was busily emptying the first brace into the crowd. As I watched helplessly, the young boy who had started them in motion toward the Charles, a kid of not more than ten, fell over, clutching his abdomen.

The "Mark Strang" in front of me pulled another pistol from the brace, cocked and pointed it. He squeezed the trigger, and with a boom an old man fell dead to the sidewalk.

Everywhere people were scrambling for cover. The man who looked just like me pulled out another brace of pistols and began to fire again—first a shot into the now-fleeing crowd that caught a handsome young man in the back and flung him face first into the mud, then a wanton shot between the shutters where a young woman was peeping out at the action on the street. I couldn't tell from the shriek whether she had been hit and hurt, or perhaps she had only been terrified.

He raised the last pistol in the brace, this time leveling it on—

A little kid, I realized, too dirty and small for me to say boy or girl, dressed only in a smock, running frantically away from him.

Instinct took over. The NIF in my hand shrieked before I was even aware that I was holding it or pulling the trigger. I had not even taken the time to reset the fléchettes, so the one that went into him was still set for temporary hallucinatory panic—not something you want to do to a man who is holding a loaded gun.

Abruptly, the loaded pistol still in his hand, the other "Mark Strang" began to scream and gibber, moaning with fear. He fired wildly at something that wasn't there, then turned and fled, leaving four bodies stretched in the street.

I didn't think it would be smart to hang around and try to explain things, especially since I did not understand any of them myself. I darted into an alley, ran down it at full tilt, and veered to the side. I could hear wailing and keening beginning back behind me, which was probably the friends of my doppelgänger's victims coming out of shock. I zigged and zagged between alleys, got myself completely lost, and made a point of staying off main streets.

At least it was only April, and the sun would go down early. For three more hours I moved quickly from hiding place to hiding place; twice I heard parties of people looking for me, but too far away for me to make out exactly where they were or anything they were saying except that it sounded like if I surrendered right now, I at least wouldn't be lynched.

I was crouching between three barrels—one rain barrel and two filled with kitchen slops and chamber-pot dumpings—when a small party of men with pistols and clubs came down that alley. By now the sun was nearly down, and I had begun to think I might stay there till it was full dark and then see what I could come up with. I was tired, footsore, more scared than I wanted to admit, and completely baffled, and for a guy who was supposed to have such a promising start, somebody the Closers would go out of their way to eliminate, I sure didn't feel like I was having much effect, at least not in any direction that I was supposed to. If I was a big threat to the opposition, you couldn't tell it from where I was squatting.

I sat all the way down and set the NIF to stun; I didn't want to murder anyone innocent, and I figured these guys were probably just a local posse.

It took me a moment to notice that the spot on which I had seated myself was foul with wet street muck and the stuff that leaked from the bottom of the waste barrels, and cold besides, and it was soaking into the seat of my pants. I gritted my teeth so as not to shiver.

"Ah, Nathan, he ain't going to turn up. He's a madman they say. He'll have shot hisself somewheres, or run into the bay, or they'll find him moaning and weeping somewheres."

"It's not our job to know where he is," a reedy, nasal voice responded, "but to look for him. And we need to look for him here."

"Well, he ain't here. And it's nigh on to dark, and the wife will be stone angry with me, she will, and there ain't no point in us being here in this empty way. You know he's got to be a madman—a Royal Customs Commissioner, to do a thing like that? First to stand about in the street when the damned Sons of Liberty are about, then to shoot—and not once, but twice, and the second time not the Sons but just a crowd—"

"Ah, the crowd was whipped up by the Sons," one of the men said, "and I told *my* son if he ever joins a mob like that, I'll by god have his guts nailed to the fence post."

"I'd watch how you talk of the Sons of Liberty," an older voice said. "They've got ears, you know—"

"And you're one of them ears, is that it, old man? They're thieves and ruffians, the type that ought to have an ear cut off so decent folks knows 'em by sight, and if you're their ear, then that ear ought to be cut off—"

There were two sharp thuds and groans, which I figured was a pistol butt being used hard on each of the arguers. "Next time I'll put a pistol ball in each of you and claim you by-god fought a duel," the sharp-edged voice I had identified as Nathan said. "We ain't here to talk about customs, nor taxes, nor the Sons of Liberty. We ain't here to talk at all, and a good thing too, because if we was drawing our pay for that, the whole colony couldn't afford you two jibber-jawers. Now what we're here for, in case you forgot, is to find a man that shot down citizens in the street. Self-defense or madman or whatever, that's for the law to decide. We're just to take him, alive if we can, and bring him in. If we find him. Which we ain't going to do by standing here and jawing."

"We ain't going to find him at all," one of the voices said, sullenly, and with the kind of tone that comes through a bruised mouth.

"We don't know that till we look, I said. And I'm the captain here."

There was a lot of grumbling, but they went off, following Nathan.

I stood up slowly; if the patrol was going west, I might as well go east.

Mark Strang, Royal Customs Commissioner? The last we'd heard from Rey Luc, there wasn't even supposed to *be* any Customs—the Empire had declared free trade, which is what you're in favor of if you're in a position of strength. It was supposed to be France, Holland, and Spain that were doing the smuggling and passing the restrictive acts in this timeline. Clearly in four years a lot could go very far wrong indeed.

I checked my transponder tracker again, but there was nothing to indicate that there was any transponder (other than mine) on Earth. Wherever Luc might be, he was at least a couple of miles away, or under or behind something that really blocked radio.

Half an hour later I found a dry, dark corner under a flight of steps behind a dry goods store, and curled up to go to sleep. Things were just plain not going well, I said to myself.

I ran over the inventory of conditions when you were supposed to call for backup. When you arrived and discovered a sizable Closer armed force. When you arrived in the wrong timeline, indicating that chronflux had carried away or destroyed the timeline we were aiming for. When you were badly hurt or in imminent danger of death, and "such condition might tend to jeopardize your mission." Nothing in any of those about being cold, dirty, tired, hungry, hunted by posses, beset by doppelgängers, or just having had the most confusing day of your life. I decided I was probably going to have to tough this one out.

You know how so often things look better in the morning? When they *don't*, it's because they're really bad and not getting better. I woke up to the crashing thunder of cart wheels in the street, right at dawn, and noticed that I was even colder, that the feel of whatever had soaked my clothes in places was indescribably slimy, and that I was a lot hungrier and coming down with a cold.

I coughed hard, spat out some phlegm, said some words that were the same in both centuries, and groped in my pocket for the first-aid kit. I jammed a self-injecting ampoule against my arm and gave myself one of my three immune boosters; for the next few days I'd have an accelerated immune response, which meant I might be sick as a dog this afternoon, and would need to eat like an ox to get energy back, but I'd be fine by tomorrow morning. For that matter, temporarily just about nothing could infect me or cause me to get cancer; if I wanted to take up smoking or whoring, and had money for either tobacco or a woman, this was the time to do it, as the humor ran in the training center.

God, I missed everyone, and I really wished I had a letter from Chrysamen. To read over the coffee and breakfast I wasn't going to get, after the shower I wasn't going to get either.

It was probably about forty degrees out. I've slept rougher than under those steps, but not much rougher.

I drew a deep breath and coughed it out. *All right, Strang,* I said to myself. *Now that we've got self-pity down cold, we work for some other possible responses, like maybe some effective ones. Let's get going on something. First job is stop looking like this, get some clean clothes, and find Rey Luc. After that, fix whatever turns out to be wrong. Merely a big problem, not an impossible one.*

The pep talk did me about as much good as a pep talk ever does. I felt better for having given it but not much for having gotten it. I shook off my clothes, decided I looked like a bum, decided I could do nothing about that yet, and slouched down the alley, pulling my tricorne down low to hide my face a little.

The trouble with alleys is that sooner or later they lead to major streets. I had known that I was moving toward the Common the night before, but hadn't realized how close I was; in just a few minutes I had popped out onto Common Street, with the wide green space to the west of me. I crossed over into the Common itself, where a group of boys and dogs were just driving the sheep in to graze, and headed for the Charles. Walking along the river might give me a chance to cover some ground inconspicuously and pick up some clues about what was actually going on. And at this early hour, other than the sheep and the boys, there was nothing and no one here.

I let myself pass close enough to two boys to hear what they were saying; they were talking about whether or not "Seth's sister" was too ugly for any man to marry. Why is it in the movies you get all the information by overhearing two minor extras, and out in the timelines you have to get it a little bit at a time. The major thing I learned was that "Seth's sister" had a nice chest and bad acne; I supposed it might be useful information in the event of being offered a blind date sometime.

Another couple of boys were talking about three public hangings coming up; none of them seemed to be mine.

The Common was a beautiful place, and without any real traffic noise, I found myself thinking that one of these days—once things were a bit more in hand—I'd have to come here at this time just for pleasure. Spring was far enough along for the grass to be bright green and a thin haze of leaf buds to be on the trees, and though damp and squishy in places, the ground wasn't really muddy anywhere except right where the sheep had been concentrated.

Eventually I hit Charles Street, which at the time was nothing more than a mud track. Nobody seemed to be walking on it this morning—it didn't serve much purpose just yet other than as a bypass for carts and wagons from Cambridge to the South Boston Bridge—and took that west to the river.

Now that I was up and moving I was warmer, and though I had no plan as yet, I had at least determined that I was going to get one. The sun was coming up fast now, and the air had that glow it gets in early spring, when it still holds the damp and cold of winter but the sun is warming it fast.

It occurred to me that, as they tell you in training and as anyone in my line learns, disguise is mostly a matter of not looking like yourself, and that can mean very simple things. I let myself slouch a lot, inclined my head forward, and in a burst of inspiration, undid the corners of my tricorne so that I was now wearing my hat wide and floppy, more like an Old West sombrero. Two hard discreet shakes, and with the brim flattened out, my translator assured me I now looked like a Methodist preacher or possibly a schoolteacher. I'd have considered going over and applying at Harvard, as a cover, but they never take Yale men there.

At least this way I would only be spotted by people who got close to me. The extra feeling of safety, plus the gradual warming of the morning, made me feel steadily better, and I picked up my pace a little.

I decided to give the transponder another shot, and this time, much to my surprise, there was a faint signal. The direction seemed to point southward, along Charles Street, opposite the direction in which I had been walking, and not having any better plan, I turned and went the other way.

The sun was getting higher now, and there was more noise of people getting to work. Probably the biggest factory in Boston, even in this altered timeline, didn't have a hundred workers in it at a time; typically people were working in little shops of three or six, a master, a journeyman or two, and a couple of apprentices. As I drew nearer to Boston Neck, I could hear more noise in general—the bank of the

Charles River had some wharves and a lot of small businesses going there.

After a bit there was a fork in the road, with Boylston Street going off toward town, to my left, and Charles Street continuing near the river, to my right. The transponder tracker obstinately pointed right up the middle of the fork.

I shrugged and decided so far Charles Street had been lucky for me, so I took the turn to the right. This meant coming into some of the new "industrial" part of the town, the part that had been built up from the new technologies that Rey Luc had introduced; to my eye, it didn't look industrial at all, with its many small barnlike structures and individual workshops, but it was in fact one of the biggest manufacturing areas on Earth in this timeline.

I noted that there was a shop that built "Engines of all Kinds" and another for "Electricks"; there would have been no such thing in Boston in my timeline, so at least I could see that Luc's handiwork wasn't completely undone.

I heard a big, slow "chuffing" noise, and saw puffs of smoke rising from the direction of the river. Pretty clearly someone was starting up one of those engines; since Luc didn't seem to be going anywhere, (triangulating off past readings from the transponder tracker hidden in my sleeve, I found that he seemed to be in just one place less than a mile away), I decided to get a slightly better look at this timeline and see how things were coming along. I walked away from the signal of Luc's transmitter a little, but it was now strong enough so that

I didn't worry about it going out, and went to get a look down by the river.

The belches of smoke had consolidated into a gray-black stream, and they were coming from a paddle wheeler. That also told me that things were still on track here. In my timeline there hadn't been much in the way of steamboats on the rivers until well after the War of 1812; here, they had arrived seventy years early.

As I came down toward the wharf, I saw that it was a tugboat—the engine was huge in proportion to the boat, and it had the kind of snub prow they have to have—with the paddle wheels on the side. But it didn't look much like anything out of Mark Twain; Greek Revival and Victorian gingerbread had not yet hit the design world here, if it ever would. Rather it was boxy and flat-sided, painted deep red (the cheap color in those days), and looked like nothing so much as a large shack on top of a cap-sized barge, with the engine and its stack of wood sitting behind the shack, and two big crude paddle wheels on each side of the ship, so close together that their vanes almost meshed. It wasn't graceful, but it looked powerful.

There was a crowd of about sixty people around the foot of the gangway leading up to the tug, and after checking to make sure that I hadn't lost Rey Luc yet (he seemed to be staying in one place), I moved into an alley and worked my way cautiously forward. A Customs officer is likely to be recognized around a waterfront, but I was wondering what could possibly draw a crowd to the departure of a tugboat in a busy harbor. For that matter, why had I heard so little noise from Boston Harbor the day before? I'd been close enough so that I should have heard more shipping or seen some masts moving—

I crept closer, staying in the shadows, doing my best to look like a preacher or teacher that was just wandering in from idle curiosity . . .

The tug captain—at least he had a coat and hat that I thought made him look like the captain— came to the head of the gangway and was promptly pelted with rotten fruit and vegetables. He ran back into the shack, and two of his men—big, ugly, dumb-looking guys—came out with muskets. The crowd started to back away, and the captain came back out, and proclaimed loudly, "I takes no sides! No sides at all! I just takes pay to move what people pays to have moved, and I follas the law!"

There were hoots of derision, but nobody threw anything, so he seemed to gather his courage. "And besides, I'm commanded by the Royal Navy, anyway! Now, I'm goin' out to bring in the *Terror*, and that's that!"

There was more hooting, but he stormed inside, and the crew started to bring up the gangplank.

Terror is a not uncommon name for a warship; this didn't sound good at all. It looked like, if I hadn't been so busy running for my life (and being mistaken for my double, who seemed to be a murdering nut, among other things) just possibly I'd have found out that things were falling apart all over. Luc was going to have some explaining to do, anyway.

I checked the transponder and saw that if I followed the street I was on now—a sign on the Brown

Dog Inn said it was Hollis Street—I should pass very close to Luc. I walked down the lane, doing my best to look the part of a wandering preacher or something of the kind, facing the now-risen sun. It was getting warm, I'd had no breakfast, and the smell of sausage frying from the inn had made the thought of some kind of lunch urgent.

A half mile later, as I was nearing the harbor again, I checked the tracker and found I'd passed him; since I had checked it just two hundred yards before, pretty clearly he was somewhere very near, though the signal was faint. The only significant building there—assuming he wasn't hiding in a storage shed or warehouse—seemed to be a big, new church that sat in a block to itself at Hollis and Orange. I approached it, checked the tracker . . . no, Luc was somewhere to the side—

It was a shock, but obvious. He was in the churchyard, which meant unless he'd been working as a gravedigger all morning, he was dead. It took me about five minutes to find the grave; he'd Anglicized his name to Raymond Luc, but it was clearly him. Moreover, he'd been killed in 1771, according to the stone, "shot down in anger/O passerby, let not your Jealousie rule you!"

I stood by that four-year-old grave and sighed. Well, first part of the job was done; a team could come out here and quietly remove Luc's body and return it to his family, if in his home timeline that was a religious duty or a matter of honor. But clearly he wasn't going to be a lot of help in the matter of getting the timeline back on track.

And even though I'd turned one timeline around

before—not many rookie Crux Ops had had that experience—the major thought running through my head was that whatever was wrong, I was just one guy, probably wanted by the authorities, no friends, not enough money to get out of town on, hungry, tired . . .

A hand fell on my shoulder, and a voice said, "Good friend of yours?"

The voice had something a little like a Southern drawl about it, and a bit like a clipped British accent, and the timbre of the voice was like gravel rattling in the throat. I'd heard one human voice like that before, though not with quite that accent, and that had been in another timeline . . . the hand that gripped me was firm and strong, too, and the man it belonged too seemed to be over six feet tall. There was one funny instant, just as the martial artist decided for me that spinning and kicking would be uncalled for, when I thought it was the man whose voice it sounded like—George Patton.

I turned and stared for half an instant; the jaw, bunched with pain from bad teeth, was the same, but the face was a young, vigorous forty-three, not the old man one sees on the dollar bill. "George Washington," I said directly.

7

"Mark Strang," he said. "Are you of the faction of Perikles, or that of Hannibal?"

"Perikles," I said, and the light went on.

No one in ATN is really sure, but we think the Closers were descended from Carthaginians; for one thing, they seem to worship Moloch, the great god of Carthage. Perikles, of course, was the great Athenian; Hannibal the great Carthaginian.

And if Washington was asking me that, it was because my double really *was* me—from some other timeline where (god, what disgusting thought) I must have become a Closer agent.

I wanted to call him "General," but in this timeline he certainly wasn't, so instead I said, "I'm very pleased to meet you, sir."

You could see the resemblance to Patton, and that was no great surprise—a lot of the old Virginia military families were heavily intermarried. I wondered, distractedly, if there would be a Patton in this timeline. Washington was taller and thinner, his face more finely formed, and of course his hair was still dark. But the characteristic heavy jowls and wide-set, piercing eyes were pure Virginia aristocrat.

He nodded and extended a hand. "You'll pardon my asking a few questions," he said. "What did Dr. Franklin learn from Dr. Luke?"

"The principle that an electric field is always at right angles to a magnetic field."

"How was King Frederick cured of his abscess?"

"With penicillin, I believe. Otherwise, he'd have died in 1751."

Washington nodded slowly. "I think we need to get you somewhere where we can't be observed, sir, and following that I might suggest a bath, a change of clothes, a disguise, and some food. In whatever order seems best."

We walked up Orange Street in silence; I knew from casual reading that Washington wasn't much of a talker, so I didn't worry about it. He'd taken care of most of what I was really worried about, and I certainly didn't expect him to entertain me on top of that.

"You might keep your head slightly bowed and appear to be striving for the salvation of my soul," Washington added. "That would make you very unlike the other Mark Strang, I should think."

"Quite agreed," I said, bending my head farther. "Have we far to go?"

"I have quarters in Essex Street," he said. "There, that looks a bit more parsonly."

I nodded. "I seem to have dropped into nothing I

expected; our last report from poor Luc was apparently shortly before he died."

"Then you're not aware, for example, that you shot him?"

"*I*—oh, my, uh, double. The Customs Collector."

"That one. It was in a duel, very shortly after Mark Strang arrived here. I was not present at the time, but I knew Luc from many years' acquaintance. It was a matter of honor, a challenge, a duel . . . and a death. A most peculiar matter, for Mr. Luc was known to be very passionate about taking care of his health, you see . . . that alone made it strange that he should engage in a duel. The claim that he had seduced the sister of Mr. Strang was, of course, stranger still; he'd always been an honorable man. There were those of us . . . those who had been deeply in Mr. Luc's confidence, deeply enough to know who he really was and where he really came from, felt something might have gone deeply wrong. Adams in particular was concerned, and wrote to me and the others at once."

"I see," I said. At that moment a cart came around a corner and passed us; as it was going by I added, "But of course in Leviticus the matter is far less clear, and surely you must agree with me—" the cart passed out of earshot. "This is John Adams?"

"That question alone marks you as our man. His useless cousin Sam is a passionate Son, I'm afraid. They're so taken with the idea of running a nation that they can no longer see how much of our wealth comes from our life in the Empire. Anyone who could confuse Sam and John is not from this time . . ." He sighed, very slightly. "As I understand it, these agents of . . . other times, other histories?"

"We call them timelines."

"Thank you. These agents of other timelines arrive with a list of people known to be important, but apparently not any idea of why they will be important. Your name was on such a list, but as an agent for the, er, friendly faction, not for those other sorts. Mr. Luc apparently was beginning to fear that his health might fail, and if it should do so, that we might be left without support."

That was pretty much what I would have expected; Special Agents generally get a station in their mid-twenties to mid-thirties, and then stay there until they die or retire. They're guys who change the world—that's their mission—but they do it as peacefully as they can, with ideas and teaching and information, and they stay with that world, often, until they die there. What they get from home is an update to their orders every six months, and—if they stop sending or call for help—a Crux Op to rescue or avenge them.

I could never imagine the kind of day-to-day courage and self-reliance that must take.

"There's no way of knowing exactly what will happen," I explained. "Whenever they can, timelines will collapse back into each other, so to separate two timelines requires enormous changes. Even then it only works at a crux, one of the places where there's a natural dividing point. And 1740–1780 is a large crux, so although there are many timelines out there where various of our people figure into the future history, so many different things could happen that it's not possible to say what we will actually do here. It's only after it's all done and the crux is over that matters will begin to settle out."

Washington nodded. "I am told this is confusing even to those of you who live with it all the time." There was a clatter behind us, and I looked around to see group of women with baskets of live chickens in each hand; as they passed us Washington added, "So it's your position, then, that anything in Deuteronomy that is not specifically reaffirmed in the New Testament cannot be binding upon a Christian?"

"That would seem to be the position of St. Paul," I said, though I hadn't the foggiest idea.

The women went by with the chickens, and we continued walking. "I'd have thought," I said, "that you'd have been in Virginia at this time, near your home."

Washington snorted. "I admit I was very tempted to retire completely after the Conquest War. I had entered a major, come out a colonel, started a world war when I was in my twenties . . . General Braddock's drive through the Ohio country and all the way to Fort Detroit had made me famous, the land grants and the knighthood His Majesty King Frederick was pleased to bestow upon me had made me wealthy—I hired a splendid man named Boone to run matters out to the west for me—and between prestige and wealth, I could settle to do almost anything I wished. I had very nearly resolved to do so, but Mr. Luc seemed to feel there was some service I could be to the new king, and since we had gotten to be friends . . . "

"Of course," I said.

"Not to mention it is very hard to say no to a

sovereign who has made one a duke," Washington added. "I don't suppose that was in Mr. Luc's reports?"

"No," I said, "it wasn't."

Washington smiled. "I've been granted the Duchy of Kentucky. I don't imagine I shall move there for ten years yet; Boone writes me that there is much to be done."

Washington's house in Boston turned out to be a decent wood-framed building with a couple of spare bedrooms and an honest-to-god bathroom; it turned out that Rey Luc had introduced the flush toilet and the shower to these folks, for which I was deeply grateful. I found myself immediately believing all the stories I'd heard of Washington's consideration for his men, because once we were there, he immediately suggested that I ought to go down to the kitchen for a meal, and that "my servant will ready you a shower, sir, and a bed and a change of clothes. I think a few hours will not hurt the business of one who has all of time at his command, and you look in need of food, rest, and some cleanliness."

The meal was wonderful—marred for me only by the fact that there was no coffee, for in this timeline there had been no resistance to tea. It was a great big slab of apple pie, a plate of scrambled eggs with ham, and a pork-and-vegetable pastry whose name I didn't catch, all washed down with a lot of tea and a nice heavy breakfast porter. The person who served all that to me was a tall, handsome, black woman, who seemed amused at the company the duke was keeping and the quantity I ate; it took me a while to figure out that I was probably being waited on by a slave. Abolition was supposed to happen fairly soon in this timeline—though if the Closers took over, it never would.

The shower, too, was a lesson in how far this century had to go—a slave had had to pump the tank full and build a fire under it—but I was so grateful for it that I managed to overlook the gross incorrectness of the whole thing. When I got back, Porter or Carrie could lecture me about it.

Besides, I tipped the guy, and he seemed pleased to be thanked. It might not have been the peak of social justice, but it was a start; at least they didn't seem badly mistreated, and I remembered from somewhere that in my timeline Washington had been a relatively decent master, making sure his slaves received an education and freeing them in his will.

I fell asleep in a clean, comfortable bed, woke up in a few hours hungry again, and got dressed rapidly. The new outfit didn't have the special pocket between the shoulder blades for the SHAKK, or the boot pocket for the NIF, so I ended up just wearing the .45 and tucking the more advanced weaponry into a little leather bag, like a doctor's bag, they'd provided for the purpose.

The servant came in and summoned me down to supper; I found that besides George Washington, there were also John Adams, and two young doctors—Joseph Warren and Tom Young—present in the room. Adams was a tough-looking little guy, despite being from one of the best Boston families; Warren was tall and handsome, and Young a square-built, muscular guy. While we were sitting down, Samuel Cooper, a local minister, came in; like Adams and unlike the rest of us, he wore a white-powdered wig, which didn't diminish his sharply etched strong features. Visually with a change of clothes any of them could have been a dockworker or cab driver, and they reminded me more of an American Resistance cell I had once known in Nazi-occupied San Francisco than they did of the stiff, posed paintings of Founding Fathers from my own timeline.

Dinner was a roast turkey, mashed potatoes, and corn bread; the available seasonings seemed to be salt and pepper. It occurred to me that this was before any of the waves of South European immigration, and therefore the diet was going to be pretty bland this trip out. Naturally no one noticed except me, and I was hungry enough to eat eagerly anyway.

I was also a little surprised at how much everyone drank; there were several kinds of hard liquor and a number of thick red wines available, and most of them were drinking mixtures of those, usually with some sugar and some hot water stirred in. I tried one of those myself and ended up sipping it for the rest of the evening. The mixture didn't seem to hit any of the other men nearly as hard.

After we'd all finished, and tea had been set out, Washington began the meeting by explaining, "To some extent it was pure chance I was here, for I am due back in Virginia in the fall, and after that I've some business in London; with the new steamships one may much more safely undertake a winter voyage, you know. But as for how we knew to watch for you, that's easily explained; your counterpart from the—did you say Closers?"

"That's them, the Closers," I said.

"Ah. Well, your Closer counterpart has been a very unpleasant fellow in many regards, but undeniably he has been popular, at least among the more drastically Tory crowd."

It took me a long moment to realize that in this timeline Tories and Loyalists were not the same thing; the King in London was a Whig, Parliament was Whig, and the Tories were thus the right-wing opposition to King George, not his staunchest supporters as in my timeline.

"Popular and inflamma-Tory," Young said, and there was a mild groan from everyone at the table. "He's made himself the darling of young men that I suppose you would call intellectual macaronis—the sort who change their ideas for exactly the reason other young men change their coats, to make themselves conspicuous and give them an importance they would not otherwise have. And like any true macaronis, they are, of course, given to calling attention to themselves by adopting what is most extreme. So where a more sensible young fellow would simply wear a wig that was too high, a hat that was too small, shoes that pinched his feet, and buckles and buttons big enough to weigh down a sail, these fellows around Strang have been vying to see who can be more Royalist than the King and more Imperialist than a tax collector. They've brawled in the streets dozens of times with the Sons of Liberty, and they've organized the King's Own

Undertakers, as they call themselves, to kidnap and murder Whigs."

I shuddered a little. "All that around someone who looks just like me. No wonder the Sons of Liberty were so quick to take a shot at me."

"They're just as bad a lot," Warren said, morosely. Later I was to realize he did almost everything morosely. Though he was a gentle and kind man, he seemed to expect the worst in every situation. "The Sons have a good sixty murders to their credit, if that's the word. It's gotten so that the Common is deserted in the morning, because people are afraid to see who may have been butchered and left there 'as an example' by either the Sons of Liberty or the King's Own Undertakers. There've been many rumors that there are Redcoat officers working with the King's Own, and I rather suspect it's true; certainly the Mark Strang we've all come to know and loathe is at the heart of it."

Cooper was nodding vigorous agreement. "But no one would have thought him mad, and what he did in Bishop's Alley yesterday was madder than anything we've seen, even poor old James Otis included."

I knew that Otis had suffered from insanity after being a major Patriot leader in my timeline; I must have looked puzzled because Adams explained, "It's that damned new explosive; we don't know if Luc introduced it through one of his many front organizations and covers, or if Strang brought it in, or perhaps it was actually discovered by one of our own chemists. It's a niter of glycerin mixed with a special white clay—"

"Dynamite," I said.

"Yes, I think that's the name it's sold under. A lump the size of a loaf of bread goes off like a barrel of common gunpowder; a small box of it can level a fair-sized house. And that's just how poor old Otis died—he was carrying a box of it into a tavern, and it's quite touchy stuff and this had gotten old enough to sweat out some of its niter. It destroyed the tavern and killed a dozen soldiers and Royal agents, and it also left almost nothing of Otis." Adams stared off into space. "It's a bad thing, you know. When you had to haul in whole barrels of powder to make something like that happen—well, then it was hard to do. With this stuff a bomb might be made and concealed anywhere, and both factions are beginning to use them in just that way." He sighed. "Otis and I were friends, you know. Without that accursed dynamite, he might be mad as a March hare and confined somewhere, but he would at least be alive."

There was a long silence at that. The candles that flickered and danced made no sound, and the dark April night outside, though it had been threatening rain as I came down to supper, held no hint of wind or rain.

"You see," Cooper said finally, "we're all more than a little disheartened, or we have been. In a bit over thirty years the world came along very far very fast. And though the information brought by Mr. Luc was what made it possible, we ourselves have done the work; Rey Luc showed us how to do things and how they might fit together into a scheme, but it was our work and our effort that brought us to understand them, and it was our further work that made them become real. We know of his influence in many places—it was he who got the King out of Bute's keeping and got Franklin appointed his tutor . . . and though George has prospects of being as fine a King as ever good old England's ever had, no one will deny that he's a little slow at times, especially when it comes to the more abstract sort of thinking, or that he is remarkably easy to lead. Mr. Luc brought out the best in him, partly by his personal contact and mainly by letting the young Prince come over here and see what sort of country he had."

"I'm surprised," I said, "that the King hasn't acted more to abate this crisis."

"No one's more surprised than I," Washington said. "For five years after his visit here, he and I corresponded frequently, and I think I may fairly say that we had become quite good friends. Indeed, Cooper, the one thing I would add is that whatever you may think of his brains, George the Third has a passionate desire to do the right thing and to know what the right thing is. I find it quite inexplicable, therefore, that in the past three or so years the King has stopped answering my letters, indeed communicates with no one in America despite all the many friends he has here, and even the London social crowd sees him only at public functions." A thought struck me; I was about to speak when Washington raised a finger. "Alas, too, Mr. Strang, from what I have been able to learn there's no possibility of a double's being substituted—too many of our Whig friends have seen him closely enough, and he has recognized and acknowledged them sometimes with a word or two. I fear he is changed; there was a brief period, you know, of fits while he was over here—"

"I had the honor of treating His Majesty at that time," Young said, "and the fits he suffered, even if they should eventually devolve into full-blown madness, were in no way consistent with any such change in him. He might be in great anguish, and even suffer hallucinations, true, but his feelings for his friends, his affections, his opinions—these would be left untouched, if I am any judge. Moreover, if he were suffering such a condition, any hypothetical Tory captors he might have would not allow him in public, and further they would have every reason to apply to Parliament for a Regency, most especially because the Prince of Wales is still a child and thus by controlling the Regency they might control the kingdom. No, what exactly is going on is impossible to say from here. It's a great pity that they didn't make their move a year earlier, in my judgment."

"Why?" I asked.

"Because then Luc would have died in London, and his last report would have come from there. You'd have been dispatched there. I'm afraid you're a good thirty-five hundred miles from where you need to be, Mr. Strang. We'll have to get you aboard a ship somehow, and not from Boston—the port's been closed by Royal order."

I looked from one face to the other, there in the wash of red light from the candles on the table, and all were nodding solemnly. It seemed reasonable enough to me.

"What's my best way?" I asked.

Adams shrugged. "The most common way seems

good enough for the purpose—and I can't think of any that would be faster. The port of Boston is closed, and so are most of the other port towns in Massachusetts and New England, but they are allowing coasters out of Providence, in Rhode Island, and from there you may easily get to New York, where we have many friends and the port is open. From New York to London, then, and good luck to you at every step."

"And Providence is only about forty-five miles," I said. "With a little effort I can walk that in three days if I have to—"

"Walk? Egad, sir. You are not the sort of maniac that Mr. Luc—I should say Dr. Luc—proved to be? Your whole timeline is not like that?" Young seemed to be peering right through me.

"I'm not sure what sort of maniac that is, Dr. Young."

"Bah! The man believed that every pleasure of life—liquor, tobacco, a good wench—was a danger to the health, and moreover he wanted us to eat more vegetables, which are of course well-known for causing flux of the bowels, and to do this thing he called 'exercising,' when any fool can look and see that it is exactly those classes which do heavy physical labor which live for the shortest time. Begging your pardon, of course, Joseph," Dr. Young said, turning to the slave who was bringing in a pot of hot, seasoned cider.

"No pardon need be begged, sir," Joseph said, and I noticed that his accent was not Southern at all, as one might have expected, but very similar to the New England accent I had been hearing here in Boston.

"It's well-known that when Master Washington freed us, he most likely added five years to all our lives."

Oh, well, *judge not that ye be not judged,* I reminded myself. I had assumed he was a slave because in my time Washington had kept slaves right up to his dying day.

"Freedom is good for people," Adams commented. "But before Young got off on his track of denouncing your medicine—I'm sure he'd have started on your morals and religion next, sir"—there was a lot of laughter at the table about that, and Dr. Young blushed slightly—"what he should have said is that one of the new traction engines is now plying a route from Jamaica Plain to Providence. The line would have been extended here by now if the Royal embargo had not been interpreted to mean that there must be no easy access to the other ports. So it's just a short stage ride, and then an uncomfortable trip by traction train, and then ships all the way. Nothing to it but a bit of discomfort and the need for some patience. Certainly no need to walk like a peddler!"

That seemed to take care of all the issues as far as they were concerned; they told me that I'd be stopping at the house of Gouverneur Morris, a young Whig in New York, for the time—anywhere from a day or so to two weeks—until I could book passage on a ship for London. They also assured me, repeatedly, that costs were covered, finally explaining that one of their sympathizers in the inn where I had first landed had quietly made off with most of the money from the trunk I arrived with. I wasn't sure they were telling the truth—whoever claimed

George Washington never told a lie, Warren was to tell me later, had never played cards with the man or watched him run for office—but it was plausible enough, and anyway I didn't have much of any way to pay for anything myself.

Dr. Warren had business in New York and would see me to Morris's house; it all seemed to be arranged. I was in bed early that night, and up with the sun the next morning. At breakfast together, Washington and I mostly talked about camping and hiking—he was a passionate advocate of getting exploratory expeditions launched to the Rockies, and my descriptions of what was actually out west just whetted his appetite for it. "No doubt there will be time," he said, "once all the current infernal nonsense is done with. I hope that by that time I will not be too old; my memories of the Ohio country when I was much younger are still fond ones, and I should like to have a chance to walk to the Pacific. And in your timeline—"

"It was done in about 1806. Of course, you've already got dirigibles. It would be hard to fly east-to-west, with the wind against you, but still, if a dirigible can make it here from London without refueling, which you all say one is expected to do any day now, it ought to be able to make it from here to the mouth of the Columbia—and you could have a ship waiting for it there."

"It's indeed a thought," Washington said. "If only I still had His Majesty's ear! But oh, well, time enough for that when the world is back on track. Meanwhile if I'm not mistaken, here's Warren with the trap."

As I tossed my bag in beside Warren's, he commented, "I see that Washington also shops at Goodwife Pelster's." The two bags were identical on the outside; nothing could have told you that Warren's contained tools for saving lives, and mine contained tools that could slaughter three thousand men.

The drive down to the Jamaica Plain station was pleasant enough; Warren and I were alone on the road for a lot of it, for with the embargo and blockade the port was not busy, and thus there was much less land traffic to and from it, and most of what there was was not urgent. This early in the morning only a few farmers going into town to sell vegetables could be seen.

From Boston Neck we could make out two of the British ironclads in the harbor, big ships with the new submerged screws instead of paddle wheels, and with turrets instead of banks of guns. They looked, to me, like kids' crude pictures of warships, the kind of thing that second-grade boys like to draw, but it was just such ships a dozen years before that had put the whole main line of the French fleet on the bottom in less than an hour.

It was a nice day again—and how often does that happen twice in a row in Massachusetts in April?—and the time went quickly. Warren, too, was interested in everything and had opinions about everything and everyone. He was one of the most highly regarded men in Massachusetts, part of the informal aristocracy of Charles Town, and though he knew everyone and everything about them, he didn't so much judge people as enjoy them. It might sound dull to listen to a couple of hours of gossip and wit about people you didn't know, unless it were really nasty and salacious stuff, Warren could not only entertain in just that way, but he could entertain while mostly talking about the good side, or at least about the minor vices. I had a feeling after a while that he just plain liked the human race, and that was why most of them were returning the favor by liking him.

It was getting near lunchtime when we reached the traction-engine station. You could see it some distance away—if I had walked all the way out onto the Neck, I'd have seen the billows of smoke in the distance, and even eight miles off you could see the big smokestack.

The traction line was sort of a compromise, a little something that Luc and a couple of cunning engineers—notably Boulton and Watt, whom he had found and recruited—had dreamed up because pretty clearly real railroads were going to take too long for the essential job of tying the colonies together and speeding up communications enough to hold the Empire together; Luc's last plan had had the first locomotives available about ten years from now, but the first need for a mechanized road had been in getting forces from New York City to Ticonderoga during the Conquest War. Thus the "traction line" had been created as a temporary expedient.

It worked a lot like a cable car, except that the cables ran overhead; every few miles there was a great big chugging multiple-cylinder reciprocating steam engine, with ten cylinders as big as wine barrels, a boiler the size of a house, and a transmission and gearing that took up a barn-sized building linking it to the running cables. Between these stations, there ran a set of wooden tracks, like railroad tracks but made of wood with just a tinplated iron top, and on the tracks were wagons and stagecoaches with iron-rimmed wheels. Because the engine didn't have to drag itself along with cargo, it could be as big as needed, and because the gears could be made so big, they could be made of wood and didn't have to be made to precise tolerances—both very important at a time when good-grade steel was made in small crucibles and the best steels were literally worth their weight in gold.

In another ten years, if Luc had lived, there'd have been Bessemer converters and a whole steel industry—the giant steam engines would make it possible to power the blowers that the converters needed—and in very little time after that there would have been a railroad from Savannah all the way to Nova Scotia. Lewis and Clark, in this timeline, would have been able to take the train to St. Louis before starting up the Missouri, probably in cars with aluminum doors and window frames, for even now Ben Franklin was hard at work on large generating plants.

Well, we would get it back on track. Meanwhile, the ride was jerky, and there was a lot of soot from woodsmoke whenever we approached stations on the way to Providence. Splitting wood and not atoms is a smelly, dirty business; the air would get cleaner around here once they started getting decent

Pennsylvania anthracite, and by the late 1800s they should have nukes and all the clean power they wanted, not to mention a bogey to help scare the Closers away (we think they're terrified of nuclear energy because their home timeline was trashed by repeated nuclear wars; if so, it couldn't have happened to a better bunch of guys).

It was still daylight when we got to Providence, and there was more than enough time to get a decent meal at an inn—I was sort of figuring if I got a spare minute in this timeline I was going to introduce the idea of a restaurant with a *menu*, but the food was good enough—and then catch a night steamer, an elegant little paddle wheeler called the *John Locke,* to take us into New York, just about eleven hours away. Unfortunately the *Locke* didn't have sleeper accommodations, and we wouldn't get into the harbor until morning, but we had telegraphed ahead, Morris was expecting us early in the day, and, besides, there was nothing we needed to do the next day, and we'd be able to sleep then.

The funny thing was that even coming from a world of jet planes and rapid transit, it all seemed like a kind of a miracle to me. Once you've walked for even a few days, your sense of distance is very different. For Joseph Warren, who had grown up with horses and sailing ships, I supposed it might have seemed like a miracle.

There were more miracles on board; the *Locke* was a luxury ship, and it had a small "tour of wonders" which included going to the ship's radio shack to meet the radioman, and to watch him try to catch one of the daily radio broadcasts from London—so far there was just one station on the air for twenty minutes every day, but in just the right conditions you could get it anywhere in the world. Home crystal sets were already down to the price of a printed book (which unfortunately was still about $45 if you were converting it in gold to dollars from my timeline). More than anything else, I figured, radio—or the Franklinphone, as it was called, was going to make a difference.

There was also a small casino of sorts; Puritan New England did not allow gambling but once they were out of Providence Harbor they could open up the tables. I'm not much of a gambler—when I've visited casinos I've stuck to blackjack or to the crap table pretty much—but Warren wanted to get in a few hands of whist, there were hot sausages, bread, and coffee there, and I could amuse myself with the newspaper or with idle conversation.

Warren and I had noticed already that his medical bag, and the bag that contained my change of clothes and specialty weapons, were pretty similar, so I piled both bags under my legs to make a sort of footstool, sat down on one of the hard-backed chairs, and began to absorb the local *Dispatch-Intelligencer*; as was common at the time, the first few pages were advertisements, which mostly told me that the changes Luc had made in the economy had really taken hold—there were ads for electric-generator windmills, crystal sets, toy "electric carriages" for children, the dirigible line from New York to Philadelphia (actually they just hooked onto the traction-engine line, and the dirigible's Sterling-cycle engine was used only for maneuvering in take-off and landing), and a variety of crude lightbulbs, though to judge from the fact that nearly everyone seemed to be using candles or gas, the new technology was more a novelty than anything else.

The other thing, though, that the ads told me was that a depression was settling over the colonies. There were many, many auctions of farms and factories, and because Luc had introduced credit buying to get the economy stimulated, many more ads looking for people to assume payments. There were many ads that began "position sought" or "land for sale," and none at all looking for workers.

It took me a couple of hours to figure all of this out because the ads weren't classified, as in our newspapers, but just fit in any old way the printer could get them to go. That was fine with me—I needed to kill time, after all, and was sort of hoping that counting ads would be dull enough to send me to sleep even in that uncomfortable chair.

The news of London was unimpressive as well; many people were sitting for the new photographic portraits, there had been many parties in the past season, and a remarkable number of rich people were marrying each other and were expected to foster happy lineages of many children of breeding and distinction. A traction engine had been built in India, and a line would shortly be opening from New Delhi to the coast.

I had just about decided that stern duty wasn't going to keep me at this any longer, and even the dullest news wasn't going to send me to sleep, as the clock struck midnight. I turned a few pages, and was about to start reading Dr. Samuel Johnson's column from London, when something across the room caught my eye.

I looked up and saw myself, leaning over the crap table. Apparently both of us had had enough skill to get out of Boston. I glanced toward Warren, but he was deep in his game of whist, and there wasn't much hope of getting him out of it without stirring up a fuss. Keeping my eye on the other Mark Strang, and doing my best to keep the newspaper well up in front of my face, I quickly scribbled a note to Warren, flagged a server, and sent the note. Then I quietly leaned forward, setting my paper to the side, and grabbed the bag with the SHAKK and NIF from under my feet.

I was about to get the NIF into my coat sleeve— this seemed like the kind of job I wanted to do without making noise—when my target abruptly collected his winnings and went out the saloon door onto the deck. Grabbing the bag, I followed him.

Fog had blown in since we had entered Long Island Sound, and it was hard to see even to the end of the deck. Had he seen me? If so, then he was undoubtedly in the shadows somewhere close by, waiting to take a shot at me; if not, then I very much doubted he was out here for any good purpose. If he was being met by a boat from shore, he might show a light, but otherwise I didn't think there was much reason for him to give himself away.

I looked both ways, again, and checked behind me, and still there was nothing. I stood and listened for a long time, but between the chugging of the engine, the splashing of the paddle wheel, the light slap of the waves on the side of the *Locke,* and the wind in the radio aerial, there was far too much sound out here for me to make out anyone quietly walking across the deck or climbing steps. He had had plenty of time, and he could be anywhere on the ship by now.

The moon came out up above, but it only helped a little; the fog was still on the sea, and though it was bright now, visibility was not much extended. I crept along the side of the main cabin, back past the saloon and toward the stern, because one direction was as good as another. I tried setting a couple of ambushes by crossing in places where my back seemed exposed but the shadows in the murky moonlight fell in front of me; either he wasn't buying it (would I? I wasn't sure) or else he wasn't behind me. I started a slow search of both decks, outside.

Of course by now he might very well have gone in the other door. At least if Warren was still in there, he had been alerted to what was going on and might be able to take some action.

I slipped farther along the side of the steamer; the chugging was driving me crazy. In the dark you depend on your ears, and I couldn't hear a thing. Moreover I had gotten to a point just back of amidships and was now near the bearings of the paddle wheels, which were screeching softly—petroleum and silicon lubricants were going to be a great thing when they came in!

"Please, sir, do not do that," a soft voice said ahead of me. It sounded like a woman.

There was an unintelligible mutter.

You know how hard it is to recognize your own voice? I couldn't be sure.

"Oh, please, sir, stop, sir, please," the voice said again, softly.

I slipped under a staircase leading up to the bridge and peered into the darkness.

"Oh, god, sir," the voice said. Something was writhing in the darkness.

I pressed closer and listened; the male voice suddenly groaned.

"That's good, sir," the voice said. "If you're in town, I can be louder there—"

The male voice muttered something, and the woman then gave her address and said, "Eight shillings, as we agreed, sir. And I did indeed make a show of resistance, but you recall, sir, we agreed I was not to make too much noise."

The muttering got surly, and there was the clink of coins.

I crept away. In any century, more people than spies are sneaking around in the dark. It occurred to me that if I had thought that poor guy sounded a lot like me, unpleasant things might have happened. At the least, we'd all have had some explaining to do.

I descended to the lower, crowded deck, which was largely open, loaded with barrels of cargo and stacks of finished wood from the New England sawmills, plus all the people they could cram aboard her. It took a lot of crawling around, and it must have been an hour, before I gave up and admitted that if my doppelgänger was there under a blanket, I could have stepped on him three times without knowing it.

I headed back up. I had seen him, I knew I had seen him . . .

Someone was crouched on the deck in front of me. As the moon had risen higher in the sky, the light had gotten better, but the fog had thickened, and now I could see only a dark outline, like a badly developed black-and-white photo. Staying in the shadows, I went nearer; I was almost on top of the figure before I saw that it was a man, stretched out at full length on the deck, peering over the side toward the lower deck. In his hand there was a pistol.

Something about the hat made me suspect, and I crept forward; when I was a bare three feet away I saw enough of the face to be sure. "Warren," I whispered. "Did you see him, where is he?"

There was no response; his concentration on the deck below was absolute. I crawled closer.

"Warren. It's Strang. Are you—"

There was no response. Knowing what I would find, and shuddering from much more than the icy spray-covered deck on which I lay now, too, I reached out and touched his face.

The unseeing eyes never blinked. He was cool to the touch, not yet cold, but that would come soon enough, and already the flesh was beginning to stiffen.

8

I crawled back slowly and carefully, though if my counterpart was watching the body, he surely would have fired by now.

Damn, and I had liked Warren, liked him quite a bit. I had this idea of myself as being tough, an ice man, bent only on revenge and slaughtering Closers . . . and it wasn't entirely true. I felt like bursting into tears; I'd just lost a friend.

But if I had normal feelings after all, I also seemed to have my full complement of desire for vengeance. We were going to settle accounts soon, I decided, and with that my brief wave of mourning was done. My heart was cold as the fog and as dark as the night, and I crawled forward, determined either to find my man or eventually have a shot at him as he disembarked.

He was nowhere on the upper deck. I even went back inside the saloon to check, with no better luck.

By now a few determined gamblers were still playing in the casino, but he wasn't among them, or among the disorderly heap of men in coats and knee breeches piled together and trying to sleep in the armchairs.

I had been around the upper deck several times, as well, and the more I thought, the more I doubted he had been there at any time that I had; one of us would have seen the other, there would have been a shot, and that would have been the end of it. That left the lower deck, where he could hide forever, and with a moderately good disguise probably get off the boat . . . or just slip over the side and swim to shore, as long as he waited until the very last minute and had someone waiting with a change of clothes and a hot fire . . . I knew in these waters in early spring you could die in minutes from exposure, but how many minutes? And would he know? When would I have to start waiting for the splash?

I shifted the small black bag in my hands a couple of times. It, too, had slowed me down, but I had no better way to carry the weapons I needed. The hand that clutched the handle tended to get raw and numb, so I'd been using my left hand, trying to keep my shooting hand in decent shape.

There's an old Sherlock Holmes line about "When you have eliminated the impossible, whatever remains, however improbable, must be the truth." There's also an old joke about a drunk looking for a lost quarter under a streetlamp, even though he lost it in the alley, because the light was better where he was looking.

If that other Mark Strang were hiding out on the

lower deck, I wouldn't find him until he tried to get off, and quite possibly not then. He wasn't on the upper deck. I doubted he would have been admitted to the bridge or stayed there so long if he'd come up with some pretext, and I didn't think he was likely to know any more than me about how to steer one of these things. And there was nowhere to hijack it to.

That left one significant space I hadn't investigated—the engine room and fuel hold. What he'd be doing down there, I didn't know, but if I could find him there, I could do something about it, and I couldn't find him anywhere else.

The best way was probably back through the saloon and down the opposite stairs, so I went forward again. I was almost at the saloon doors, and just passing around a little wind barrier they had to protect the deck chairs in nice weather, when something moved in front of me. I stepped sideways silently.

"Please don't hurt me," the voice said softly. It didn't sound like the working girl it had been before; I thought it was probably the steward, and who else—other than us agents?—would have been out on deck at this hour?

"The key," a voice said. It sounded like my own voice on the answering machine.

"Yes, yes, sir, but there's nothing down there, the passenger valuables aren't locked in the engine room sir—"

"The key," it said again, and I knew the voice for my own. In the dark I could not make out which shape was whose, but sooner or later they would separate, and if need be I could stun them both, and then revive the steward—*after* I made sure my counterpart would never wake up.

Doing my best to keep it silent, I turned the catch on the black bag and reached inside, feeling for the NIF, which should be lying on the right, with the SHAKK on the left. Something hard and the right size for a handgrip met my hand. I began to draw it out slowly, but something felt wrong.

With great care I set the bag down on the deck and braced, but it took a hard pull that was nearly impossible to keep silent.

Neither of the figures noticed; there was a jingle as one handed a key to the other, but the hands were hidden behind the nearer one, and I still didn't know who was who in the dark.

I felt with my left hand, and then bit my lip in pain. Something had seared into my left hand . . .

I forced the case open wider and felt more carefully, looking out for blades, to confirm they were there, not to cut myself on them again—

And I found them. There were bone saws, scalpels, and now that I felt more, bottles of medicine in there. I had taken Warren's doctor bag by mistake, and god only knew where my SHAKK and NIF were now.

I wanted to scream and throw the thing around in a rage, but I bit my lip, closed the bag, and set it down on the deck. Time enough to pick on myself later.

My left hand wasn't cut badly, but it was slick with blood; I wrapped it in a corner of my coat and squeezed down hard to stop the bleeding.

The two figures finally parted. I drew my Colt from its shoulder holster; this wasn't so finely discriminating a weapon as the NIF, and I would want to be right about who I shot. Unfortunately, the builds were similar, the light bad, the fog thick—

Abruptly the more distant of the two figures brought up a pistol and shot the other in the back. The steward fell with a scream, wounded and probably dying—when you're hit in mid-back like that, in a world without antibiotics or blood transfusions, you're a goner.

My alter turned and ran. I shot at him twice, unable to hit him even at the close range because I could barely see him, and I couldn't seem to adjust for the roll of the deck—

And he shouted, "Help! Murder! Murderer on the deck!"

My real position was instantly clear. There was one fresh corpse and one dying man on that deck; the dying man, if he could talk, would describe me. And I was standing here holding a smoking pistol.

I turned, darted into the shadows, and fled down the stairs, jamming the gun back into the shoulder holster as I went. Nobody was going to be listening to me if I tried to explain.

There were screams and shouts from above, and I realized they had found the dying steward and Warren's body. That would at least slow most of them for a moment; I needed to get under wraps here somehow or other.

The problem, of course, in this chilly April night, was that every blanket that could possibly be found on that deck was in use. Moreover, my clothes were too nice and too clean—a leg with stocking showing anywhere, or my relatively new and decent shoes, almost anything of the kind, could easily betray me as not belonging where I was. And this was the kind of America where if they bothered to take me into New York for trial—the captain no doubt had the authority to hang me right there—the trial would be next morning and the sentence carried out ten minutes later.

I squatted as deep into one shadow as I could get, between two bundles of blankets that seemed to be a sleeping couple, probably a farmer and his wife taking some choice part of the crop into the big city . . . lucky bastards, I thought, be content where you are, it's a big nasty universe—in fact it's millions of big nasty universes—and if you can find love in just one place and time, stay there.

That made me think of Chrysamen, which was distracting if I thought about her as a person and discouraging if I thought about whether it was time to call for a rescue yet. The mission wasn't quite in danger, just me . . . and if I died, the signal would go off automatically. I still had the button in my pocket, but I didn't yet have a good excuse to push it.

There were lanterns being lit all over the place above, a lot of people were beginning to order each other around, and some of the sleeping bodies were beginning to stir on the deck where I was, not yet very aware, but their consciousness sort of crawling to the surface to see what the noise was about. I couldn't stay where I was, and there was no diversion readily available, at least none I could think of—best to get moving before they came down here with the lanterns.

I had known my counterpart had come down here with the key to the engine room, and you couldn't miss your way to that—the deafening racket as you got closer to the stern was unmistakable. As swiftly as I could move without making noise, I headed for the stern, stepping over bodies, pistol already drawn because it was too late to worry about looking suspicious, and I wanted it handy.

The noise grew louder, and now there were no bodies on the deck—no one could have slept there.

In the moonlit shadows, there was something on the deck, something too small to be a person, and yet it had what looked like two human arms flung out from it. For one horrible instant I thought it was a human torso, that my counterpart had dismembered one of his victims for some obscure reason, but then I saw that it was too flat to be a body.

I crept forward and found a complete set of clothes at the rail—clothes that would have fit me perfectly.

I stared at them for a long second. Had he stolen a uniform and boldly dressed in it right here, was he naked for some reason—

I looked over the rail to the dark, brooding bulk of Long Island, still farm country where it wasn't outright wilderness, and my thoughts came together with terrible speed. I leaped to the engine room, found it locked, beat on the door, and shouted for a moment without any response.

There could be no more than a minute to spare. I yanked the Model 1911A1 from its holster, thought,

Don't jam now! and laid it against the lock and bolt. I wanted to make sure a single round would do the job—I had only the round in the chamber, one fresh magazine in the Colt, and two magazines in my pockets; when you're trying to change all of history it's a good idea to make sure you have enough ammunition.

I pressed the muzzle hard against the surface, to get the round angled to shatter the lock and, with a little luck, then cut the bolt as well. The trigger squeeze was slow and smooth, the kick against my hand was ferocious as a little pressure backed up into the barrel (and amazingly, it didn't jam as I'd half expected it to).

There was more shouting behind me now, and they'd be here in seconds. I kicked the door open—it bounced a foot or so open and then bounced back. I shoved hard with my shoulder, against some resistance on the other side.

It was what I might have expected. The engineer was in there, and both stokers, and all had rolled against the door from where the bodies had been piled on an overhead fuel bunker. All three of them had round holes in their faces, the size hole a pencil might make if you jabbed it hard into a watermelon, and all three of them had baseball-sized chunks torn from the backs of their heads and sprayed on the walls; there was a smell of cooking meat where one such chunk had smeared across the hot face of the boiler.

Apparently my Closer doppelgänger also liked the Colt Model 1911A1.

All that I saw in a short glance, in the vivid red

light pouring from the firebox, so that even now in my memory I see it all in reds and blacks, the shadows deep and hard and everything else stained shades of red and orange in the flaring, dancing light. It was a scene out of hell, and yet none of it was interesting, at least not compared to what I was looking for, not at that moment. I was looking for something in particular, and unfortunately there were twenty or thirty things it could look like . . . a lump of clay, a black box, an irregular package, an old barrel, but it would be—

There. On the side of the boiler there was a silvery cylinder, about the size of a can of tomato juice or a two-pound can of coffee, stuck onto the iron surface with what looked for all the world like black roofing tar. It did not look like it belonged there.

I had seconds to work, and chances were I was dead anyway. Since that other Mark Strang had gone over the side like that, into water cold enough to kill you in minutes—even if he had a wet suit and scuba gear at his disposal, he was in a hurry. And if he was in a hurry, he hadn't set the timer for very long.

So, with no time for anything better, I did something I *really* don't recommend if you find a bomb— I grabbed it with my bare hands, braced a foot for an instant on the burning-hot surface of the boiler, and yanked that silver cylinder with all my strength.

There was a sucking, tearing noise, and it came off as if it had been stuck on with very old bubble gum. I pivoted on my remaining foot, put my other foot down, and was about halfway through a crude pitch-out when I realized there were two big goons with pistols in the doorway. They raised the pistols, staring at me; I held the bomb in front of me, and said, "Dynamite," with as much control in my voice as I could manage.

Their eyes got wider, but their pistols didn't move. I began to walk very slowly toward them, and said, still keeping my voice level and slow so that they would understand what I was saying, "I don't understand the fuse on this thing. It may have a clock inside, or go off when it is bumped." On my third step I was pushing the bomb toward the point where their shoulders overlapped. If they had wanted to take it from me, I'd have let them, but they backed out the doorway.

Out of the blazing heat and red light of the boiler room, the air rushing out around us making yet more fog, we must have looked like three shadows in a complex dance. I had lost my night vision from my time in the boiler room, and I was stumbling just a little, taking short steps and trying not to fall in the sudden dim, blue fog. My hands were hurting incredibly, and I knew that the cylinder was burning them; if that had been a modern high-pressure boiler, I'd have had third-degree burns if I didn't just lose my hands, but fortunately a wood-fired low-pressure boiler doesn't get much above the boiling point. It was merely like grabbing a pot of boiling water off a stove with your bare hands and then slowly walking twenty feet with it.

I knew I wasn't far from the aft rail, anyway, and as I continued toward the two big guys, they parted before me, and when they slid sideways to be out of my way, that told me about where the rail had to be.

This time there was nothing to prevent my pitch-out; the cylinder rose over the railing in the smeary, gray-red light, etched against the fog, faded and blurred in outline, and was gone into the fog; an instant later there was a splash.

I turned to face my captors, holding my hands over my head. I could feel my hands stinging in the salt spray, and I didn't want to think about what that indicated; I would have to give myself one of my two remaining injections of nanos to heal that, and I wasn't at all sure, offhand, whether the kit with those was in my pocket, where I hoped it was, or in my bag—which was god knows where.

The two men closed in gingerly, and one said, "You would be the Mark Strang wanted in Boston for wanton murder?"

"I am in fact his twin brother, Ajax Strang," I said, "but I know how much like a lie that sounds, and you might as well take me in, for I'm sure I'll have to prove it in front of a judge sooner or later."

"And was it your brother who murdered Dr. Warren and Steward Little?"

"It was."

"And the engineers?"

"Yes."

"And where is he now?"

"His clothes are beside the railing back there," I said, "and I can only assume that he has gone over the side and swum for Long Island. It's very cold, but if he has confederates ashore—and I am all but certain that he does—he can probably live to tell of it."

"Mr. Strang," the shorter one said, "since you

have already said you don't expect us to believe you, I will only say that of course we don't. If you'll please keep your hands up, sir, then we can—"

The light was so bright, even through the fog, that my first thought was that lightning had hit, and my second was of a nuclear bomb. I was facing away from it when suddenly the fog flashed in my eyes, and it made my eyes hurt and my head ache; the men facing me were facing the light, and they were temporarily blinded.

I guess that was why they didn't shoot me when I flung myself to the deck on my stomach, ignoring the agony of my burned hands slamming onto the hard surface. The truth was that I wasn't thinking at all; I just knew something really bad was about to happen.

In the time we had been talking, the *John Locke* had gotten more than a mile from the point in the Long Island Sound where I had heaved the bomb overboard. Sound travels at twelve miles per minute, or about a mile every five seconds; I had a long breath or so, there on the deck, to listen to the screams of fear and pain from those who had been awake and looking the wrong way, to watch the boots of the men who had arrested me take a few aimless pain-filled steps around on the deck, and to feel the swollen agony of my hands on the rough, cold, salty deck. I even had time to say to myself that at any moment the sound would come and that I had better get my hands over my ears to prevent ruptured eardrums.

I felt my elbows begin to press on the deck to move my hands to my ears—

I had forgotten that sound travels much faster in water, the concussive effect from an explosion is nothing but a giant shock wave. The deck below me slammed up into me with terrible force; it felt like being pressed against a door that was being taken down with a headache ball, like being a mouse flung into the air by some sadistic kid and then hit like a ball with a baseball bat.

There was a long dark second of knowing nothing, and then it was terribly, unbelievably cold, and I couldn't breathe. With all my strength I lashed out in all directions, but things were holding me, my movements were dreadfully slow, and—

My hand broke out of the water over my head, and I realized I was floating, with a big bubble of air between my shoulder blades trapped under my coat. I stroked down with my arms and raised my head, just like they teach you in Boy Scout swimming classes, and sucked in a big gulp of icy air. It was wonderful stuff, even though it set me coughing, so that it was three or four more bobs upward before I got my breath for good.

Even in that short time I had become so cold that my arms and legs were numb, but I managed to tread water and, using my stiff, burned hands, get my pants off. Fortunately they were just knee breeches and two hard yanks were enough to tear out the buttons near the knees, though it skinned my already burned hands under the salt water, and I came close to fainting. With one more yank I got the belt off, and with another the pants came down. It took forever to knot the legs into a loop—maybe a whole minute or so—but then I was able, with a hard kick in my treading water, to whip the tied breeches over my head, filling them with air, pull the open waist down into the water, and stick my head between the tied legs. The pants inflated beautifully, another thing that worked just like in Boy Scout camp, and now besides the air in my coat I was being held up by the air-filled "collar" formed by my pants.

That meant it no longer took any muscular effort to keep my head out of the water. I began to kick, slowly, looking up often, trying to make for the black bulk of Long Island by the shortest way I could, though in truth from my position, with my eyes only inches above the water, I could only see that some parts of the horizon had a dark band of land above them, and not which of those was closer. I had not kept any sense of direction between the explosion and finding myself in the water.

I figured that two thousand strokes of my legs ought to bring me to land if I kept pointed in the right direction, and so I started kicking, resolving to count to three thousand before pausing to take stock. This was not a good time to start the kind of thinking that leads to seeing the world as futile, let alone for noticing that if there are billions of time-lines and hundreds of millions of galaxies in every one of them, one life doesn't matter much, and I was cold and tired, and that my hands really hurt. Pain kills endurance—that's why in collision and combat sports you try to land some blows on your opponent even if those blows couldn't be effective enough to win, just so that the poor bastard gets tired faster.

Two hundred and fifty strokes later the shore was about where it had been, my hands hurt more, and my legs were beginning to ache. I shifted to a sidestroke kick and kept going. Do this twelve more times and then think about it. Jeez, the water was cold . . . good thing I was in shape, but even so I could easily have had a heart attack hitting this stuff at this time of year. . . .

The night had finally turned clear, or maybe the shore breeze was tearing the fog away. The moon was incredibly bright, with no competition from the ground, and the stars seemed to blaze rather than twinkle. It was dark enough so that I could see the colors of the stars easily . . . so nice and dark, and now that I was keeping a steady beat going with the sidestroke, I was warming up quite a bit. I could almost just go to sleep in the nice water for a bit.

What was the count? I thought I had counted six hundred a while back, but maybe it was only five, or then again perhaps I'd missed a hundred a couple of times and it might be a thousand. How could you keep track when it was so boring? At least it was . . .

Warm.

There are three major warning signs for hypothermia. You stop feeling cold. You stop being able to concentrate on even simple, important tasks. And you have an overpowering desire to sleep.

And once you do, you never wake up.

Really, I was doing pretty well; during World War II a lot of men died of hypothermia in less than ten minutes in the cold water of the North Atlantic, and I'd probably hung on for half an hour or so, so far, and I wasn't really beaten yet, just tired—

Back when I was a kid my brother Jerry and I used to go see movies about World War II every chance we got. That was before Jerry was killed, of course, but then he'd been out of college a year or two before . . .

He was killed with Mom and my wife Marie. I remembered it vividly; I was so tired, and if I dreamed of that, I'd have nightmares, I knew I would even though I was so comfortable . . . so comfortable even in the cold water of the North Atlantic where my ship had gone down but Humphrey Bogart would be coming along any minute in the rubber raft with some hot soup for me . . . or was it Katharine Hepburn? Or would he have Katharine Hepburn for me?

That made me laugh so hard that I sucked in what felt like half a lungful of water, which set me to retching and coughing. The blast of pain in my chest and the heaving of my guts brought me back to consciousness enough to realize how much I had drifted. I was back in the real world, even if not very coherent. There's something about getting close to dying, and realizing it, that brings you right around, if you're not completely gone.

Had I been kicking? I didn't know and began to kick harder to try to make back the time—that wasn't right, I knew it wasn't right, I'd tire myself out but I couldn't think—

I churned onward; maybe the effort could raise enough heat to ward off the last stages of hypothermia, and at least this way if I sank, I would go down fighting. I avoided thinking about Dad, Carrie, Porter . . . about Chrys . . . about warm beds and big bowls of hot cereal and soup . . . there were an awful lot of thoughts to fight off, when you came right down to it.

My left foot felt like it burst into flames, so much so that I yelled, and it set me to coughing again, and in the convulsion whatever had gotten my left foot promptly got my right, and now both of them were in agony. I doubled over an instant, putting my head all the way underwater, and the diving reflex cut in and panicked me, groggy as I was, so that I lurched wildly, thrashed frantically, and then stood up to get a breath . . .

I had coughed and spewed half a dozen times, getting the last of all that out of myself, before I realized. I was standing in chest-deep water, and only two hundred yards off there was a stony beach with pine trees behind it. I lurched forward in the water, stumbling over submerged logs and boulders, and finally staggered up onto the gravel, my pants deflating around my neck as I came out of the water. I made myself keep going—I needed food, shelter, something—and just beyond the trees I found a winding wagon track, probably leading to some farm or small town.

It was a warm night, and now that I was out of the water, shivering and walking were doing some good.

How long I staggered, I don't know, but the sun was up when I finally came around a bend and found myself looking at a fallen-in barn and an empty house. There was at least a roof on the house, and I staggered in and found a corner with a big pile of leaves in it, reasonably dry.

Finally I allowed my burned, peeled, bloody hands to fight into the pocket of the breeches and find one of my two remaining ampoules of nanos. I jammed it in my arm and lay back, panting; they would rebuild me, but they took so much energy from the body that I had been afraid that while I was moving they might make me collapse, and even now I was afraid they would be the final push into hypothermia and death.

Something came into the room; my vision was getting dark though there was bright sunlight pouring in through the door. It got closer and I leaned down to see. . . .

I was down on my chest, I realized, face-to-face with a live chicken. It had black feathers and a red comb, and it was turning its head from side to side and clucking a little, now and then, wondering if it remembered people or not, and perhaps thinking that people used to put out corn for it. I reached very slowly forward—I doubt I could have done anything quickly—and it came a step closer to see if maybe I was about to throw the corn. The expression of stupid curiosity, of being focused only on the hand as maybe something to feed it, might have made me laugh if I'd had the energy.

There was a practical difficulty or two to consider, I realized, as I grabbed the chicken by the neck. I could make a fire but not trust myself to tend one, and the field-butchering lessons from training school were kind of hazy in my mind, and anyway I didn't have hours to pluck it—

And then the one important thing I needed to remember from training school kicked in. The nanos in my bloodstream would last about twenty hours. During that time if I were cut, the wound would close up within hours, and if I became infected with anything, the infection would quickly die out. It was like having a super-immune system, though paid for at a huge cost in body energy. But right now, with the nanos fresh in my bloodstream, I could drink out of sewers, eat roadkill, and lick every used bedpan in a hospital, and nothing would happen to me—

The thought is father to the deed. My hands clenched once and broke its neck, and after that I don't remember much, or at least I prefer not to remember much. I woke up late in the afternoon with the sun going down, blood and feathers all over my face, and an amazing mess of discarded bones, feathers, beak, and feet scattered around. I seemed to have lost five pounds, which I figured was probably the body consuming whatever it didn't get from the chicken. I yanked the now half-dry breeches on and staggered out into the yard.

There was still a bucket in the well, so I cranked it down and up—it was work but not difficult. My hands were covered with new pink skin and quite a few other places seemed to be fresh and healthy new flesh as well; I noticed that some of my fingernails had grown an inch during the night, probably the places where I'd hurt a fingertip or cuticle, and when I looked down at my feet I saw that not only were all my toenails really long, but apparently the nanos had sensed that I needed calluses there, and I had the kind of hard, horny feet you get from going barefoot in all weather, though again all the flesh was pink and new.

When the bucket reached the top, before I quite took a drink, I caught sight of my reflection. There were still blood smears everywhere, and a feather or two that I hadn't brushed off. My hair was a tangled, uncombable mess, and where the nanos had rebuilt skin on my face they had also caused big tufts of whiskers to grow out. And I was so happy to be alive, and feeling well, that I was grinning like a complete idiot.

"That's *Mister* Geek to you," I told my reflection.

9

It wasn't so much knowing how to get to New York that was the problem—after all, I was on Long Island, on the side facing the Sound, with the water a scant few hundred yards off. All I had to do was face the water, turn left, start walking, and keep walking.

My guess was that the *John Locke* had blown up at about 3:45 in the morning, local time, and since it was due into port at about 5:30 A.M., I was probably thirty miles, as the crow flew, from Manhattan, which was all there was of New York at the time—the whole settled area was what's just Lower Manhattan today, Greenwich was not only still a village, but it was separated from town by farms, and the other boroughs were pretty much farmland and little villages. According to the information they'd dumped into me, in this timeline Boston was not only still the biggest city in the Thirteen

Colonies, but would stay bigger longer. The faster things grow, the more they concentrate near pre-existing sites, and thus it would probably not be until the middle of the next century that New York would become America's largest city.

All of which meant that there weren't going to be any buses or trains along soon, and even when I got to Brooklyn I would probably have to wait a while for a ferry.

That put me in mind of another problem, and I checked my coat pocket. I still had the purse of silver and copper coins, and there was enough in there to get me food, lodging, and a ferry if I was careful. It would be nice to afford new boots as well, but maybe Morris would be able to lend me a pair or to extend a loan . . .

It did seem pretty bizarre that with the resources of almost two million Earths, the ATN was borrowing petty cash from private citizens. Maybe I could do something to get everyone reimbursed. . . .

If your feet have ever been in shape for barefoot walking, you know there's still a limit to how much of it you can do. After seven or eight miles, I was getting footsore and, moreover, skirting around villages was getting to be a hassle. I figured I was far enough away, and my clothes were at least dry, so that people wouldn't immediately wonder if I'd been on the *Locke.*

I was in luck; the next place along the road, a little tavern called the Dog and Pony, had fresh bread and sausage and decent beer for not too much, and was willing enough to let a traveler sleep in the yard for part of the afternoon. I got fed and rested, borrowed a scissors, and trimmed my nails. For a copper coin I rented a basin and razor and made myself all but presentable; if I had just had shoes and stockings, I might merely look like I needed new clothes.

The owner was a little surly guy who didn't seem to have the slightest curiosity about me; as I finished another beer for the road, and was tucking some bread, cheese, and sausage into one of the coat's big pockets for later, though, he asked, "You'll be going up to New York Island, then?"

"I will," I said. "I've friends with money up there."

"If you don't mind working your way, the stage is coming, and I know they'll have need for a porter; bunch of folks swum to shore up the coast after the boiler blew on that *John Locke* yesterday, and the money to pay the passage for the rich folks just went by t'other way this morning. I know Fat Richard that drives the stage is short a porter-boy, for his usual one broke an ankle, and with so many well-off folks, even if not much floated to the shore, there's bound to be need for a porter-boy coming back, especially what with some of them bound to be injured."

"That's a great opportunity," I said. "How soon do you expect him?"

"I expected Fat Richard an hour ago. That means he either broke a wheel and won't be here today, or more likely he was held up getting all the quality-folk"—he said *quality-folk* the way my father used to say *terrorists*—"into that stage, with them all fussing and some of them hurt and wanting special arrangements."

I nodded. "So it might be worth waiting around for an hour."

"Aye. And if you'd like to dig up a potato bed for me, I have an old pair of boots you might have for it, that I think would fit you."

We checked, the boots fit, and I got to work on that stony patch of ground. One nice thing about the times, there was no paperwork to fill out, and if you weren't fussy, there was at least some kind of work. I remembered reading that it was only after the Civil War that it could be proved that anyone ever starved to death during an economic depression in America; before that the countryside was always close, and most people could do enough work to get themselves a space in the barn and a little food.

When the stage pulled up it was the silliest-looking contraption I'd ever seen. Luc had introduced vulcanized rubber to this timeline a while back, so it had inflated tires with wooden spokes, like what you see on old Ford Model T's in our timeline. That meant a lot of the shock from the bumpy, rutted road was being taken up by the undercarriage, and to make that work in turn there was an elaborate double system of springs, much more complex than on any old-movie stagecoach, with individually pivoting and counterweighted arms rather than axles. So from the wheels up through the suspension it looked like a moon buggy.

Above that it got weird. The passenger compartment was small and looked like it was about half the size it should have been for the wheelbase; it was shaped like a can of ham lying on its side, and held on to that silly suspension with a system of guy wires, as far as I could tell.

In front of this thing was what looked, more than anything else, like a bicycle built for four, or two bicycles built for two welded together side by side, in which each front cyclist pedaled the front wheel directly, like the way a kid's tricycle works, and each back cyclist pedaled the back wheel directly. All four of them sat way back, so that the rear cyclists had their heads only a couple of feet from the front of the stagecoach behind them.

Or, I realized, three cyclists. The rear seat opposite me wasn't taken. And just as abruptly I realized what the other duty of a porter-boy must be. Well, I didn't mind working, and it beat walking for speed if not for ease.

A few minutes later introductions got made. The guy on the left front was Richard, "driver, captain, and company man," as he described himself. He was fat only by comparison with the other two, and I'd actually have said he was just muscular. I suppose it's all relative.

I sat behind him. The one who sat on his right was Abel, the guard, who had a short carbine strapped over his shoulder and a pistol at his belt. To my right was Seth, the conductor, who grinned at me as we got onto the seats; there had been the minor task of carrying one man with a broken, splinted leg to the outhouse and back, but there was no one getting on or off at the Dog and Pony, so I didn't have to load any additional bags.

"It's a clever porter that signs on where the guests have lost their luggage," Seth said.

I smiled back at him. "Except for some work on my legs, I think of this as a free ride."

"Wait till we climb that hill down yonder, from Whitstown to Flushing. That's when you'll see how free this was!"

I nodded and laughed, and then the driver said, "All right, now, gentlemen . . . we're all introduced, our passengers are all aboard . . . now, porter-boy, Strang, have y'ever did this here before?"

"Not at all."

"Right, then you're as fitted to the work as Abel here and better than Seth, for him's learned it wrong. Y'see where my left foot is here?"

"Yes, sir."

"Well, now you see where your own is. And see that your own comes back to that place when mine comes back. Not just afore, not just after, and not pritnear, and if y'do get it wrong—and ye will, ye will, ye've these two t'show you how to get it wrong—don't you try to catch it up, but take your new mark and mind you keep it where it is."

"Got it, sir."

"But will y'do it?"

"I'll try."

"That's what I was afraid of hearing, ye're just like the others."

"We ain't moving at all while we talk, Richard," Seth said.

"True enough. And . . . one, two, *stroke*."

If you've ever ridden a bicycle built for two, you've got an idea of what this is like; your legs work pretty hard and it takes a while to get in sync so that you're pushing forward but not doing all the pushing. This was both easier and harder—harder to stay on Richard's beat, but much easier to tell when you were off it. In half a mile or so, I wasn't exactly an old hand, and I could tell my muscles would complain later, but I was pulling my own weight and then some, and we were clipping along at something like four miles an hour or better.

The other men settled into the rhythm comfortably, once it became clear I wasn't going to be impossible, and soon we were bouncing along that dirt road, the little scoop seat at my back thumping my butt, the pedals pushing against my legs but not painfully hard. I could probably, if I'd had a decent pair of running shoes, have run the distance in a bit less time, with maybe a little less overall effort, but it was interesting, anyway, to see the little villages roll by and to swing by the occasional farmer out doing his spring plowing.

I even saw one steam tractor, an immense chugging thing that slowly crawled across the field on big steel rims, which got everyone talking for half an hour; Seth and Richard were very much in agreement that it was the wave of the future, that with steam you could plow deeper and faster, and so forth, but Abel inclined to the view that the horse was cheaper, oats grew faster than wood, steam tractors did not make more steam tractors, and anyway no one had proved to him that plowing deeper really brought that much more wheat.

"You've all got strong views on it," I noted. "Are you all from farming families?"

"Aye, each of us," Seth said. "Alike as can be in that way. We're all third or fourth sons, there was no more land to take us, and the frontier is a long way away. Oh, we dream about it, but mostly we work. The pay's good, and the Flushing Line is a good outfit, you know, and so it's not so easy to decide to pack it all up and head for Ohio or Kentucky. Nothing keeping us here but decent pay, but that's a lot, especially when a man's got a family."

In my timeline, there had been almost no settlements across the mountains yet, and many people who weren't in line to inherit a farm had been angry about the frontier being closed to them. It occurred to me that even after the Revolution, only a tiny minority of people had ever packed up from settled regions and moved west; the only difference in this timeline—but it made a big difference in terms of peace and quiet!—was that the normal force of family and community, and not the authority of the state, was perceived as holding people back.

I wondered what was happening to the Indian nations, and whether they'd get any better deal out of it this time. Supposedly there were going to be treaties of alliance and development and all that, but the fact was ATN was in a war, they wanted timelines to develop fast economically and technically because more sophisticated timelines made better allies, and people who just wanted to live the way they had been living tended to get stomped flat.

We claimed we had allies who had joined ATN while still in the Stone Age, but the truth was that once we found them, they didn't stay Stone Age long. And even now teams were jumping farther and farther back into the past, despite the enormous expense, to get industrial civilization going earlier and earlier in more and more timelines, and thus to create allies who were ever more advanced in science and technology up at the 2700s A.D., where the fighting was going on.

That meant that if you were, say, a Polynesian in 800 A.D., in any of billions of timelines, with hardly any risk at all that the Closers would attack your timeline in your lifetime . . . you were not necessarily made better off when ATN agents showed up and leapfrogged Japan into the Industrial Revolution, bringing steamships out to the South Pacific hundreds of years early. Very likely you died of disease, or you quite possibly got shot by not-yet-fully-culturally-sensitive Japanese, or failing all that, anyway, a pleasant life went out the window.

I wondered just how much good we actually did . . .

I also wondered why I was having such thoughts. I figured it must be partly having the luxury for thought—these were not guys who talked a lot unless there was something to talk about, the work was repetitive and strenuous but not killing if you were in shape, and so I had my mind and eyes free. It was a nice spring day, and those are the best kinds of days to be outside with nothing to think about that has any immediate relevance.

The villages were getting larger as we got farther south and west, and the country was more settled. In a little while we had reached the point where there were no more woods between the farms, as such, just one farm after another shading into villages and back to farmland, and the road was actually a little crowded—that is, there were people, wagons, pedal stages like ours, and so forth in sight all the time. I took a deep breath at that; it occurred to me that my counterpart was out there some-where, and that given that he was me he'd not believe I was dead until he saw the body. Therefore, he'd be looking for me, just as I was for him, and whichever of us saw the other first would have the advantage.

The hill outside Whitstown, leading up to Flushing, was everything Seth had implied it would be. When you push a wheel directly with pedals, if there's any resistance at all, the resistance has all the leverage. For my own sour amusement I started to figure it out. . . . The stage behind us probably weighed 1500 pounds loaded, we and the pedal gadget probably 850, and on a 5 percent grade like this that worked out to probably (near as made no difference) a backward drag of maybe 120 pounds. Okay, so each of us has one foot pushing at any given time, thirty pounds against the foot—except the wheel multiplies it. If the pedal radius was about half the wheel radius, that would come to—

"I worked it out once," Seth said, "and I make it that we're pushing sixty pounds on a stroke."

Well, he'd had more than one chance to do this, I thought to myself. Richard said, "Just hold your stroke as even as you can; this part is where ye earn your pay. And remember at least ye won't get pedal-kicked as we do comin' down."

The push went on for quite a while, but there was a reward I wasn't expecting at the top of it; I had wondered why everyone was emphasizing getting to

Flushing, and I hadn't realized that it was the end of the line. As we neared the top I saw that the woodsmoke marking the clear spring sky was not from a village, but from a power plant, and that there was a traction line starting from here.

I still had all the bag unloading to do, but all it was was work, and Seth, as conductor, helped a little. Besides, a coach full of shipwreck victims doesn't have a lot of bags and certainly doesn't have anything very heavy.

The passengers inside the coach were pretty quiet—not surprisingly, since I'm sure many of them were still in shock. Three were injured badly enough to need carrying, and that was the toughest part of the job, not so much for the weight as the caution I had to put into it.

"You're good with the public," Seth observed. "Stick with work like this, and you might make conductor some day—though it's not so easy as it looks."

I grinned. "I've other business, but it's good to know I could take this up. Though I doubt I'd make conductor quickly—it looks like there's a lot to learn." No matter where you go or when you go, you'll never give offense by telling a guy his job looks difficult.

"Well, that's what Richard told me when I was a porter-boy and he was a conductor," Seth said, grinning. "Good luck wherever you're bound."

By now it was almost dark, but there was still a seat on a passenger car just starting out on the traction line, so I rolled into Brooklyn that evening just as it got dark. A quick walk down by the wharf assured me that the ferry would start again at first light and told me how much cash I had to hang on to to get across to Manhattan; there was enough left for a bed and two meals at a tavern nearby, though if I'd had anything worth stealing that I couldn't keep under me, I'd have thought a long time before staying there. As it was, the fleas attacked pretty fiercely at first, but I was so tired that it didn't matter to me, until morning anyway.

Breakfast was a big bowl of boiled potatoes and beef, plus all the corn bread I could cram in, which was quite a bit—the nanos had presumably expired, but I was still paying back the energy they had consumed.

It was chilly and gray but not raining when I walked down to the wharf and caught the ferry. The East River was as gray and flat as the sky, and there was no wind this morning, so we went over pretty quickly. Less than four hours after I'd gotten up, right about midmorning, I was on the wharf in Manhattan, completely broke and knowing only Morris's address. It was even less impressive than my entrance into Boston. I hated to imagine what arriving in London would be like.

Well, nothing much to do for it; Morris, like most of the rich people, lived up higher and away from the water, so I started the short walk from the wharf up French Church Street to Broadway. There was more brick and stone than in Boston, and in general everything had an air of comfortable prosperity; I remembered that in my timeline Thomas Paine had said that the British moved the war to the Middle Colonies because there were more Tories there, and there were more Tories there because more men had more to lose. I could believe it, looking around me; here were thriving businesses, big new houses, all the signs of growing wealth in a city, and a lot fewer beggars than you would see on the same streets in my timeline. Hardly anything makes a city more attractive than enough work for everybody . . . I hoped that the progress we had created here would at least continue to provide that much.

The only problem with all this was that I was still broke and ragged.

I had just rounded the corner onto Broadway— and that was really a surprise, for Broadway at the time was a wide, tree-lined mall, thick with elms and chestnuts just budding out—when something caught my eye, and I quietly slipped over toward the trees and the traffic on my right to get a good look without being seen.

Sure enough, there I was again . . . it was my double, this time getting into a cab a block away, headed the other way on Broadway from where I was going.

Instantly I was turned around and headed for the wharf again; I wanted to know where he was going and what he was up to. Besides, I was fairly sure that he had not yet spotted me, and one of the best ways not to be spotted is to be behind the guy, not in front of him . . . if I didn't let him go, then he couldn't surprise me later.

I could have saved myself most of the walk; he finally arrived at the Exchange, at the foot of Broad Street, not three blocks from where I'd gotten off the

Brooklyn Ferry. He didn't stop there, however, but turned to the left and headed for the wharves.

I had little trouble following him in the crowd, for his one-horse cab had actually moved more slowly than I could walk in the crowded streets, and there were so many people down around the markets that it wasn't difficult to stay concealed. Even after he got out of the cab, I wasn't afraid of losing him, because he was making such a direct path through the crowded market stalls and down to the wharf that there was kind of a cloud of disturbance around him—he seemed to have no problem with just shoving people out of his way.

When he reached the wharf, he headed straight for one big, modern liner, and I realized I was about to have a major problem here—its stacks were already puffing smoke as she built up a head of steam, and from the look of the tides coming over, I guessed they'd be sailing about noon.

The liner was the *Royal Hanover*, and it was another strange contraption, a product of the way that Rey Luc had goosed the technology of this timeline along. There were four tall, thin stacks that looked more like the stacks of a Mark Twain–kind of riverboat to me than anything for an ocean liner. Each of the stacks had two wooden masts running parallel to it, a scant foot or two away; presumably those held up the stacks in high winds, since they were all bolted together, but just as obviously they could be used for rigging sails in the event of an emergency.

The *Royal Hanover* had what was pretty clearly a hybrid between paddle wheels and screws; probably the better metals developed so far weren't available in quantity enough to make drive shafts that wouldn't buckle under the load, so it wasn't possible to just put a bladed propeller on the back. But paddle wheels are pretty inefficient in that you're moving most of the wheel out of the water most of the time. So they had compromised by putting a huge cone-shaped wooden screw on the stern, with hundreds of slender wooden blades arranged like a shallow spiral staircase.

The whole ship had been hung with so many fake columns and pilasters that it looked like a storage room at a theater where they did a lot of the Greek tragedies.

And, from my standpoint, the most notable feature was that there was a man at the gangplank checking tickets and signing people in. The ship would probably depart within three hours, and when it did, there went my best chance to track my doppelgänger—not to mention that he would get a head start of several days in London. I didn't even know if there were any more berths available on the *Royal Hanover* . . .

I had just about figured that out, and sidled up one little alley while doing it, when I saw the other Mark Strang come down off the ship again. He checked a pocket watch and talked with the guy taking tickets, then set off in a considerable hurry— probably getting some last-minute thing for the trip, or maybe just finding a quiet corner to send a message back to his superiors in one of the Closer time-lines.

I watched him go, and a thought dawned on

me—a beautifully simple thought. I wanted to be on that ship. And there was no problem at all with that, because I already *was* on that ship.

I let another five minutes go by, to make this convincing, hoping desperately that he wouldn't turn out to have gone somewhere a block away and already be coming back. Luck was with me for once, so when the five minutes had passed, I strolled up the gangplank.

The ticket taker, of course, took one look at a man in a ragged coat and breeches, ruined shirt, no hose, and obviously old and worn boots, and got ready to heave me back down the gangplank. I walked up very close to him, and then said, "Do you recognize me?"

He stared for a long minute, and then said, "Mr. Strang, is it? What on Earth are you doing in them clothes, sir?"

"Keep your voice down," I said, keeping mine very low. "You know I'm a Customs agent, of course, but in fact I also do His Majesty's business"—and I dropped my voice very low—"as a mumble mumble rhubarb. Lord Harumph takes an interest in these matters, you might say."

He nodded and laid a finger beside his nose. "Ah. We carry many such passengers lately."

"I'll warrant you do. Well, I shall be coming on and off a few more times in the next few hours. Most of the time you will not see me—believe me, sir, I am good enough at my trade for that!—but should it happen that you do see me, it would be a very good thing for your King and country if you did *not*, if you take my meaning; just, er, wave me through, if you could. I just wanted to make sure you had a good look at my face so that you could—"

"Recognize without questioning. Of course, sir, go right aboard and do whatever you need do. But we still do sail at 12:15 sharp, sir, so make sure you're aboard."

"I shall certainly make sure I'm aboard," I agreed. "Thank you so much for your understanding."

"Er, for that matter," he added, "I should assume then that you have means a bit, er, beyond those of your occupation?"

"You may assume it."

"Well, then, sir, I shan't worry about the deposit you've put into ship's safe; just see that a man comes round to pay the *Hanover* when we make port, and see that he, er—"

"Is able to compensate you for your trouble and assistance. Very well, and thank you!"

Not only had I gotten aboard, I had just opened an unlimited credit account with the bad guy's name on it. I was pretty proud of myself.

It took no more than ten minutes to find a good, out-of-the-way corner and get to sleep under a pile of canvas there. With any luck at all they wouldn't be using the sails this voyage—this might make a good place to sleep for several days.

I stayed down there, getting hungry but being cautious, until long after I had felt the ship start to move.

10

It was late afternoon when I finally let myself emerge on deck, and I was careful to come up slowly. Unfortunately, I couldn't very well ask, "Has anyone seen me around? Where am I?" and I really did not want to meet myself—not yet, anyway. I had had some time, besides sleeping, to do some thinking, and I had a better idea of what I wanted and needed to do to get the mission accomplished.

In the first place, there *had* to be something that the Closers had done besides just dispatch my counterpart to stir up trouble in Boston. I mean, I'm a bright, talented guy and all that—who should know better?—but I am *not* Superman, and this guy was exactly as capable as I was, but not any more capable. He couldn't possibly have created a situation teetering on the brink of war just by covertly financing a few hotheads on both sides, stirring up hatred here and there, and that sort of thing. That's a harassing action, not the main process.

Moreover, I'm not a subtle guy, the Closers are noted for liking brute force, and yet somehow whatever was being done was being done invisibly. . . .

That meant the Closers had somebody a lot more subtle and shrewd than I am on the case, and most likely that person was in London. So almost for sure the other Mark Strang would be going there to meet him.

Now, that left me three options. The first one appealed to me because it was action and it was simple: kill my alter before he got to London and take his place at the rendezvous, then play it by ear and try to penetrate the Closer operation that was probably active there. Easy to do, and I'd supply my own alibi doing it; as soon as the body was over the side and out of sight, there would be no evidence that anything wrong had happened.

Two, stick close to my alter, spy on him, follow him, and eventually figure out what was up; then use the knowledge when I got to London. That other Strang might even get away, though I kind of hoped not; he was pretty clearly not the biggest fish in this particular pond anyway. That was the prudent and intelligent thing to do.

The third thought, which I kept pushing to the back of my mind, was this: the Mark Strang they had looked so much like me, and had so many features in common with me, that he could not have been from a timeline at all far from my own. Chances were that he and I shared a lot of background, and that meant perhaps that we shared many values.

It was far too much of a gamble, but in principle—after all, a Crux Op on mission is only evaluated by results, not by how he gets them, I told myself, and then had to shove the thought away, but it kept coming back.

In principle it might be possible to turn that "other me" to our side. He could not be so very different from me, and if he was not, then his heart should go to the ATN, as mine had.

Just where that piece of lunacy was getting into my brain from, I really could not say. My best guess was that I was thinking of the many discussions of values that Chrys and I had had in our letters; her timeline believed in changes of heart very deeply, and many of their favorite stories and plays had villains who reformed at the last moment, usually for the sake of sheer pity. I thought those were lovely fairy tales. . . . but then she thought our stories, in which violence finally settles the question, were naive because violence usually just means more violence.

If I could win by changing his heart, it would please Chrysamen a great deal.

I suppose if I'd been stuck with him on a desert island or something, with no clock running and without so many lives at stake, I might have considered it or even given it a try. After all, it couldn't hurt that much to try. . . .

But there was just too much at risk. And the fact was that I hated Closers, hated them for all that they had done, and to see a version of myself working for them was altogether too much. Whatever might please Chrys, if it were just up to me, I'd have already fed my doppelgänger to the fish, and if I'd been able to put him in alive, and watch a group of small sharks gradually consume him, I'd have stood there laughing with glee while I watched.

So, since there was that idea I couldn't get rid of, which seemed dumb, and the thing I wanted to do, which seemed rash . . . and the most prudent course—I decided to go with the most prudent. I would let him live, spy on him, and see what I could learn.

And *then* maybe if I was lucky, I would feed him to the fish.

So when I came up on deck, I was mentally prepared for the worst possible case—I'd pop out and he'd see me—but no such thing happened. I had noticed, and had heard from some of the men in Boston, that my counterpart was a little more decadent than I, had more of a taste for liquor and fine food, gambled with more enthusiasm, and so on. Warren had assured me he had a reputation as a "whoremaster," which is what the eighteenth century, with its keen sense of calling things by their right name, called what we call a "stud."

On the other hand, unlike me, he hadn't shown much interest in books or etchings or anything of the sort. Boston at the time should have been a spectacular place for finding all sorts of Early American crafts and arts—after all, Paul Revere wasn't being distracted so much by politics and was getting to concentrate more on his silversmithing—and if I had been stationed there on a long-term basis, my house would have been full of such things. This version of myself, though, seemed to own neither art nor books.

So I figured with nothing much else to do on shipboard, and not being all that good at entertaining himself, my counterpart would probably be attending the "rum and gambling in the forward saloon" that was scheduled. Meanwhile, there was a great big tea in the rear saloon—and in the fine old British tradition that would mean a full-fledged buffet meal.

I filled my plate four times, leaving it on my counterpart's bill, and each time crouched in the corner, looking as crazed as I could manage, and wolfed it down. It wasn't so much a matter of having lost my manners, though I was hungry enough not to be too fussy, as not wanting anyone to look too closely and perhaps later ask my counterpart how he had changed his clothing or his behavior so quickly.

At any rate, the mutton sausage, corn bread, and sweet cakes were all quite good, and I managed to slip a lot of the last plateful into my pockets for future reference.

Since the afternoon was very fine, and I suspected my other self of being the kind that did not come out till dark, I let myself enjoy a brief view of sunset from the stern. It was cold out there, and I was still pretty ragged, but it was nice to get a breath of fresh air, and once you're out of sight of land the sea is about the most restful thing human beings have ever found to look at, even when it's wild; a lot of the Romantic painters were fond of it for just that reason, and standing here on the rolling deck, realizing that some of those painters had already been born, I found myself hoping that this timeline would still have its Romantic period.

I had just decided that I had best get back below-decks when the steward came by and exchanged glances with me; then he smiled and said, "Sir, I might mention that if you want to be inconspicuous here, your dress as a beggar is a giveaway. No man dressed as yourself could afford to be aboard . . . "

I nodded. "Unfortunately it's the only disguise I was able to bring with me from the city."

"I might arrange something; several of our sailors are tailors as well, you know, for on long voyages there must be such, and they draw a bit of extra pay for it. I could look about and see if someone might be found to make you another set of clothes. . . . something to conceal your appearance, so that you did not look yourself."

"It's a magnificent idea," I said, and I had to admit it was. The steward was undoubtedly going to mark up the price by several hundred percent, and he knew there were deep pockets to pay the bill. "But the tailor, or yourself, must not bring the clothes to my cabin—I have reason to believe that certain people who are no friends to the King are searching my cabin every time I am out of it. There's a pile of canvas—I believe it's the auxiliary sails—just below us here, is there not?"

"You've a sharp eye, sir."

"Sometime when you see me up and about, place the clothing just under the port, aft side of that pile." It was the farthest corner from where I was sleeping. Even if he happened to synchronize it by my doppelgänger, that should be all right. "It need be nothing fancy; indeed the main thing that would help is if it concealed my face, and looked like something a man might wear on shipboard. I should be happy to pay full price for old clothing if it got it to me the sooner."

The steward couldn't quite keep his eyes from lighting up at that point; the deal just kept getting better. "In that case, sir, I think we might well have something under there tomorrow morning."

"Absolutely splendid! Your King will be grateful!"

"If he ever hears of it, I suppose, sir. Will you want anything else?"

"Hmm. Now that you mention it . . . I will be in the forward saloon for much of this evening, dressed, er, differently from this fashion, shall we say. I would like it very much if a large gin punch— very sweet, with the gin doubled—should find its way to me. Make that two, actually . . . but only if you can find me one other thing . . . "

"Yes, sir?"

"A fellow gets lonely on these damned voyages, and the service from which I draw my pay is under-standing, but not *that* understanding. Do you sup-pose there might be, among the women on board, someone who would like to be my companion for this evening, one who would come to me and make it appear as if she were drawn to me, and to, er, do my pleasure for the night? If you could draw on some of my private money, which is in the ship's safe, to pay for this and arrange it—so that, you see, I need not be conscious of handling money . . . "

"Why, surely, sir! I should be delighted. I've one with red hair, plump, and nice in the chest, and another that's young and just learning, very thin and dark—"

I knew my own tastes well enough to say, "Thin and dark should do it. But anyway, if it is arranged, see that she doesn't mention money, that she merely acts as if she were fascinated with my person. It's a whimsy I like to indulge."

"And a very good one, sir, and popular. I've handled such things before. Indeed if you like she can play the virgin."

"Oh, that won't be necessary. Let her be, even, a little coarse in her approach. But see that I have two of that sweet gin punch first—say it's from an admirer. Gin, you see, tends to enhance my prowess."

"It can all be as you've said, sir—"

"And naturally while you are in the safe I should expect you to take some handsome fee for services rendered and arranged. Shall we say one third of whatever the young lady gets?"

"I get that already sir, but you mean in addition?"

"I do indeed. My employer, you will see, shall make all good—as we enter port, I'll give you a note to send to them that will bring them at once to the dock with the gold required." Another thought occurred to me. "Oh—and if you'd be so kind—I have reason to believe they watch me constantly and closely when I am 'myself' and not while I am in disguise. Therefore, if you could avoid speaking of any private arrangements whatsoever when I am not in disguise—"

"Of course, sir. Very good indeed, sir, everything will be as you ask." He was bowing and scraping, and I think he was fighting the urge to rub his hands together with sheer glee.

We parted company then, and I went below to

catch a nap before the night's festivities. Things were looking very strikingly up.

When it was dark above, I slipped silently back to the deck and began to do some real exploring. I needed the other Mark Strang to be out of his cabin for a while, and then I needed him to be in there and not likely to come out. Sending him a load of gin (his head was like mine, and gin goes straight to mine—and in a warm sweet punch like that he'd have no idea how much of it was hitting him), and then a hooker, ought to guarantee the latter part, and the setup ought to keep him out of his cabin long enough.

We'd learned a lot about picking locks at COTA, and this one wasn't tricky; the main protection for shipboard cabins was that you were at sea for almost three weeks, and in the event of theft they could search the whole vessel, thereby at least finding the property and quite possibly also catching the thief. Though pricier metals could be used on the lock, the technology wasn't at all far advanced; a little jiggering and the end of a knife was enough to flip a couple tumblers and let me pop the thing open.

Now, here was something strange . . . I'm a pretty neat guy, and always was except during the half year or so after half my family was blown up in front of me. It isn't so much that I try as that it comes naturally; everything tends to have a place, and it's easier to put it there than elsewhere. So I was more than a little startled to find that the little chamber was a complete and utter mess, with clothes, books, papers, and whatnot strewn everywhere, covers from the bed on the floor, and even a plate with a mostly eaten dinner on it sitting in the middle of the unmade bed. Moreover, I've never smoked—I hate the smell—and there were two overflowing ashtrays in here, along with a stale smell of tobacco. All that since just this morning? I wouldn't make a mess like that in a week.

My first thought was that I had broken into the wrong chamber, though I'd been very careful about confirming it from the passenger list . . . but no, a quick search turned up the complete giveaway—a .45 caliber Colt Model 1911A1. There weren't any of those in this timeline yet, except the one that I was wearing (which might or might not work after the swim it had had—sometime tomorrow I was going to have to strip it and clean it thoroughly, and even then I had no way of knowing how dry the cartridges had stayed), and the one my counterpart had brought with him.

That, too, seemed pretty strange. Me, I don't go anyplace, not even to the toilet—hell, especially not to the toilet, it's a classic place for a hit—without that good old piece of Army iron. If I had to jump out of a burning building and the choice was between bringing my .45 or bringing my underwear, there's no question. After all, you can shoot perfectly well without underwear.

But apparently he had gone unarmed to dinner, and was very likely getting drunk there and messing around with a girl he'd never seen before. This other

Mark Strang really did not have my instinct for self-preservation.

More searching turned up a few familiar Closer weapons. There were three more of the "tomato juice cans," adjustable bombs a lot like ATN's PRAMIACs—you could set an explosive power anywhere from about "big firecracker" to "ten megatons." There was a long, thin wandlike thing with a tall sight, a bulge at the middle, and a rest that fit over the big muscle of the upper arm. I'd seen them in training; you extended the sight to eye level, gripped it by the bulge, and squeezed the bulge to fire. It hit whatever was in the sight.

It was a slightly better weapon than our SHAKK, in several ways, and we were trying to get it reverse-engineered and improved still further.

All that I had found out so far was that I was in the right room and that my other self was a Closer agent. I had been searching thus far in the little bit of moonlight that came in through the porthole, going by feel until I found something in the mess and then holding it up to look at, but now I pulled the curtain over the porthole closed, jammed some clothing against the crack of the door, and lit a candle.

I almost gasped, but if there had been any possibility that this was the wrong room, or that the other Mark Strang was from a timeline close to mine, all the doubts were erased now. There were small hooks for pictures on the side of the room opposite the porthole, and the other Strang had used virtually every one of them, all for pictures of the same thing.

My wife, Marie.

She was the same one, and clearly he had branched off my timeline sometime after the marriage. I remembered a couple of those pictures from my own dresser drawers and albums.

It had been nine years in my subjective time since Marie had died. I had been a very different man at the time—one of those all-around guys, brainy but an athlete, too, nothing ever too difficult for me or even really hard, married to the best-looking woman I'd ever met . . . I had been one of those guys for whom the whole world constantly goes right.

We had flown home at my father's expense, as the whole family always did, for a Fourth of July gathering at the big house by Frick Park in Pittsburgh. Marie and I, Carrie, and her twin brother Jerry were all to fly back that Sunday, so we were all getting into the van; Marie and I had only that morning broken the news to the family that Marie was pregnant.

Mom was driving, Marie got in, Jerry got in, Carrie was about to get in, Mom turned the key—

The van exploded.

The bomb was so big the van flipped over and rolled down the lawn, slamming most of the frame and floor up into the ceiling.

Carrie was flung back against me, her legs gone below the knees, one arm severed and torn to a bloody mess that was later found in the bushes.

I got my belt off and made a double-bind tourniquet for her legs, used hers for the stump of her arm, and stopped the bleeding. She lived, and being tough as she was, she found a way to go on.

When I finally looked up, it had been maybe twenty seconds since the bomb had gone off.

Dad had run by me, but when I turned to follow him I fell—somewhere in getting hit by Sis's flying body I had broken my ankle. So as I pushed myself up off the blood-slick pavement with my hands, I could only look toward the van, where the blast had flipped it and rolled it down the lawn. It lay on its side, flame and smoke pouring from it. The underside was toward me, and I could see how it had been slammed upward, bending into the body everywhere it wasn't tied down.

Dad, forced back by the heat, was dancing around it like an overmatched boxer, trying to find a way to the still-open side door now on the top of the van. From where I lay, I could see it was hopeless—the frame had been bent and jammed up into that space, and even without the fire he couldn't have gotten anything out through there.

He said he saw something or someone moving in there in the long second between when he got there and when the gas tank blew. The coroner said, though, that to judge from the shattering of the bones that remained afterward, there was nothing alive in there at the time; he thought Dad was probably hallucinating, or perhaps had seen a body sliding down a seat or falling over on its side.

Anyway, if the coroner was right, Mom was probably crushed against the ceiling instantly; Jerry was impaled on a piece of chassis that must have ripped up through the seat at the speed of a bullet, entering his body somewhere near the rectum and breaking his collarbone on the way out. His whole body cavity must have been torn to jam before the first time the truck rolled, and the sudden pressure loss would have meant he was unconscious before he knew what happened.

Marie's skeleton was twisted and coiled. The coroner thought that the whole seat had been hurled against the ceiling, fracturing her skull, breaking vertebrae in all three dimensions, ripping both femurs out through her leg muscles, rupturing many of her internal organs. The coroner said chances were she was dead before the van rolled down the lawn.

But Dad saw something moving in there, just before the gas tank blew, and if Mom and Jerry had both received unquestionably instantly fatal wounds . . . what did that leave? Hallucination, a body falling over, or . . . ?

And yet Dad said he saw something moving in the van, before it burst into flames, before it burned completely, while he danced around it trying to find out what, or who, had moved, and while I crawled miserably down the lawn, my clothes still drenched in Carrie's blood, and long before the fire trucks and rescue crews got there.

It had sent me into that very special part of hell known as severe depression. I had spent half a year doing nothing, staring bleakly, trying to wish the world away.

But I had eventually come out of it. Gone forever was the trendy, brilliant young academic I had been; I had not looked at my partly finished dissertation in art history in a long time. A chance came for me to carry a gun and get even with Blade of the Most Merciful, the Closer front that had butchered my family.

And I found that I was not the same fellow at all. There was a cold black core of glassy, frozen hate in my heart, and I took a deep pleasure in hurting the kind of people who needed hurting. Ex-husbands who beat up their wives, loons who attack singers, losers and creeps out to hurt someone famous, that sort of thing. I came to appreciate the deep, booming thud my boot could make on a deserving human rib cage.

The scar in my heart that was Marie came to me sometimes in dreams. Sometimes I thought, just for a moment, that our child would be in third grade, if Marie had lived to give birth. But the pictures of Marie were mostly off my desk, mostly out of my living quarters . . . not because I chose to forget, but because that was the past, and the past needs to be kept behind us, so that it doesn't devour the present and future before we get there.

It had taken a while, though. And part of what had helped had been when I had stumbled through the rabbit hole in time that let me find out that my real enemies, always, had been the Closers. During my time in the other timeline, when I remembered Marie, it had tended to be with a certain fond warmth—just after I had pulled the trigger on a Closer, just after another one of the self-styled Masters of all the timelines had been blown apart. I kept one picture on the wall as a remembrance and never looked at it.

This was more than just a remembrance. This was a shrine.

And in a strange way it went with the sloppiness of the room. I hadn't even bathed most of the time that I was in the deep depression after the murder. Had this version of myself had not ever really come out of the catastrophe, not learned to go on? God knew he was active enough; he had none of the depressive's inability to move. Had he lost Marie in the same way? Had he lost her at all?

It was a complete mystery, and not one I was likely to solve by standing there and staring at it, I decided.

The great thing about sloppy people is that when you toss their rooms they rarely notice. The bad thing is that often there are just a few objects—and you don't know which ones they are—that they knew the exact location of, and if you get one of those out of place and they notice, they've caught on. It's so much easier to get a neat person's place back together.

I had been pretty much around the horn of things to look at. He didn't have anything written down, but then I would not have either. I wanted to sabotage his weapons, but the only one I understood was the .45; a thought occurred to me, and I traded him my wet and probably rusting one for his clean, well-maintained one. At least he was taking care of his gun even if he wasn't making his bed. For good measure I swapped him ammo, too.

There was nothing else. It was about time to go, I figured—and then I heard my own voice. "It's over this way, so just come on and be a good girl."

She squealed and gave a high-pitched giggle; I

would have put her at two years past puberty at most.

I had had a plan for this in mind since the first instant I had been in there. I blew out the candle, yanked the clothes away from the door, jerked the porthole curtain open, and slid swiftly under the bed. I might have to count on the other Strang to fall asleep, but I'd heard him stumble a time or two as he approached, and his speech seemed a bit slurred. And if his body was like my body, he would be sound asleep right after sex anyway.

Though no matter how you try, it's kind of hard to maintain any mental dignity while you are hiding under a bed spying on yourself.

The door opened, and I could see his boots and her slippers. "A light so you can look at me?" she asked, and he said no.

I'd've felt a little funny about laying a kid prostitute in front of twenty pictures of Marie, myself. And there wasn't much to report about all that. He wasn't especially nice or especially rude, and I wasn't all that sure that he was excited at all. He told her what he wanted, and she did it, and that was about all. When I thought about it, during my bodyguarding days there'd been one "working girl" who had hired me to protect her from her ex-pimp, and paid me partly in exchange of services, and that was about what it had been like—sheer biological relief and not much attention paid to the partner.

About as soon as he was done she was yanking her clothes on and out the door; there wasn't a lot of romance around here to spare.

I waited till I heard him snoring, then crawled

forward very slowly and carefully, a hand and a knee at a time, until at last I could stand and look down on the sleeping, drunken man. There was enough moonlight through the portal to see that his face was wet, I suppose from crying in his sleep, and that a trickle of snot traced its way over his upper lip. The room smelled like an old locker room, and it was oddly cold and clammy, and not just from the April sea air.

I could have killed him then and there, any number of clean and quiet ways I knew, and I'm not sure he'd have cared. But I needed to know where he was going, who he was meeting, and why; and more than that, to my slight disgust, I found I pitied him.

I slipped through the door as quietly as a shadow does, closed it, and turned to breathe the clean sea air. When I got back to my pile of sails, I found that the steward had already put my change of clothes in there, and once again I was to be dressed as a scholar. At this rate I might have to think about finishing my dissertation . . .

I spent a few hours moving quietly from corner to corner, finding ways to listen to conversations. I wanted to get whatever idea I could of what impression this other Mark Strang had made, and of what people were expecting to find in London. I learned nothing about either subject; mostly I discovered that the two prostitutes the steward had smuggled aboard were busy, that the man mixing gin drinks was busier still, and that the celebrated "wit" of the period wasn't much of anything to listen to cold sober. After a while, with everyone else asleep, I went back to my pile of sails and got some sleep.

11

In a line of work like mine, you can learn to relish the dull times, even the *frustrating* dull times. The steamer took twenty days getting across the Atlantic and swinging around the south of England to come into London, and I would honestly have to say that I enjoyed most of it. I spied a lot on my other self, and mostly I found that he was bored and depressed, he didn't appear to be communicating in any way with anyone in this timeline or elsewhere, and he did pretty much the same things every day— ate, exercised enough not to lose muscle tone, began to drink late in the afternoon, and then either spent the evening at cards (he cheated, just a little, not so much to win I think as to make the situation a bit riskier) or drank himself into an early stupor and went to bed.

That helped me considerably, because he didn't usually go into the aft saloon, where the main meals were served. He ate at the gaming tables or sitting in a chair in the forward saloon, and he ate only enough to keep himself alive. Meanwhile, I was free to go wherever he didn't—deck promenade in the afternoons, a big breakfast before he got up, a huge tea while he got his start on the afternoon's drinking. I suppose that of the crew that tended to the passengers, about half thought Mark Strang was that morose, silent man who appeared to be working hard at drinking away some small personal fortune, and the other half thought Mark Strang was that burly man in scholar's clothes, hat brim always pulled low outdoors, who liked to sit in corners and read, and ate immense meals.

As to which of us was really which—well, I leave that to the philosophers. I know who *I* was, anyway.

The last day of the voyage, we entered the mouth of the Thames and a steam tug, one of those paddle-wheel contraptions like the one I had seen in Boston, came out to drag us into London Harbor. The afternoon was fine, but I had sent my counterpart a lot of rum punch, a lot of gin punch, and the girl the night before, and he was still asleep in his cabin. Just for fun, once he was really asleep, I had slipped in and done some some random damage to his Colt, then carried off his hypervelocity gun, since when he woke, to a series of surprises he would know I had been there anyway. We'd all fired them at COTA, and I thought it might do better things in the hands of the good guys than it would where it was.

So he was asleep belowdecks when the bum boats came out. Those were little boats, mostly operated by women, that came out to sell trinkets, tourist stuff, fresh fruit, and anything that people might want at the end of a sea voyage. More importantly, from my standpoint, they generally carried off mail.

I had my envelope and letter ready to go, the address selected after listening to half a dozen gentlemen discuss various difficulties in their lives, and the first bum boat to pick up mail and leave was carrying that envelope. The steward glanced at me, and I grinned at him. "That's the letter that will get your gold fetched here, sir. You should find that I've been more than generous. Now, let me add, it is desirable that I not be seen leaving the vessel, and to that end, I shall contrive to appear to be drunken and ill in my cabin. If you could refrain from waking me—pretending to wake me, that is—until half an hour after our gangplank is down—"

"Not a problem at all, sir, the *Royal Hanover* is a busy vessel at such times, and I'll have no time—I'll see to that."

"Thank you," I said.

The toughest part of the whole thing was finding a good time to go over the side on the side away from the gangplank; when there was finally a chance to do so quickly and quietly, I had been pacing around nervously there for half an hour. At least this time I had been able to change back into my rags, and had swiped the equivalent of a GP bag from my counterpart so that my scholar's clothes and weapons stayed dry. The water was not just cold but filthy—London's system for handling sewage was to let the rain wash it out of the streets and into the river, and the city was huge by the standards of the day, and, of course, though steam was coming in, there were still large numbers of horses.

I dragged myself out underneath a pier, nearly retching from the smell, and began to look for some stairs or a ladder up, preferably farther away.

There was a loud clatter and some shouting; after a bit I heard my own voice, bleary, raw, hungover, and in a rage. The note I had sent had fetched a detachment of Royal Marines with the note that I was wanted for murder in Boston, and had added debt-skipping to the list of offenses. Moreover, it had added that I was a dismissed Royal servant "still trading on His Majesty's name for financial credit."

My badly hungover doppelgänger was being arrested; he would be in jail for a while, and given how much I'd spent on his account, would undoubtedly be remanded to debtors prison. I had little doubt that he'd break out of there in short order.

Meanwhile, I was free and armed. Unfortunately, I also stank, and the little bit that had been returned to me from the ship's safe wouldn't get me far. Still, it should cover a room at an inn, a meal or two there, and the most urgent need—a bath and a shave at a barbershop. Getting all of that should take the rest of the day, but I was no longer in quite the hurry I had been in.

A little shopping allowed me to find a place where the bathwater was fresh and hot and the soap newly made and soft—a big consideration if you visit any version of the eighteenth century, believe me. It's not to be assumed that you will get bathwater that hasn't had other people in it, or get it warm, let alone that you will get any kind of soap that you want touching your skin. But this place was quite nice—they'd been hoping to get the sailors off the *Royal Hanover* and had been beaten out by a special price reduction on used hot water down the street—and very willing to make a deal.

It takes a little getting used to, to take a bath in front of everyone who happens to be in the barber shop, but once I got past the modesty issue (which I did by ignoring it till it went away), it was marvelous to sink into hot water and take a good stiff brush to my skin. There had been baths available at a very high rate on shipboard, but though the Closers were paying for it, I had not wanted to take the chance of being out in public, out of disguise, in such an exposed position for so long. So I had had no bath since the one in Boston almost three weeks before, and I'd had a couple of saltwater swims and a good dunk in sewage in the interim, not to mention wearing the same clothes through much of the time. I was good and ready for this bath, and it was about as wonderful as experiences come.

Afterward, dressed, clean, and relatively presentable, I set out to see what the biggest city in the world had to offer. For an art historian, the effect was very strange, for much of what there was to see in the city was still something you'd recognize from Hogarth, Rowlandson, or Gainsborough, but in three dimensions, with full color, and vividly noisy and smelly—but at the same time there were great thumping steam-driven factories, small Sterling-cycle cars rolling in the streets, a few electric trolleys, and in the great squares, electric lights just coming on. It was a scrambled mixture of everything; as I watched, the *Great George*, first of the Royal Navy's new dirigibles that were eventually to cross the Atlantic, passed over the town—the newspapers on the ship had said it was due to begin field trials. There were telegraph offices in all the better-off districts, and it was very much like seeing bits of London in the 1920s wander into a collage of the London of Tom Jones and the London of Sherlock Holmes. Every so often I'd note some landmark from my own time—St. Paul's, or the Tower, or one glimpse of Westminster far away—but mostly it was as confusingly different as Boston and New York had been.

There were a dozen Whigs that Washington and Adams had told me to look up, and after I had strolled around a little, just for the pleasure of being off the ship and somewhere relatively safe, I stopped a boy and asked him what street I was in. His accent practically screamed "Cheapside"—it was the old Cockney accent, not the one you hear today but the one that you find in Dickens's novels—but I managed to gather that I was on Threadneedle Street.

A moment later I felt like a complete fool, when I passed the Bank of England, a landmark at the time and so much a part of London that it was like having been on Pennsylvania Avenue in Washington, D.C., standing in front of the White House, and asking where you were. Oh, well, fortunately this was a century in which lunatics and the feeble-minded were turned out to wander around, when they weren't being beaten, tortured, or exhibited to amuse the gentry. No doubt the kid merely thought I was one of them.

That realization, anyway, allowed me to know where I was going at once; the coffeehouse where I stood the best chance of meeting any of the people I was looking for (and where I could at least get a newspaper and see what was currently going on) was very near St. Paul's on Ave Mary Lane, a place called the Chapter House. The Society of Honest Whigs, Society of Supporters of the Bill of Rights, and a host of other reformist organizations met there; I was supposed to find Joseph Priestley, the noted scientist and friend of Franklin (and where in my timeline he'd discovered oxygen, in this one he had discovered valence and the periodic table; at least in my timeline I'd have understood what he'd done).

Failing to find Priestley, I was to look for Catharine Macauley or for Thomas Hollis. All of them were from the radical wing of the Whigs, but where in my timeline they'd had very little influence, here they were leading figures in the city, at least as important as Adams and Warren were in Boston. After conferring with them, I'd try to figure out what to do next.

Chapter House was severely crowded, which I might have expected in the evening, and no one had seen Priestley or Hollis; Catharine Macauley would have been conspicuous, as the only women in there at the moment were serving.

Besides coffee, Chapter House served sandwiches and various kinds of cold dinners, so I decided my best bet was to get some dinner and wait out the evening; there was an excellent chance of catching someone I wanted to meet. I found a table—a little circular thing barely big enough to hold a plate and cup—with an armchair, sat down, and waited for one of the girls who waited on customers.

From her, I got a *Times* and a *Daily Advertiser*, both used (which meant they were that day's paper but about one-quarter the price of new), plus a plate of bread, cold sliced beef, and cheese, and then she went off to get me a pot of coffee and a cup.

When she got back with that, I slipped her a coin to do some inquiring around and to make sure that if anyone I wanted to see came in, I'd know about it.

Then I settled back to enjoy myself. So this (despite modifications) was the London of Dr. Samuel Johnson, Goldsmith, Hogarth, Adam Smith, Rowlandson—and with added features like electric lights and flush toilets. It was really a pity that I couldn't tell anyone, back home, or have them believe me if I did tell. I could have traded on this in the English or art departments for a good long while.

The *Times* had mostly news of Court, most of which was that the King made very brief appearances but seemed quite concerned to make sure that his old friends knew he was merely busy, not ill and not avoiding them. This led to all sorts of odd rumors which were lovingly reported as almost fact.

The *Advertiser* was radical Whig, and it was much more sharply critical, but since the King himself had been quite Whiggish till recently, and no one knew what had caused the change, there was a certain strange tone in all the stories of trying to get the King to come back to his senses.

In neither paper was there the faintest pretense of objectivity, and I appreciated that fact quite a bit; you might not get the truth from your newspaper, but you would never mistake your newspaper for the truth.

The coffee was very strong by my standards, like barely filtered Turkish coffee, and gave me sort of a caffeine buzz; the food was generally good if very plain. A man could get to like London, I decided.

I had been half-listening to the conversations around me—two young men discussing horse racing and which brothels in town offered the best bargains, a couple of men arguing about electricity and phlogiston, one grumbling owner of a theater explaining for the tenth time to a playwright that if there were not enough songs, the police could close him down and therefore the play was not acceptable without more songs.

There was a certain odd silence for an instant, and I looked up from a theater review in the *Advertiser*—it looked like Sheridan's *The Rivals* was a big hit in this timeline, too, with Mrs. Malaprop much the same, but now parts of it took place in a traction-line car— to see the other Mark Strang.

"Brother Ajax," he said calmly.

Over his right forearm, which he held level in front of him, he had a newspaper, and under the newspaper, only I could see that he had a .45 automatic pointed right between my eyes. "Why don't you invite me to sit down, and while you're at it, avoid moving in any way that makes me nervous?" he added.

I moved my hands farther away from my body;

the gesture was invitation, surrender, and above all else a way of demonstrating that I didn't have any weapon right to hand.

Of course if I had, I'd have used it already, and chances were he knew this.

He sat down, and I noticed, glancing around, that everyone in there was staring at us. They'd probably never seen a set of twins who looked so much alike. So far, so good; right now I really wouldn't want to be alone.

While I had been reading it had gotten dark outside, and though the coffeehouse was now fairly brightly lit, the light came from dozens of candles and some gaslights, so that it all flickered strangely; the clouds of tobacco smoke in the air were thick, warm, heavy, and oppressive, and I suddenly became aware that for all of its comfort, the place had the unmistakable stench of bodies that didn't wash often enough, at least not by the standards of my time in my timeline.

The thought that came to me was that I knew him, literally like I knew myself, and if our situations had been reversed, knowing this was an effective and dangerous Closer agent, I'd have been happy to pull the trigger.

I could not imagine that he was going to be any kinder about it to me. The only question was whether he wanted witnesses, and if he didn't, and told me to come with him, I wasn't going to have much choice.

So there was a good chance I would die in this place, thick with its human stenches, or not far from it, in a history where I didn't belong . . . a timeline where there was no Chrysamen, no Dad or Porter or Carrie, and where there would never be.

I'd have felt sorry for myself about it except I was too disgusted—to get caught at a table in a public space, reading a newspaper—and that made me too angry; life had been all right before Closer bastards had wrecked it, over and over again. Even then, there might have been some purpose in knowing that I was fighting them, that I would get my licks in . . . and now I was face-to-face with the fact that I was at least as much on the other side. Moreover, that other side seemed to be winning . . .

It made me crazy with rage, more furious than I'd been in a long time, angry and reckless and willing to do almost anything.

Almost.

I looked at that automatic, under the folded newspaper in his hand. I knew I had carried it through a couple of good swims in salt water, the one thing that was mostly likely to ruin it, and that I'd done no maintenance before I switched guns on him. I knew his ammo had taken a similar dunking, but it was good modern stuff that shouldn't have been too badly bothered.

That afternoon I'd also taken a handful of dust from under the bed and sprinkled it into the works, spitting on it to make it stick. But I had not dared to damage it more than that and possibly give my presence on the ship away before I had the full benefit of my head start.

Clearly I had just lost my head start, and although I'd done my best to make sure that gun was unreliable, the Model 1911A is tough. It wasn't *that* unreliable. It looked like it was his call, and all my anger would do me no good at all.

"I do want to say, Brother Ajax, that the bit of billing all that to me—and then sending the Royal Marines to arrest me—was pretty good; I'd have been here much more quickly if you hadn't come up with that one. As it was, I finally understood why the steward had been acting so weird around me for the whole voyage, and not only did I get matters straightened out with the Marines, I also got the steward carted off for stealing my gold, and gave the Marines my deposition. I should guess they'll be hanging him tomorrow morning, or, if you like irony, perhaps they'll let him off with transportation to the colonies. We're alike enough that I'm sure you rather got to like him; just think about him at the end of a rope, and the way the neck makes a crunch like a breaking chair, or perhaps imagine him in some nice swamp in West Florida or Georgia, chopping brush and living on bread and water. Oh, am I making you angry? Well, it's just possible, just very possible, that I'm rather angry myself, Brother Ajax. I think you had better come with me."

Suddenly, as I got up and carefully kept my hands away from my sides, and waited while he got my bag, I noticed that for all the bad smells and dim light, for all that most of the people in there were talking about things that didn't matter to me . . . for all of that, I really liked Chapter House. I wanted to stay there.

Mostly because as soon as I was out of it he was going to blow holes in my body until I was dead.

And I'd used that particular weapon often enough to have a really good idea about what kind of holes they'd be. Little and smooth going in, big and raw coming out.

It was dark when we went out of the Chapter House, and he didn't bother to hire a lantern boy; instead he just told me to turn left and walk, then to turn into a deep alley. I started to wonder if maybe it was dark enough to make a move, and then realized that I just didn't know; bad idea to try unless I knew it would work, since there was no real point in getting shot early.

Then again, if he was thinking, he might realize the best way to get me for sure would be to get me somewhere reasonably concealed—like where I already was—and to leave me thinking that he was going to do something else, or had something he had to find out from me . . .

And then just pull the trigger by surprise.

If I knew for sure that it was about to go down— that I was a few feet from the place appointed for my death—I would draw and turn and fire, maybe taking him with me, counting on dark and luck and the rust that might be in the weapon, if he hadn't cleaned it yet, or the dirt that might jam any of the working parts—it was a lousy gamble, of course, to bet on a gadget to fail when it was made to stand abuse, but it would be the only thing to do if I were six steps from him pulling the trigger.

But if I weren't . . . if he intended to keep me alive for a while . . .

There was no way of knowing. And with no way of knowing, in that uncertainty, I couldn't do a thing, except notice everything around me and keep looking for a logical way out of it.

My feet were slipping in the slimy mud of the alley, and it was getting cold back here, where the buildings were so close together that the sun probably never shone in here. There was a strange smell I had not quite recognized, and then I stumbled a little, and he barked, "Hands up!"

My hands stabbed at the sky and threw me so far off-balance that I nearly fell, but at least I knew now that he could see me moving, and that if I was going to get out of this one, it wouldn't be by pulling the .45 from its holster.

I had to appreciate that the guy was as smart as I was and knew me pretty well. He had figured out that if he asked me to extract my .45 and drop it, I'd want to see which of us had a better reaction time. But if he made me hold my coat open and reached in to get it, he'd risk getting a foot or fist in the face and a quick test of one of the nifty pistol disarms I'd learned at COTA.

So it was better to leave the gun where it was. He could always take it off the body later.

It was how I would have thought of it.

Okay, shooting him was out. Temporarily at least. I didn't think he'd appreciate idle chat, either. Better just keep doing what he said.

"Feel the ground in front of you but don't bring your hands too close to your body. I'm wearing infrared goggles now, and I can see you even if you can't see me."

Damn. In the instant that he must have been putting them on, I could have turned and bagged him. But of course—he was good enough to not let me know.

I felt the ground in front of me. I found something with a blade—

"Don't even think of throwing that, but hold it in your hand."

The knife was big and heavy, something a surgeon might have used in that day and age, when they amputated legs and arms with no anesthesia and, therefore, speed was the most important thing.

I held it by the hilt, just as if it were good for something, but in my left hand; if I got a chance with my shooting hand, I wanted to take it.

"Just in case some eighteenth-century Sherlock Holmes should realize that it's odd for a man to hold a knife in the hand he doesn't use—and the position of the shoulder holster would give away that you are right-handed," the other Strang said to me, "perhaps you should move that to your right. Do it slowly. And yes, I do remember that you, or I, or we, are a lousy shot with the left hand. While you are at it, turn over very slowly and sit, so that you are facing me."

I did as he said.

"Now take that left hand and feel to your left a few inches," he said.

I did and I found something under my hand— something thin, and warm, and wet. A little more feeling around and I knew that what I had was a human leg, a small, slender one—and that though still warm, it had begun to cool. I felt slowly up the leg and found knee—and then a ragged place where it was severed at the thigh.

My stomach was heaving, but with no more expression than if he'd been telling me where to catch a bus, he said, "You can find the rest of her around, near your hand, if you're interested in examining her further."

"Who?" I gasped out.

"Does it matter? No one you know. I promised her a few small coins to come back here and do what I wanted. I didn't have to offer her much because she was so young. Then we walked back here, and I asked her to close her eyes and tip up her chin, as if I were going to kiss her. I got her larynx on the first stroke, so she gave no cries; then I cut her up. I think she died fairly early in the process, actually, so I suppose if you're worried about suffering, there wasn't much. You *do* worry about suffering, don't you?"

I felt sick and sorry. I wanted the .45 that was so maddeningly close, right there on my shoulder. I wanted to empty it into him, again and again and again, especially into the face and head, until I had erased any resemblance between us.

"You do, don't you?" he repeated.

"Yes, goddammit, I do, and this is fucking horrible, and I'd be damn glad to see you hanged for it." It might not have been the smartest attitude to take with a guy who had a gun pointed at my head, but it was about the only thing I could manage to say. Throwing up might have been a more accurate expression, but I was too angry and too focused on finding a way to get at him.

"There was a time when I cared about suffering a lot, too," he said. "I can remember it, pretty much the way you remember the pain after the wound is all healed; you know it hurt very badly, and you know you don't want to do it again, but no imagination or memory can really bring it back for you."

"Why?" I asked. "Why would you do something like this to someone you don't know? Damn it, I know you, and I didn't diverge from each other more than—"

"Just about nine years ago, both our times, I think," he said. "So you're thinking we should somehow only be nine years different. But think how different that can be. Your wife . . . mine, too, for that matter . . . your Marie . . . her remains are in a cemetery somewhere near Baltimore, I imagine, near her parents' house?" There was a long pause, and then he said, "You can answer or I can put a shot into your leg, and have my .45 back up and aimed at your head before you can get yours out."

"Yes, she's buried there." Knowing what my counterpart was, I had not wanted to share with him anything of myself.

"Much better, much better. Well, then, she's very different now, nine years later, isn't she, from what you remember? A box of decaying pieces, formerly burned. That's quite different. And your sister Carrie—"

"You made your point. So we're different. So nine years can be a lot. So *why*, dammit? *Why* did you cut up a little girl and then bring me to her body?"

"Because when I finish talking—ah, but you won't know when I'm done—I'm going to shoot you, and leave you here with her body, and then go summon some men from Bow Street, who will come out, discover that I have slaughtered my twin brother Ajax Strang—it was so good of you to come out with that alias and explanation, for one of those detectives on the ferry survived and as a result there are now warrants out for both of us—discover, as I said, that you are dead apparently after you did all this to a little girl. Your case will be closed, and mine will be resolved by a Royal pardon, and then there we are, all safe and sound. You will be dead for a good reason, I will be alive for the good reason that you are dead—"

"But what did *she* ever do—"

"Oh, what did that steward ever do? And yet by implicating him and leaving him in the lurch, you've either sent him off to die of malaria in the American South, or just possibly to his hanging. And what did the people you've shot on your past missions ever do? They got in your way, or they shot at you . . . it seems very fair to me. Pretty clearly, the only thing anyone ever 'does' is to be in the wrong place at the wrong time—and then, presto, they are in a crime, a war, a terrorist bombing, and wondering what they ever did, without realizing that if it hadn't been them, someone else would have been wondering."

Now there was a long, long silence, and finally, very softly, he said, "I want to be understood. You may consider that appalling, but I want to be understood. But you remember what you—or I—used to say back when we were teaching Intro to Art History. 'Art is man's way of explaining himself to himself.' So what we're getting to, here, is the art part. After all, who can resist a chance to be really, really understood . . . "

"I don't think I want to understand you," I said, my guts still filled with disgust, still trying to find a way to a weapon and an even shot at him.

"Perhaps not. But you're going to hear an explanation of it all, from me, now. As I said, I don't know when I'll get this chance again. Which I think you will understand whether you want to or not. And then, once it is explained, I'm going to kill you. So I would say, offhand, that either you can be dead right now, or you can hear me explain, and then be dead. The choice, really, is all yours."

Well, if nothing else, he had made his point very clearly. "Explain away," I said, "and take all the time you want."

12

He drew a deep breath and sighed. I felt the cold stones of the alley pressing up against me, the foul black mud oozing in through the seat of my trousers, and the blood congealing on my hands, and let my eyes roll up for just a second to see a few stars through the narrow slit the top of the alley made in the blackness.

I suppressed a shiver and resolved to stay alert. There was always a chance, if only just a chance, that he would slip, or I would get a chance . . . but only if I was alert at every second. And just now the only tool for staying alert was probably listening to him, little as I really wanted to do that.

When he finally spoke it was like a whisper. "The last time you and I were the same person was Christmas Eve, Mark. The Christmas Eve after Mom, Jerry, and Marie died. Do you remember it?"

"Yes." I could hardly forget it. That night there

had been an attack on my father's house that had been stopped by the guys from Steel Curtain Guards, the bodyguard agency that had been watching us survivors. It had been hard, bloody fighting, in which I had taken no part—because I had been hanging around the house uselessly, lost in another world, living in my bathrobe and eating cold cereal, bathing only when someone insisted, leading the half-dead life of the severely depressed. Somehow, having missed the chance to put a bullet into one of the terrorists responsible had been the final step; I had wanted to live in order to kill them, and that had brought me back from that cold wilderness of despair.

"Well," he said very softly, "in your timeline, I understand, you started to change at that time. But the timelines bifurcated because the Masters stepped back through time to intervene at that point."

The Closers call themselves "Masters." It's just part of their charm, I guess, because of course it implies that all the rest of us are slaves, or meant to be slaves. I didn't like hearing the word used that way, coming out of my mouth, but the guy was still holding that gun on me.

"They came back and made the attack succeed. All the Steel Curtain guards died in the fighting. Then they came in and . . . well, they took me and Dad and Carrie away to one of their bases. And they made me an offer. We could all die, or we could live in a different world. One that had Marie, Jerry, and Mom still alive. One where we three had been killed."

"So you all went," I said. I felt disoriented, dull,

and heavy, and I mustn't feel that way—not if I was to have a chance of getting out of this. "I can understand that."

"No, that's one of the parts I don't understand," the other Strang said, and for the first time he didn't seem to be angry with me or about to kill me, and there was a little, desperate edge of sanity in his voice. "Dad chose to die. Carrie chose to die. I don't know why they did that. They . . . *left* me."

As far as I could tell, though he had nearly sobbed, the .45 in his hand had never wavered.

"And then the Masters took me to another world-path . . . I was a wreck by then, I don't mind telling you that . . . "

"You were—I mean I was—well, both of us were a wreck *before* you were kidnapped," I pointed out.

"Hunh." It was a strange little grunt, with more recognition than anything else in it. "Yeah, I sure was. You're right, of course. Anyway, what happened then . . . well, they took me to a world where there had been no bomb, but I'd been shot in front of the family as a 'warning.' And where they were all glad to see me . . . I spent several days doing nothing but cry from being so glad to be with all of them."

I could understand that. My eyes were getting a little wet. But it also occurred to me to say quietly, "You realize, of course, that they probably produced that worldpath for you to move into. Another Mark Strang died so you could have his family."

The other Strang had been raised the same way I was, and Dad had always had that big poster hanging in the downstairs hallway, that quote from George Orwell that to write anything worth writing you have to be able to "face unpleasant facts." He didn't hesitate long before he said, "Of course that's what they did. I gave it very little thought at the time. And it made very little difference after I figured it out. Well, actually, that's a lie. Two lies. I didn't figure it out, Marie did, and then it made a big difference."

"She didn't like the way you'd chosen."

"Of course not. They'd shot her husband. And I wasn't the same guy. I wasn't the 'real' one. The 'real' one didn't have shattered nerves. The 'real' one didn't have nightmares. The 'real' one hadn't . . . betrayed everyone in the family." There was a funny tone in his voice, something that it took me a while to place because it had been so long, and then I realized there was a strange little whine in it—something I hadn't heard in a very long time.

What he was doing, unconsciously, was imitating the way Marie talked when she whined. Not that that was often, I hasten to add, but Marie and I were married right out of college, and we were two people for whom nearly everything had nearly always gone right. That gives you a pleasant disposition—you're used to people "being reasonable," which is what most of us call it when we get whatever we want, and you generally assume that if there are hitches or delays, they are temporary. But it also means that *if* it does become clear that you are not going to get what you really want, you think there's something drastically wrong with the universe.

When things didn't go well for long enough periods of time—and after all, when you work on archaeological digs together, normally the past has not been obliging enough to leave you exactly what you wanted it to in perfect condition—Marie and I had both reacted less than perfectly. I got sullen and irritable, and she whined.

It occurred to me that with a real grievance as deep as the one she had in this other Strang's timeline, she might have developed that tone that I heard maybe once every other month into a constant, grating, nasty sort of sound that could easily drive a guy half-crazy . . . if he wasn't already half-crazy to begin with.

There had been a long silence. He had said he wanted to be understood and that when he was sure I'd understood everything he would shoot me. Was it better to give him some sympathy and see if I could make him hesitate, or to play stupid and make him explain it again?

There was a cold, unpleasant something dripping off the timber wall behind me, and it was slowly soaking my collar. I wanted out of there; I decided to gamble on sympathy.

"Well," I said, "it wasn't entirely your fault. You were a wreck, you'd been through hell, you'd seen them kill everyone, and you just wanted some comfort from your family—"

"Exactly," he whispered. "But bad as the situation was, they couldn't leave well enough alone—"

"They?" I asked. "You mean—"

"The Masters. Yeah, they won't like what I say next, and you know we all wear a recorder, so they'll hear it. I don't care now, but they'll make me care later."

There's physical courage and there's moral courage,

and they are not always found in the same people; there are men who can face gunfire who can't resist peer pressure, and people who can face being martyred more easily than they can deal with a high diving board. "Then tell me while you still can," I said.

"Right." He sighed. "They claimed they were keeping their promise to make it all right again. They . . . intervened. They did things—and threatened to do more . . . to make all of them, Mom, Dad, Jerry, Carrie, Marie, behave like I wanted them to. I tried . . . that's the thing I most want you to believe, and it is true, I tried to tell the Masters that what I wanted them to do was to stay out of it, let the family find a way to accept me as I was, as who I was, to understand that I hadn't ordered it, hadn't realized what was going to happen, that I just needed a lot of help, and I needed it from them . . . I don't know. I really don't know."

"You really don't know why they didn't listen," I said. It was obvious enough to me, but I'd spent a long time hating Closers and not having to do anything about them but kill them when they turned up. Hatred, like love, requires you to focus a lot of energy and attention. I knew their style.

It had not been enough to create a potential agent for them by restoring his family to him. They had to make that as painful as possible, so that when they bound him to them—as they were bound to do, when you make a deal with the devil he's never giving you a loss leader—this other Strang would experience it as a horrible pain that it was impossible to escape from. The "Masters" don't want love; that's freely given and unpredictable, it makes people loyal, but it doesn't make them slaves. No, they want pain and fear. Those are reliable. Once they've made one of their slaves feel that—and then do their bidding—the slave is really theirs.

From that standpoint, better still if the slave hates them. Hatred breeds understanding, and a good slave understands his Master.

I had the fresh body of an innocent child beside me as all the evidence I needed that this other version of me had come to understand them much too well.

"So you lived in a house where they were being forced to turn into robots," I said, "probably growing to hate you more and more, while they were being forced to act like they loved you, probably forced to do things you knew they wouldn't naturally do to 'prove' they loved you . . . "

He did sob, then, but he also extended his right arm just a little and braced the wrist with his left hand, as if he might start firing then. There was still no chance for a move. My buttocks were getting numb from the alley, and the smell of that poor kid's blood—and there's an amazing amount of blood in even the smallest human body—was somehow getting stronger with time, so that with every word he spoke I was weighing those self-justifications against the consequences here beside me.

"At first it mattered a lot. I kept trying to find ways around it, ways to tell my family that it was me, that I was a prisoner as much as they were. That didn't work at all; the Masters always intervened to make them agree that they accepted it and believed it, so that I couldn't tell whether I was getting through to them, couldn't even tell how they really felt because all of them, always, were stiff with anger and fear at being made to say things. It isn't just a matter of torturing them so much that they deny their own real feelings—it's more than that. Torture people enough, force them to play a part for long enough, and they *have* no real feelings.

"And it was then that they came to me for the rest of the deal." He groaned, then, and if I had not been thinking very hard about the fact that he had made choices all along—he could have decided to defy them, he could have decided to die, no matter what condition he had been in, all he needed was one instant's courage, and they'd no longer have been able to get at him—I might have felt my heart wrung by that groan. Or perhaps I might if I hadn't been sitting there in cold mud waiting for him to blast a series of holes in my body. Or if I hadn't been sitting there smelling and almost touching the corpse of his victim. It was a very convincing groan . . . but nothing could have been convincing in the circumstances.

To this day I wonder if he realized that. Maybe the groan wasn't for me, but only to convince him.

"So they made you one of their agents."

"It was that or see everyone tortured to death. And then . . . well, there are things they make you do in training camp. Things that some men and women just won't do. Things that sort of . . . strip you down. Get you to your core. Get you to where you understand what you're really made of."

At that moment I began to hope that he *would* pull the trigger.

No such luck; he continued. "I refused things, at first, and they had no concern at all, they knew I would refuse, they expected me to refuse so that they could show me what would happen if I did.

"And I started to change, to *really* change. Or rather I started to become myself. I found things out."

There are times when you can't stop even your stupidest impulses; I asked, "What things?"

"Oh, the same things you found out, Mark, working for the other side. That you're good with weapons and with your bare hands. That you like to kill human beings. That you enjoy causing pain. That when you push deep enough down into the core of either of us, all you find is hate."

I fought down the urge to scream and leap at him, kept myself in place, but I don't quite know how I did that. It seemed important, so I managed it, is all I can say even now.

I drew a long deep breath and made my voice stay flat and level. "You're wrong," I said. "You're absolutely wrong. Think about yourself. You just wanted love from your family—"

"But that's not at all the same thing as loving your family," he said, and there was a nasty, gloating *smile* in his voice that made me—

Hate him. Want to kill him. *Listen* to him.

I began to be afraid that there were things worse than dying.

"You see," he went on, "to love is to be vulnerable, to let them hurt you again. And you and I, we know, we've been hurt enough. We have all the pain we need from that bomb going off. We don't need any more of that. And think about how good it is to see a human head blow apart. Think about having—what do you call us, the 'Closers'? It's a silly term, Mark, they didn't 'close' anything off for me, they opened doors in myself I'd never have known were there. I might be injured or feel pain and sooner or later I will die, but I'm no longer vulnerable. That's the discovery their worldpaths made. The greatest gift of all is not love, but hate. Think about yourself for the last few years. You've killed and killed, fought and run and fought again, lived on adrenaline and strength. Have you really felt alive anytime you didn't have your finger on a trigger? Don't you find you'd rather see a man's head blow apart than hold a naked woman?"

I sat and listened, and I tried hard to think. And strangely enough what I thought of was not my lost wife, brother, and mother, not of Carrie and Dad never seeing me (or me them) again, not of wondering what would happen to Porter, but of something Chrys had said to me. *"Mark, sometimes you turn my stomach. I don't like them either, and I'm glad to do them harm, but spare me your bloodthirstiness, please . . . I don't see any reason to rejoice in pain and suffering."* And she had said that in the middle of a fight . . .

It had made me angry that Chrysamen, who I liked so much, who I wanted to understand me, had said that. I'd been really annoyed to feel so—

So *ashamed*. Because she had been right. And because I had known it and been unable to admit it.

And just now it seemed so important to be able to say that to her, to say that she was right, I was wrong, and that I would try to do better, not for her or because she'd like it, but just because she had seen what I should be, instead of what I was, and that I didn't want her to understand me as I was nearly as much as I wanted her to call that good part of me out into the open.

And now chances were I wouldn't get a chance . . .

He was still talking, too. "There's a sense in which I'll never get you to understand. What it's like to hold the little pain control that can send Marie into agony in your hand, and tell her exactly what she's going to do for you; what it's like to have her do it, see that look in her eyes like a beaten dog, have her obey perfectly and then give her a jolt anyway . . . and see her accept it without resentment or surprise, because she's learned that that's all she's for—"

My hand was about to leap for my holster when a pistol roared in the alley, and I heard the other Strang cry out in pain and surprise.

My hand finally leaped to my shoulder holster, but the light was dim, he'd been careful to sit in a shadow, and that first pistol flash had all but blinded me—I fired at the sound the other Strang was making as he scrabbled through the alley, but I heard the shot scream off something hard and fly harmlessly away. The muzzle flash revealed one of his legs pulling away into the shadows, and I fired again, but it did nothing, and he got clean away.

"Are you all right, Mr. Strang, and just which Mr. Strang am I addressing?" a voice asked. It was a young male, with the upper-class London accent, and it had the kind of pleasant sound to it that you get by a lot of training in public speaking.

"You've got the one that was being held at gunpoint," I said, "and I'm about as well as can be expected. The other one got clean away, I think—or if he's around, he's lying low, and since I haven't moved and he hasn't fired, I would guess he ran for it. Probably because he doesn't know how many of you there are."

"Well, then I'll chance a light," the voice said. A lantern unshuttered just twenty feet away, and I stood up and moved toward it—not quite fast enough to avoid seeing the little dismembered and mutilated body beside me. My heart sank like a rock, and I thought again I might throw up; my counterpart had done that as casually as I might have cleaned my .45 or prepared a cover story.

There are people that there is no shame in hating; hate might not be all there was at the core of me, I hoped it wasn't after seeing him and what it had made of him . . . but I didn't have much feeling for him except hate.

"I think I actually hit his pistol," the man who had rescued me said. "His shooting hand may be a bit sore. I was aiming for the hand, but . . ." He shrugged.

"Even at the distance, hitting the pistol was a damned fine shot," I said, meaning it. The brace of pistols I saw across the man's chest were simple dueling pistols, better than anything that had been around in the 1775 of my timeline, but not at all as accurate as even a Civil War revolver would have been. It was also a very lucky shot, and luckier for me than for him.

The man was quite young, about twenty-five or so, and remarkably handsome. His hair was thick and dark, his eyebrows heavy and arched, eyes wide with intelligence, and he had the kind of jaw and chin that Hollywood never finds enough of. "Well," I said. "You know my name—"

"But you don't know mine," he finished, and stuck out his hand. "Sheridan, Richard Sheridan. Sometime agent for Mr. Priestley, my literary career not yet being thoroughly under way, and my political career thus far a matter of humor."

I nodded. "And did you hear much of what we were talking about?"

"All of it. I had followed you in here because, before your counterpart pulled that gun on you in the Chapter House, I had in fact just determined that you were the Strang that I had been sent to find, the one that Colonel Washington had asked us to look for and to assist. Unfortunately it was not until he began to extend his arm to shoot you that I had a clear shot; that gun glinted distinctly in the starlight, and then I could do something. Till then I could only wait. I trust you won't hold the intrusion on your privacy against me—or the fact that I was fascinated."

"Considering how matters turned out," I said, "I have no complaints."

"Well, then, at least one mystery has been resolved, as far as I am concerned. I'd been wondering for quite a long time, sir, about certain aspects of our work, and I do believe I've heard them answered tonight. So there are a multiplicity of these 'world-paths' that he refers to, and in each of them history is different—"

"We call them 'timelines,' but you've got the idea," I said.

"And plainly there is war across them, as comes naturally to man," Sheridan added.

"Yep. Or at least there's war. I don't know that I want to think of it as 'natural.'"

"As you wish, sir. And apparently there is one faction that wishes to see all men their slaves, and another that opposes them? And you work for the liberating faction? Am I right in that?"

"You've got it."

"Well, then, sir, I am very pleased to make your acquaintance. Most especially because you have just unraveled a mystery regarding the King and his strange behavior."

"Glad to hear it," I said. "Can we get out of here?"

"Of course, sir." He held the lantern higher, which was a mistake, because it meant that behind me, he saw what my double had done to that poor kid prostitute. Sheridan's eyes bulged, his jaw went slack, and I just had time to take a step back before he threw up all over the place.

I didn't blame him at all . . . but I was also very careful not to look back.

"I thought you'd heard everything," I said.

"I knew it was back there, but knowing and seeing are two different things," Sheridan said, sighing, and then, drawing a large handkerchief, he wiped his tongue. "There's blood on you, a great lot of it. Let's go to my house and get ourselves a change of clothes, a good scrub, and some coffee and brandy. There's a lot to tell you about, and I would rather not discuss it in this setting."

We stayed in the shadows while Sheridan flagged down a cab. I had been trying to think of who he was for a while, and then I remembered the theatre reviews in the paper. I asked him, as the cab pulled up, "I do presume that you are the author of *The Rivals*?"

He was delighted and clapped a hand on my shoulder, then grunted and pulled out a rag to wipe the nasty smears from his hand. "Yes, I am. So the thing has had some success in your timeline as well?"

"Or something by someone like you, with the same title," I said, carefully. "That's one of the confusions of this kind of travel; you don't actually meet the same people that were there in your own history, you meet the people they would have been in the history you are visiting."

"Perfectly clear," he agreed, grinning. "Remind me to avoid discussing such murky matters and stick to clear subjects like theology and political intrigue."

The cab was fairly nice inside, and I felt a little guilty about spotting up the guy's upholstery, but clearly this wasn't the time to argue about it. The little space inside would have seated about one and a half modern people on each side, so the ridge between the seat cushions dug into one side of my bottom a little uncomfortably, but it was so pleasant to be in a seat outside the weather that I wasn't complaining much.

The cab ran on a little Sterling-cycle engine that was hooked to something that looked a lot like the derailleur rig on a ten-speed bicycle. The Sterling engines were one of Rey Luc's more clever introductions; they're known by a lot of names in a lot of different timelines, and in fact here they were called "Dr. Luke's Patent Engines." It's a simple gadget and perhaps the real miracle is that, like the hang glider, telescope, horse collar, or paddle wheel, they weren't found back at the dawn of civilization in every single timeline.

It's about the most efficient kind of small engine you can make without precision machining. Any piston engine works by heating some fluid—a liquid or gas—so that it expands in the cylinder, pushing the piston out; in gas and diesel engines the heating is done by burning the fuel inside the cylinder, which is why they are called "internal combustion" engines. In those engines you get rid of the hot gas by venting it to the outside, which is why there are a lot of days when you can't see very far in Los Angeles.

In steam engines, of course, you have a boiler to make hot steam, the heat gets supplied by some kind of fire somewhere, and the steam either gets vented, or else you cool the cylinder somehow and get some extra energy by having the steam contract and suck the piston back down—thus providing a power stroke in both directions.

The Sterling engine goes the condensation engine one better. One way or another, it brings the cylinder alternately into contact with the heat source and with something to cool it. You get power on both strokes. Usually you don't even bother with putting water in there—air will work just fine as the working fluid.

In this century, Ben Franklin's student—the Joseph Priestley I was supposed to meet—had invented the electrical process for making aluminum. The stuff still wasn't cheap . . . but it so happens that aluminum is about the best stuff in the world for Sterling engines. It's lightweight, it holds pressure at the right temperatures, and it conducts heat rapidly, which is important since the faster you can heat and cool the cylinder, the more power you can get out of the same size engine. Thus chances were pretty good that by the time this timeline had automobiles and airplanes, they'd be running on Sterling engines.

Besides, they're kind of fun to watch. The easiest way of all to make them work is to have the cylinders spin around a stationary crankshaft, so that the motion of the engine itself brings the cylinders close to the heat and then moves them away from it. It doesn't turn out a lot of rpm's, but there's a lot of force in every stroke, so it has to be geared *up* to the speed you want to run at, not *down* like our automobile engines.

Thus Sheridan and I got in on one side of the cab, and the driver up top got Sheridan's address and threw a fresh scuttle of coal onto the fire on the roof of the cab. The whirling cylinders were attached to a big ring, which in turn was on an axle that drove a little wheel that stuck out to the side away from the door—and that little wheel turned a belt that turned a wheel almost as big as the cab itself. It looked like a cartoon of a mad inventor's dream.

It also had a suspension that would be thought a little crude for a toy wheelbarrow, and the London streets jounced and slammed us as we went, but I had to give it credit—we zoomed along at almost 20 mph, and at the end of the ride, at Sheridan's house near the Drury Lane Theater, we were certainly less tired than we'd have been walking the same distance.

Sheridan's house had such modern conveniences as flush toilets and a shower that didn't require human pumping; I decided once more that Rey Luc had been one hell of a guy.

After we were clean and dressed again, the doorbell began to ring; pretty soon some of the city's more prominent radical Whigs were sitting around Sheridan's fire, many of them looking a bit morose. Since it had long since been decided that this would be a "conscious" timeline—that is, many people right from the first would be aware of the war across the timelines and of their place in it—I didn't have much trouble with spreading the knowledge around farther. Sheridan, for reasons I couldn't fathom, had me tell most of the story of my adventures here, as if he really wanted to make sure that everyone knew everything.

There was a long pause, and then Priestley said, "In fact, Dr. Franklin has told me about matters of the kind several times. I'm quite sure Mr. Strang is telling the truth. And you are absolutely right, Sheridan, you've put your finger on just what this implies. We have our puzzle solved, but now we must decide what needs to be done."

"Your puzzle?" I asked. "Perhaps it's your turn to fill me in."

"Indeed it is, Mr. Strang, and if we've hesitated, it's only been because for these past few weeks we've been unable to speak of this in front of strangers. Perhaps you should tell him, Fleming, since you were the first witness."

The man who spoke was dressed differently from the others, and though his accent was not Cockney, I knew at once he was from a lower class than the other men. It took me only another instant to realize it was a very slight Welsh brogue, one he had been at pains to suppress. "Well, sir, it's really a pretty simple story. I was working at the new Queen's House—Buckingham House, it was, the place His Majesty moved his family to after his coronation—and it was a simple job, as I'm a pinner by trade and all that had to be done was to fix up a few joints to get a wainscoting to hang straight upon its wall. And that was when I saw the King go stamping through and shouting back and forth with his lords—shouting like a madman, I might add, sir—and he kept talking about one room, some upper closet in the St. James Palace, the old royal residence where good old King Fred lived and his fathers before him. Now, it happened I knew that wing as I'd worked there before, and there was some furniture work to be done there just a bit later that week. So naturally I kept my eyes open while I was there . . . and what I saw there, just walking about a bit during dinner and nobody watching—was the King again, the King in a small room, sitting up in a stiff chair, and his eyes wild and glaring—not like the King I knew at all . . . his skin all blotchy and not healthy-looking at all . . . and yet, sir, I knew he was downstairs at the time, receiving an ambassador."

"It makes sense, then," said Priestley, shaking his head. "Strang has supplied our missing piece."

"*What* missing piece?" I asked, feeling stupid.

"Well, if there are these timelines or worldpaths or whatever, and if that can result in your having a double . . . why not our King? And my guess would be that the one Caleb Fleming saw up in the tower in St. James is probably the one we used to have, the one who had been so splendid in the first years of his reign and then deteriorated into the vain and unpleasant creature that we now deal with. I think your enemies, your Closers, have switched kings on us."

13

The question of what to do about that took almost a day of discussion to settle, and unfortunately this was a century that truly enjoyed discussion, so there was very little hurrying them along. The first question, and the one that between Sheridan's imagination and Priestley's scientific precision took the longest, was the question of why the original George III was still alive. Fleming, with his common sense, eventually came up with a simple enough explanation—it would have been all but impossible to smuggle anything remotely resembling the corpse of King George III out of the Court of St. James at any time of day or night. That meant not only that they couldn't kill him, but in all probability they couldn't let him die, either; his body was bound to be detected before they could cover it up, and "once it is known that there is a double for a king," Sheridan said, "depend upon it, there will always be rumors that it is not the real King that sits on the throne. And this King they have brought us has made himself exceedingly unpopular, sir, with every class of society. Let the word get out, and the people will rise up to put the rightful King back on the throne."

"Then couldn't you just put rumors out and let matters take their course?"

Tom Hollis, who was an alderman, shook his head. "Nothing is certain, and both sides know that. Right now it's better for them to take the chance that he won't be found, or that their replacement King will come to look different enough from the original with time. But if there were serious doubts out there, while it might result in their getting caught, it also might make them decide to gamble—and even if they do get caught, if the rightful George III is dead, well, we don't win either."

It was a standoff, obviously.

Just as clearly, there had to be very heavy Closer penetration of the Court and quite possibly of Parliament as well.

"Our best bet," Sheridan said, "is to get the King out of there, into the hands of the Royal Navy, and thence to America. From there he can rally support and bring down the false regime. I'd suggest Ireland, but the Irish hate us; the French would be happy to lock up the King forever . . . and the false King undoubtedly has already extended his influence back into his ancestral domain of Hanover. Indeed that explains why, after so 'British' a start, the monarchy has become so suddenly 'German' again. No, it's America, the Navy, and then the Army that can save the King and kingdom."

"Agreed," Hollis said. "Once he's aboard ship somewhere we will be in far better stead, but how to get him to a ship?"

Priestley had been staring off into space, and now he smiled. "And the problem would seem worse than that, would it not, gentlemen? London is a port on a river, and the larger warships cannot get past London Bridge. We would not only have to free the King from St. James—a very heavily guarded place indeed—but we would also have to get him down to the river, and then downstream to a large enough warship to get him to America, with a real possibility of being killed or captured the whole way, and with the whole city in an uproar after shooting starts at St. James." His smile got bigger and wider, and he stared farther off into space; he looked like a grinning idiot.

"Dr. Priestley, if I didn't know by your manner that you had some idea in mind for resolving the whole matter, I'd punch you in the eye," Caleb Fleming said, firmly.

"And we'd hold you down so he could do it without interference," Sheridan added. "What in the sweet name of god do you have in mind?"

"Well," Priestley said, "how many shots are left in that remarkable gun of yours, Strang?" Sheridan and I had retrieved my bag from the checkroom at the coffeehouse and found that it was intact; one test shot had brought down a seagull three miles away, convincing everyone that it would do what I said it would.

"If I'm reading the Closer hieroglyphs right—and maybe I am and maybe I'm not—I'd figure it at 331," I said. "That's enough to kill every guard around St. James and blow the doors down, if you just want to go in by brute force."

"And its range?"

"Around six, seven miles, about the same as the SHAKK I'm used to," I said. "I wish I knew exactly."

"No problem at all. I was merely wondering if you could hit Buckingham House from St. James Palace."

"Ah . . ." I thought for a moment and then recalled from trips to London that, at least in my timeline, St. James and Buckingham Palace were not at all far apart. And this would be much easier, because the Buckingham house wasn't nearly so built up yet—not yet a "palace," at all. "There should be no problem at all," I said.

"Well, then," Priestley said, "if you'll permit me to be more overoptimistic than my position as a scientist would warrant, strictly, then I do think we can manage the whole matter pretty handily. It will merely be extremely dangerous and difficult."

"What isn't?" I said.

I noticed Sheridan scribbling frantically when I said that, but since Priestley was then launching into explaining his plan—something that turned out to take a couple of hours—it was not until later, at dinner, that I found myself with time enough to say to my host, "Er, by the way, Mr. Sheridan—"

"Do call me Dick," he said. "And may I call you Mark?"

"Er, sure, no problem," I said, "I'm from a very informal time myself, but what I meant to ask—"

"It must be delightful to be from an informal time. More of the goose, sir? I think this is quite the tenderest we've had."

It was very good goose, in fact, so I took some more before trying to press the subject any farther. "Now, anyway, Dick—"

"Oh, yes, the informality definitely makes a difference. I feel much more closely the sentiments of true friendship with you, sir."

It didn't surprise me to remember that in my timeline this guy had been a member of Parliament, and a prominent public speaker, for more than thirty years . . . or that he'd had a relatively successful business career as well.

"Now, Dick," I said, "one way in which we are *extremely* informal is that we quite often use an expression that I'm sure you'll understand." I helped myself to a bit more mustard and spread it on a terrific piece of steak, figuring that if I was going to offend my host, I might as well do it while fully appreciating his food.

"And that expression would be?" he asked, looking mildly amused.

"The expression would be 'cut the crap,'" I said, "which means—"

"Oh, I know what it means, it's current in my stables," Sheridan said. "I suppose, Mark, you intend to ask me just why I have been taking notes on what you've been saying. And you don't think it's because I'm a spy, because others with a like chance to see me have plainly seen me doing it and not asked me."

"Uh, yep, that was the question." I smiled as nicely as I could manage; I really didn't want to offend him, but I really did want to know just what the hell he was up to.

He snorted and shook his head. "Well, you know, this house and a good part of what else I own is all a matter of *The Rivals* having succeeded. Now, it so happens that I've another comedy I shall be presenting soon . . . a splendid little thing called *The School for Scandal*, which is even more a work of genius than the previous—"

I nodded. "In my timeline it was thought to be so." And then, smiling broadly, I added, "And your modesty is very becoming."

"Modesty, sir, is for men who cannot assess themselves accurately. Or perhaps for those who assess themselves too accurately. In any case, it has no place in the temperament of the artist, who needs to see clearly. At any rate, it is good to know that my *School* will, as it were, bring in some handsome tuition. But that can only be the start, you see . . . there's also the matter of becoming wealthy enough to buy myself election to the Commons in an appropriate district. That is going to take money, for all that it will make a great deal once I am in."

It occurred to me that in my own century when artists lived on grants and Congressmen on graft, I'd never seen anyone combine the operation, but there was no logical reason not to. I nodded approvingly, figuring it was the best way to get him to tell me the rest.

The gaslights flickered, and his smile deepened into a smirk; I had a vision of looking at—for lack of a better expression—a handsome devil.

"Well, then, has it not occurred to you that your life is the stuff of which melodrama might be made? And that once victory is won we are going to be public with what has happened, no doubt you recall that since you explained it to us? Well, sir, I do believe that with the right actor to play the role of yourself—and with a Bibiena or two, which I think I can command the price of, to paint the scenes of the time you come from and the wonders of twenty-ninth-century Athens—that you will do very nicely. I should be happy to cut you in for a share of the profits except that the thought did occur to me . . . "

"That I'm on duty, and, besides, you'd have no way of getting them to me," I said. "Oh, well, it's an entertaining thought, I guess. And if I do happen to make it back here, I'm expecting to be shown the town," I added.

"Nothing would give me greater pleasure. Well, we'd best get on to coffee and the trifle; they will be here soon enough."

And that was the nearest thing to business we discussed during that last dinner. There really was nothing else to talk about anyway. Priestley's plan would work or it wouldn't, and the preparations were already made and things set in motion. We might as well enjoy the pleasures of a sweet dessert over coffee and a good, comfortable stretch by the fire before we started off on what might be our last night alive.

So we had our coffee and dessert, and we talked about comedy and Molière, and about Hogarth and Rowlandson, and why some centuries have better cartoons than others, and if it wasn't what I had come to this time to do, it was certainly the kind of thing that the century delighted in, and it was what I needed to do.

We had just let it get comfortably quiet, and I was letting myself daydream a little about Chrysamen and the letter I would write to her when I got back, when the delicate little clock on the mantel chimed quarter of eight with its brass bells. The two of us stood and picked up our small kit bags—very small considering how much traveling we had ahead of us—and started for the door. At that moment the whistle on Priestley's steam-engine coach sounded outside the door.

"'Harper calls, 'tis time, 'tis time,'" Sheridan said. "And 'When shall we three meet again?'"

I followed along after him, muttering, "'I coulda been a contender.'"

"I beg your pardon?"

"A line from another sort of play . . . one your timeline hasn't come up with."

"Ah."

Priestley and two others were waiting in that coach; others were to arrive out at St. James by trolley or on foot. We had forty-five minutes to get there, which in the crowded streets of London was not as much as it seemed.

The whole way there, Sheridan kept muttering, "'I coulda been a contender.' Fascinating sort of rhythm it has. 'I coulda been a contender.'"

I had a feeling I had intervened more than I intended in these people's culture. And since in this timeline Marlon Brando would probably never get born, the chances of having him play me seemed pitifully slim.

The coach jounced and thumped its way across Blackfriars Bridge and through Southwark, its carbide-gas headlamps stabbing into the darkness ahead of us. It was an experimental model that Priestley was hand-building for some nobleman—he and Watt had some kind of rivalry going for who could most revolutionize industry, I gathered, and this gadget was part of it. It was probably one of the most recognizable moving objects in London, and we were counting on that fact.

The two men Priestley had brought were strong and burly, and they had something you didn't see much in that century—deep suntans. Chances were they were officers of some regiment. They were being kept in the dark about all of this. If things went wrong, they couldn't turn us in, and if they had an alibi of ignorance, it might save them from the firing squad. So we didn't speak to them.

After a long interval one of them raised a window, leaned out, and asked something of the engine tender. When he came back, he said, "As you had guessed, sir, there are now three coaches following us with their lights out."

"Steam, Luke's Patent, or horse-drawn?" I asked.

"Luke's Patent, all three, sir."

That was a nuisance. Steam carts could have been put out of action with a hole in the boiler, horse-drawn by killing the horses. Now I would need to fire enough shots, and make them go into the right places, to put that very simple and clever steam engine out of action.

We wound deeper into the tangle of streets that

was Southwark; the area was in fact one of the older parts of the city, Shakespeare's theater had stood there, and it had been old then, and so there were plenty of alleys and niches. We wanted somewhere truly narrow. Priestley's coachman had grown up down here.

We hoped his memory was accurate.

Finally, as we wound down a narrow, dark alley that we were assured had an opening on the other end, pursued by all three carts, I opened the bag, got out the Closer weapon, and then opened the window. I climbed carefully through the window, grasping the little ladder that was supposed to let you get to the roof, and climbed up, hoping all the while that the little brazier that heated our Sterling engine wouldn't tip on me.

Crawling past the coachman, I sat down on the tail. The coach bounced horribly in the rutted streets, and I really needed both hands for the weapon, but eventually I got the sight folded and pulled out to a comfortable height, and the rest of it unlimbered so that it rested in my forearm. I was ready to shoot.

Some twiggling at the scope control let me find the setting for infrared, and now I could plainly see the rims of the cylinder assemblies on the three coaches following us, since those rims were heated in the braziers.

Moreover, by a little fine adjustment I discovered that I could see the wheel hubs, for the friction produced just enough heat to illuminate parts of the axle and wheel assemblies to the weapon. That finally gave me a thought.

There had been a lot of stories back at COTA about the fact that the number displayed did not seem to correspond accurately to the number of shots a Closer weapon would still fire. This probably meant that we didn't actually understand how the weapons did what they did. You could use them like a SHAKK for a while; then they would begin to whoop, and you had to throw them away or they would go off like grenades. Their power source was clearly not the little baby nuke that a SHAKK carried—Closers didn't even want to share a timeline with nuclear power, let alone carry around a little direct-power reactor with them—but just what it was was another good question. Possibly an anti-matter device of some kind, but those were at least as radiation-prone as the nukes; was it only fission and fusion the Closers were afraid of? Or maybe somehow they were making atom-sized black holes and drawing power by throwing matter into them; according to that theory, the "whoop whoop whoop" noise was triggered when the Hawking radiation got too intense, indicating that the black hole was about to blow apart. It seemed quite impossible to say, anyway; all we knew was you could shoot for a while, then it would begin to malfunction unpredictably, and then finally it would start whooping and blow up.

Anyway, it wasn't whooping yet, and it had not yet malfunctioned in any other way. I thought for a long instant about just how long and dark and winding this alley was, and then waited until I got a clear view of the last coach pursuing us.

This wasn't exactly *The French Connection*—none

of these buggies could do any better than about twenty-five miles per hour and all of them were bouncing around in the muddy London alley as if they'd been Jeeps racing through Baja. I was going to have to count very heavily on the homing properties of Closer ammunition.

I finally had a long breath of clear view of the last carriage. The rim of the cylinder assembly on top glowed where the brazier heated it. The brazier itself was one bright mass of light in the infrared scope; the occasional glimpses of the bearings were like fireflies.

I sighted on the rim and squeezed off one shot. There was not the slightest recoil against my forearm—even the SHAKK has a tiny kick—and god knew how the ammo was doing what it was doing, but it hit that whirling iron rim and apparently steered right around through it, peeling it off like the skin off an apple.

I saw that in my peripheral vision as I aimed and fired at a wheel bearing; an instant later the coach slumped sideways as its wheel came off, and it plowed into the side of a building. Then I turned my attention to the coach nearest us, from which two pistol shots had just roared in quick succession—the boom you get from a .45 is unmistakable, so I knew my counterpart was in there—and gave it three quick shots, one each for the rim of the cylinder assembly, the bearings on one wheel, and the bearing on the main drive wheel. The coach fell into pieces and slammed another wall.

We were gone before I got a shot at the middle coach.

It was as if I had felt a silent hug from Chrys—they were jammed in the alley, immovable coaches in front and behind, with a very real risk of fire that they would have to fight (not because they were nice guys but to avoid losing their whole party and baggage)—and I had not fired a shot at one of them. So far as I knew, though they might be shaken up, they were all still alive.

It was a strange feeling, though; a few days ago I'd just have shot all the coachmen and enjoyed every moment. I wondered what kind of fighter I would make without a love for the taste of blood . . . and wondered what I had ever seen in the taste of blood.

It was a fine night, and I wasn't needed back inside the coach, so I sat up with the engine tender, a dour and silent Scot who was supposed to be highly reliable but about whom I also knew nothing. After a while we rolled across Westminster Bridge.

In my timeline, that's an impressive experience—everything is lit up, and Westminster itself is a grand sight, especially at night with the light coming from underneath. But in this timeline there were just a few crude arc lights that were used for special occasions, and this wasn't one of the special occasions. We rolled over the dark Thames, the engine chuffing away beside me; it was heavier than a Sterling and a little bigger, but it was whirring along at a much higher rate of speed and as a result the transmission was just that much more effective and modern; the driver was constantly yanking the clutch in and out and trying to find a better top gear. Priestley claimed to have had it all the way up to thirty miles per hour twice, though never while being officially timed.

We rumbled and thudded over the cobblestone pavement of the bridge, and now we were well on our way. We could assume that warnings had been radioed or sent by runner all over the city, and that we were being treated as the main body of the approach. With luck, the body of men moving silently down Swallow Street would attract much less attention; the group that had gathered by St. George's Hospital and was now coming quietly up Piccadilly would likewise gather no close inspection.

We hoped, thanks to the attention we had gained with the shooting we had done and the ruckus in Southwark—tied to such a conspicuous vehicle—to find them ready, waiting, and excited to see us. And since there was no official business tonight, and the King had become so secluded, whatever force there was, hidden or visible, would move to get between us and Buckingham.

They would probably not worry much about St. James Palace, though undoubtedly some would be left on guard there. None of the royal family except the rightful King was there, and after all if he started to escape, there would be time to move forces back into place. It was only a matter of a few hundred yards, and St. James Palace, in those days, was surrounded by open ground. The King could not possibly get away.

Or so we hoped they'd reason. These "assisted" timelines were disorienting—the wrong things were there at the wrong times—and that was what we were counting on. The *Great George*, if things were still on schedule, had already slipped off her mooring post near Bethnal Green, and was cruising through the sky toward us. If she could meet her date, Priestley assured us, the naval officers he had talked with had figured out the mechanics of the rest of the escape.

We were betting that they wouldn't think about the aerial route, that it would still not seem quite logical to them.

St. James's Park was dark as pitch, and though we knew it was popular spot for assignations, if anyone was making love out there they were doing it quietly. We were taking the swing to the south and west of the park, aiming to put ourselves between the Palace and Buckingham. The carbide lights blazed out ahead of us, making the trees throw strange shapes into the darkness, and the moon lit the more distant shrubs, bushes, and hillocks as we went on through the night, but no sound came to us over the relentless noisy pulsing of the engine and the roar of the coal-burner.

As we rounded the corner to turn toward St. James Palace, I stretched out almost prone, with my head next to the driver. The engine tender had picked up a Pennsylvania rifle, and I heard the windows sliding open under me as Priestley, Sheridan, and the nameless officers readied themselves. We had been making plenty of noise and running with lights on; we had shot it out with Closers less than fifteen minutes before. We expected half the Royal Army at any moment.

We turned the corner and it was just as dark and

quiet as it had been before. Through the trees, which did not yet have their leaves, we could see Buckingham House and St. James Palace, and there were a bare few lights burning in each. There was no trace of the armed opposition we were expecting, and even less of the armed irregulars that were supposed to free the real King and get him to the roof for the *Great George* to pick up.

There was nothing but silence and the darkness, the sputter of our lamps, the chugging of our engine, the grinding of our wheels on the pavement. We might as well be driving into a stage set.

Then suddenly there was a single man in front of us, waving his arms frantically and shouting. The steam-carriage slowed and swung wide; I flipped the Closer weapon to infrared and scanned for any possible ambush, then shouted to the driver that there was no one else. We slowed to a stop just beyond the man, and he ran up to the coach window.

"Dr. Priestley! Mr. Sheridan! Mr. Strang! Sirs, it's bad news, the worst, and for the love of Christ put out them lamps if it's not too late already!"

Without waiting for Priestley's barked "Do it!" the driver killed the lights; the engine tender began to stoke the now-idling engine, getting it hot and ready to run fast if we needed to.

"Sir," the man said, still panting, "Sir, listen, we're betrayed, I think. Or some such. They got our main columns, sir, they got us in the street far from here—"

"Who got you—"

"The King's Own Scots Machine Guns, sir, and the King's Riot Cavalry, them new forces, they met us in the street, sir, it's a massacre, there must be hundreds dead, and they knew right where and when to find us. We didn't get near to St. James's, sir, you're here without friends, and you've got to turn and run—"

He coughed violently, and it was only then we saw that his shirt was stained with blood. "Good Christ, man, are you—"

"Dying, I think, Gov'nor. Had to warn you or we'd have—"

The men were hauling him into the carriage; I crouched upright and began to sweep the landscape with the spotting scope set on infrared plus visible light boost.

Below me I could hear the muffled cries of frustration as the man died despite their best efforts; he was hit in the lungs, might have made it if he hadn't run a mile to get to us, or so Sheridan said that the small, pale man, who turned out to be a surgeon, had said.

I swept twice more without seeing anything. If they had found some way of getting at us, they must be invisible. I turned the scope back toward St. James Palace.

There were at least a hundred guards moving swift and silent as shadows out of St. James Palace— men who were moving in a quick, stealthy "buddy rush" that meant they had to be the First Virginian Rangers, one of the deadliest forces in the Royal Army—tough frontier riflemen who had scouted for Braddock in the War for Quebec and later raided far behind the lines in France itself.

I whispered the news down to the men below; we

had no more than half a minute till they got here, and they weren't moving like they were looking for us—clearly we hadn't killed those lights soon enough, or maybe a glow was showing from somewhere on the steam engine. There was no time to get ourselves turned around and in motion the other way; we would have to stand and shoot.

And nobody at COTA had ever told me—maybe nobody had known—how you got a Closer weapon to fire on full auto.

"This looks like business," I whispered to the men below.

14

The carriage squeaked and shook as the door opened. One of the two nameless Royal Army officers, a tall, thin man with a beaky nose and a strange, piercing stare, got out and walked silently toward the oncoming force. He had gone about twenty paces when the first rank of the oncoming Rangers froze; then all of them did. Then he whistled a strange little tune, and one man in the middle stood up and whistled something back.

There was another exchange of whistles. I was beginning to wonder if maybe we were going to hold choir practice here or something when our man, and theirs, ran forward and embraced each other. Silently, the Rangers stood up; just as silently, our little party got out of Dr. Priestley's steam coach and walked over to join them.

"I suppose this destroys my pretense that people don't know who I am," said the officer who had ridden out with us.

"If I admit I don't, will you explain what's going on?" I asked.

The Ranger officer laughed. "We damned near attacked and killed our commanding officer. This is Colonel Dan Morgan, and we were wondering where the hell he was when we got orders earlier tonight."

It rang a bell, again . . . Dan Morgan. In my timeline, he and Benedict Arnold (back before Arnold had changed sides) had nearly taken Quebec for the Americans.

It didn't take long to explain the situation, oddly enough; the Rangers would go wherever Morgan said they should, so he simply said that the guards inside St. James Palace were holding the real George prisoner, that the George in Buckingham was a pretender and an agent of a foreign power, and suddenly we were about to make the attack with the best infantry we could possibly have had.

I got myself positioned near the front. God knows I'm no soldier—I've never served a day in any uniform other than a security guard's, and "right face" means about as much to me as "keelhaul the poop deck"—but given a nice simple job like "stay out front and shoot anybody who isn't on our side," I could handle it.

We relied on deception for the first step; Morgan and Major Marion walked up to the door and asked the captain, his lieutenant, and his top sergeant inside that wing of the Palace to step out and look at something. Two paces from the door, they abruptly pistol-whipped them and flung the doors open.

The Virginians next to me were on their feet in a silent bound and running for the Palace doors. We were going in through doors in the side of the tower, not through the main part of the Palace, but this did not bring any special relief—there were lots of windows from which we could be fired on.

It didn't take the guards inside long to recover. There was a muzzle flash from a window. A man running beside me stumbled and fell. An instant later I heard the bang.

I popped a shot through the window and heard the wet sock of a hypersonic round going home and turning bone, flesh, and brain into red jam. I scanned other windows, fired at the barrels.

It was a Closer weapon, all right. Our SHAKKs, if you point them at the muzzle of a projectile weapon, will set their projectile to home in on the open muzzle, scour its way up the barrel destroying it from the inside, and finally smash the round backward through the firing chamber to destroy the weapon. The poor bastard who's holding it might lose a finger if he's unlucky, and the way the weapon blows up in his hand isn't going to be any fun, but he's around later to complain about it.

This was a Closer weapon. Aim it at the weapon and it finds the brain of the person who is holding it.

I squeezed off eight shots and eight of them died. That probably meant three more Virginians, or so, got to the door alive.

Once they were inside, there was no stopping them at all. These were men who were used to fighting with knives in the dark, unexpectedly, out in the middle of the forest. Given lights, untrained opponents, and plenty of others to watch their backs, the Virginia Rangers smashed their way through. The guards inside began to throw their weapons down, first in ones and twos, and then by the dozen, until suddenly this tower of the Palace was ours.

I raced up the stairs to where Colonel Morgan and the rest were talking excitedly to the King, who looked thin and ill but functional. "I am so glad to see all of you," he said. "Now we need only get my family and we can—"

There was a loud crash from downstairs, and the thunder of gunshots. I darted out and was halfway down the stairs when I saw that a counterattack was under way; grenadiers were trying to force their way in down a long hallway, and were being held back by Virginians crouched behind overturned tables. I popped two of the grenadiers with rounds from the Closer weapon, and that seemed to make them retreat.

A Ranger strode up to me, his soft leather boots thudding strangely on the hard marble surface below him. "Sir," he said, "we have a major problem. It looks like there are troops coming out of Buckingham, and some of the forces that went out to suppress the mob in the streets are returning as well. We're going to be cut off and surrounded very quickly if we don't get moving soon."

He probably wasn't supposed to salute a civilian advisor like me, but what did I know about that? Besides, he was standing there looking like I should know what to do. "I'll let the Colonel know," I said. "Meanwhile make sure everyone is ready to move."

He nodded, so it must have been the right answer.

I raced back up the stairs—this was four flights of marble steps, past a dozen paintings that really ought to have had some attention and more fine furniture than you can imagine; there's plenty of exercise in my job, but, though you travel, there's no chance to sightsee.

When I burst back into the room, I discovered several people—Morgan, Priestley, and Sheridan among them—looking very carefully at the floor or off into space, clearly trying to appear to be listening to the King and actually trying to come up with some overwhelming argument.

"It's quite impossible," George was saying. "I can't leave my family to the mercy of these scoundrels, and most especially I can't leave my eldest son—and heir!—to their attentions. So we *must* cross over to Buckingham House and rescue them."

"Your Majesty," Morgan responded slowly, "I am sorry to repeat myself, but we just don't have the forces. We'll be lucky to hold the roof till the *Great George* gets here, if it gets here, and after that it's anyone's guess. I would go after the Queen and your children myself if I possibly could, but we can't risk doing it."

"It's no longer a risk," I said. "It's impossible." Quickly I told them about the troops pouring out of Buckingham and the returning forces from the city.

The King turned and looked out the window, across the low middle of the Palace on the opposite side of the inner court, toward the city itself. Flames were showing in places, and in others there was the unmistakable distant twinkle of muzzle flashes. There was fighting raging across the city tonight.

Major Marion said, "I do believe those troops were sent with orders to hang any Whigs they could take, without trial."

"Oh, God," George groaned. "These bastards have my subjects killing each other."

"Exactly, Your Majesty," Sheridan said, very smoothly—maybe too smoothly, I thought. "This is why we need to get up to the roof, so that when the *Great George* comes we can whisk you away to—"

"Nonsense," George said, just as firmly. He was thirty-seven and looked younger, despite his years of captivity; there was something about the set of his pouty lips over his cleft chin that made you think of a stubborn small boy and feel like spanking him, and yet at the same time his clear, slightly outsize eyes seemed to be looking at and weighing everything, constantly searching for the right thing to do. That was just the way he was; once he locked onto an idea, there wasn't much use in trying to talk him out of it. I was to realize later how hard he worked to make sure he locked onto *good* ideas.

Unfortunately, hard work has never guaranteed success. "The Queen must be frantic with worry, especially since she has had cause enough in the past to fear for my sanity, and it's impossible not to reassure her on this point just as quickly as I can. And then, too, has it not occurred to any of you that they have the Prince of Wales? If I die, they will have a perfectly legitimate Regency that they control. In that case all the effort you have made will be wasted."

The other obnoxious feature of the King, I realized, was that every so often he would hit on something he was right about, and those ideas would be a thousand times harder to shake him off of. I had just had the sinking realization that this was shaping up to be one of those operations they pick through at COTA ("Now how could this blunder have been avoided? Given that the situation was already a disaster, what could they have done?"), when three panes of glass blew in at us. The other side had gotten riflemen onto the roof of the wing we were facing.

Everyone took cover, and Morgan dragged George to a fairly safe corner. I took a look outside, saw a few of them, and popped them with the hypersonic weapon. Sickeningly, I realized that "popped" was more than just COTA slang—these guys went to messy pieces like squeezed pimples.

There was firing now from windows on all sides of the tower, but there were muzzle flashes all around as well. We were surrounded and cut off.

I heard Morgan pointing this out to George, who made an impatient, hissing grunt, and said, "Then do the best you can. I'm at your disposal, sir, if anyone has a good idea."

By now I was running from window to window, trying to get riflemen whenever they fired. I had probably killed twenty men, besides the ones killed in the first rush on the building, and every one of them had doubtless been quite certain that he was dying for his country—that is, he would have been if he'd had time before he was torn to bloody rags. In the whole city there were probably not actually twenty people consciously on the wrong side of all this—it was all over a deception and a misunderstanding.

Damn, but my counterpart and his cronies were talented. I was going to have to find them and reward them. . . .

Morgan gave a low whistle, and I crawled to his side. He'd been using one of the new bolt-action Pennsylvanias, with a sniper scope, and I'm not sure he hadn't killed more men than I had with homing ammunition. When a frontier marksman like Morgan pointed a gun, something died.

"Strang, the news just got worse," he said.

I could hear the crashes, booms, and screams far below as the Virginia Rangers held the ground floor—for now.

I peeped out the window and saw. The Palace was beginning to burn.

"They're lighting it," he said, answering my question. "It's probably worth it to them just to get rid of us, get rid of the real King—and with any luck this way there will be plenty of bodies to hide his among—"

"Yeah, and I'll be burned beyond recognition," George said, crawling over to join us. "I don't suppose there's anything useful I can do except not die, just now."

"That will be useful, and it may be quite an accomplishment," I said. I looked up and managed to bag a man with a torch before he could apply it to the house; it made the others hesitate. Dan Morgan's rifle barked, and another of them fell. The rest broke and ran, but after all, there were fires already burning that we could not fight, and the air was fast getting thick with smoke. The way gunfire was echoing in the stairwell suggested that we weren't going to hold the ground floor much longer, or the floor above it—too many doorways, too many windows, this was a palace, not a castle or a fort, and it had not been designed to take a siege.

"We're going to have to retreat to the roof in any case," Morgan said. "I hope the damned Navy turns up with that airship, or we've really lost."

It's hard to describe how well the Virginia Rangers handled the retreat—I was too busy to see much of it, it was so confusing that no one could have managed an accurate picture, and besides, it breaks my heart to talk about it. But they managed to bring along their wounded and even most of their dead, and they made the enemy—who should never have been set up to be the enemy!—pay dearly for every step, room, and hallway.

It took the better part of half an hour, while St. James Palace blazed around us. I guessed that in this timeline Buckingham would become the important one much faster and sooner.

Whenever I could get a glimpse out the window, I did, and I hated what I heard and saw—it looked like much of modern London was going to burn down before this was over. How much of that was obstruction of fire companies by the struggling factions, and how much of it just the fact that the cities of the time were flammable and fire-fighting techniques were crude? I don't suppose we'll ever know.

The lower floors of the tower itself were on fire by the time that those of us around the King were getting him onto the rooftop, and the strong updraft was going to turn the place into an inferno at any moment; as soon as a draft broke through with enough force, the whole tower would become one big chimney, and we'd all be cremated. The only positive thing you could say about it was that the fire was now so hot that the enemy couldn't close with us.

Besides myself, Priestley, Sheridan, the surgeon, and Morgan and Marion, there were eighty-three living men on the roof. Rifle bullets were pocking the surface of the roof as sharpshooters tried to kill our men up there, but a shot across a burning roof is extraordinarily tough from below—the smoke and flames are in the way of your aim and the strong, unpredictable drafts will distort your shots. It was frightening, but most of them were not even managing to hit the roof.

The noise between the shooting, the burning, and the screams of the wounded and the dying, was completely deafening, and that was why we didn't hear the *Great George* at once. It was only when she turned on her spotlights that we actually realized that rescue was at hand.

The *Great George* was a dirigible, but if you start picturing the kind that were around in our timeline from about 1890–1940, you won't imagine anything like it really was.

To begin with, it was right at the edge of what

was feasible for its day; it had an amazing all-aluminum keel with good pine ribs, but it couldn't have fully round ribs the way a full-blown dirigible does, so it was flat on top where spacers were put in to keep the ribs in the right position. So it had a strange "flattop" look, which was exacerbated because for fire safety the six big gas-fired Sterling engines were put on *top* of the ship. So start by imagining a dirigible with the top half cut away and with wooden propellers up on trusses, so that it looked like there were six old-fashioned farm windmills sticking out of the top.

Then, too, there wasn't anything they could use cheaply to make that much hydrogen, and though they had vulcanized rubber and latex, they didn't have enough to cover the gas cells inside the ship—so they compromised by using producer gas, the stuff you get by passing steam through a bed of glowing coal. It's a fifty-fifty mixture of carbon monoxide and hydrogen, both of which are lighter than air, and both of which will burn.

Besides, keeping the gas in the cells warm greatly increased its lifting power, and the ballast of water and coal underneath helped keep it upright and on course. And finally, since to make producer gas you burn the coal in a sealed vessel, there was less risk of sparks—the engines simply burned the same producer gas.

So in addition to all that other stuff, imagine the same object with a big, heavy aluminum vessel, the coal burner, the size and shape of a large apartment building Dumpster, hung under it, and two tanks of water attached to the sides of that.

It was a dreadfully silly-looking gadget, even before they painted a big Union Jack on each side and an image of George III on the prow, and even before they put the little hanging pilothouse with all its Georgian gingerbread and columns up under the prow, with what looked like a steamboat cabin hanging behind that, where the troops and passengers went.

And just to top it off, there were the half dozen machine guns (big crank jobs like the early Gatling guns) and tiny cannon that studded the catwalks around the outer edge.

It looked, in short, like what an airship would have looked like in a science-fiction movie of 1875, if there had been any such thing.

It had to be just about the most beautiful thing I had ever seen, and I was yelling and hurraying like everyone else. It made a big, graceful turn, and as the people inside realized which side it was on, a fusillade of shots screamed out toward it.

Gravity is not on the side of an upward-bound bullet, but it is on the side of a cannonball moving downward. The cannon on the *Great George*'s starboard side boomed and roared, one after another, and the other wings of St. James's, already in flames, flew to pieces, taking the sharpshooters posted there with them. The cannon boomed again, dirt roared up from one clump of bushes, and bodies lay there like broken dolls. We saw dozens of men flee from their spots on the lawn and grounds; the thought of becoming a choice target was simply too much for them.

Give everyone involved credit for guts; the airship had to sit there for several minutes while just about its maximum possible load of people walked across narrow gangplanks to the entrances on the top, sometimes carrying other wounded people. Getting the King across made him good and furious, for he fully intended to be the last off the roof and had to be swayed by arguments that if we lost him, we lost everything. And the last few of us running across the gangplanks had an experience that I'd just as soon have missed—fleeing across something twenty inches across, rocking up and down, bridging the gap between a burning tower and the rocking airship. There were hand lines about ten inches above the gangplank, and believe me, I held on to them.

I was only stupid enough to look down once, and notice how much my gangplank was dancing around above the blazing wreckage below. Then a stray bullet, from somewhere far off (they were too afraid to get close) burst through the gangplank less than four feet in front of me; had I been there, I'd have been injured or killed. I looked at the bobbing airship, her underpowered engines desperately trying to keep her in position, and at the burning tower that was now shedding blazing pieces into the court and open yards below, and at that bullet hole, and thought, *Boy, am I lucky.*

The laughter from that thought carried me right on across the gangplank, scuttling like a monkey climbing a shaking stick, clinging to the ropes for dear life, bent over and coughing.

They just cut the gangplanks free—they had spares and there was no way that anyone was going to untie them at the other end—and we started to rise into the night sky. Producer gas is flammable—it's a fuel, after all, and it's what the engines were burning—but it doesn't blow up quite so easily as hydrogen. Even so, the crew had been climbing around madly, with all the healthy Rangers pressed into service along with them, getting sparks put out before they could burn through the heavy canvas fabric.

The heat from the fire had warmed the ship steadily, making it tough to keep *Great George* level as the gas cells on the side nearer the fire warmed more; the moment they cut loose, the captain dropped a load of ballast, perhaps in the hopes of nailing some of the people running in under to shoot at us, but mostly just to get us up above the flames and the sparks.

It was a strange sensation; there was almost no forward motion, and the starboard side, which had been nearest the flames, distinctly rolled upward as the whole great airship tilted on its side. The propellers were fighting to catch the air, and all of those of us who hadn't yet gone down the tunnels through the inside to the gondola or the pilothouse found that we had to grab whatever was handy and cling to it.

The black smoke was all around us, so at first there was just a sensation of rising through the choking cloud, and only my own grip on a line in front of me and a peg beside me seemed real.

Then we broke from the smoke, and sweet, clean air filled my lungs. I sucked in a few wonderful breaths, coughing and hacking the dirty taste of smoke off my tongue and lips, and then began to breathe more deeply. It was a cool night, and our ship was warmer than usual; we had a lot of lift, and the ship climbed swiftly into the icy, clear night sky.

It felt wonderful to be alive.

The men around me, most of whom had never flown before, were exclaiming and pointing. I sat up on the little platform that surrounded the main hatch, my bottom on the tiny wooden deck so that I was looking through the railing, and got a good look around.

The Moon and stars were far brighter than they ever are above a modern city, but there were odd palls and wisps against them, and as I got to my feet, I saw why. The city had caught fire at four points—besides the blaze at St. James Palace, which would probably burn itself out, there was a fire in Southwark (guiltily I thought about my wrecking of the Sterling-engine coaches, and how proud I had been not to have killed anyone in stopping them; just possibly I would have made hundreds of families homeless before dawn, despite my being so carefully humane. It seemed like intentions ought to count for something, dammit).

The other blazes were on Piccadilly, about halfway from the hospital to the Palace, and on Swallow Street, clear up by Hanover Square. They were clearly getting out of hand already; this was going to be one of those truly bad fires in the city's history, maybe as bad as the one in the 1660s. London would be a different place in this timeline because of what had happened tonight, and that, too, made me sad.

And yet the rightful King was now at large. Moreover, word would be out in the city right now, and the rumors would have the city ready to rise on our behalf when we needed it to.

If it hadn't all burned to cinders, of course.

I stood for a long time and watched the silvery Moon shine off the dark Thames, and the streaks of smoke from the great, leaping fires. Airships are too quiet and fly too low; every so often I could hear the shrieks of those fleeing the fires or the crash of houses coming down. It was going to be very bad, I figured.

The Rangers were slowly filing down the hatchway behind me, a little sheepishly because they weren't the sort of men to get lost in the scenery quite so easily as all that.

The airship came about and began to work its way southward; to fly into any sort of head wind would have been very difficult and slow with her enormous cross section and relatively weak engines, but she did well enough at heading south into Kent to get herself over open water. I looked around once more, at the Moon and stars, at the dark land below unmarked by any farmyard lights as yet, and then again at the distant, burning city, and shivered with the cold of the early-spring night so high up.

When I finally descended through the long tube that wound between the gas cells—the big, spherical balloons that held the lifting gas—to the outside catwalk, and then walked along it to the gondola, I was chilled to the bone, and bothered, too, by the strange new sensations I was feeling about having been in a fight. I wasn't just tired and sore, as usual, but there was also a feeling of sadness at the lives cut off. It was hard for me to shake the feeling that someone might have loved someone I killed, or that someone might have treasured a house I had accidentally set fire to. And the Palace of St. James was absolutely irreplaceable; they'd lost some of the finest art their timeline had, and a library of rare books besides.

I wasn't sure, just then, that Chrysamen's improvements in my character were actually doing me all that much good. There was still a long fight ahead of me, and feeling bad after the last one is not a positive sign. I would have to talk with her about this.

Or about anything else in the world. Hell, as long as it was with Chrysamen, we could talk about raising parakeets, recipes for stewed bananas, or common indoor houseplants, and I'd love it.

As I came into the gondola, the King turned to me and smiled. "Oh, there you are, Mr. Strang. Please join us—we're having a sort of a council of war."

"Sure." I discovered there were a bunch of people around a tiny desk with a map, and an empty chair, but no one was sitting on it—probably because the King wouldn't sit when so many others were standing, and no one else would sit in the presence of the King.

The captain, a quiet, polite man named Richard Pearson, was showing us all how it looked on the map. "Now, we can set down several places in Kent," he began. "There we can unload the Virginia Rangers, at least their wounded, but I would think the whole lot of them if possible—they're extra burden and there isn't much we can do for them aboard, nor anything much they can do for us while we are airborne.

"Now, after that the matter begins to get genuinely complicated. As pure theory we are carrying enough coal and water to get us across the Atlantic, but of course we cannot take that chance with the King in so dangerous a situation—the first crossing of the ocean by dirigible, and not even in the easy direction, with the west-to-east winds, as we had intended. When Admiral Howe first informed me of the situation and our mission, he stressed to me that he would have some ship or other meet me in the Channel, but as yet I've neither the name of a ship nor a position for one; our man on the radio is trying to raise the Admiral in order to get some orders on the subject.

"Once I've deposited His Majesty with whatever vessel will take him across the sea to New York, then I would say . . . I beg your pardon?"

The King had turned to whisper something to a young officer.

"Ah, no, Captain Pearson, excuse *me*, please," King George said. "I was indulging in some calculations of my own. I am told it will be more than an hour before we touch down in Kent?"

"It will indeed."

"Then if I can get pen and paper, I can send off a load of letters with the Rangers—each of the letters containing some little thing that only I might remember about some lord or politician, plus the vital information that it is indeed I who am at large. That should fix that usurper on my throne."

"It should indeed, Your Majesty," Sheridan said, grinning. "And it might well allay some of the worrying of your family—"

"Or delight William, the young scamp," the King muttered, but he was obviously pleased to have everyone think his idea was a good one. We found him a surface to write on, a pen, and paper, and he set to work.

The empty field in Kent where we set down was broad and dark, but Captain Pearson had seen the highway from above, not far from there, so that the Rangers would be able to move quickly once they disembarked. The King had managed, writing as quickly as he could, to come up with fifty-nine messages, plus a short open letter to his subjects, and these were divided among the Rangers, who undertook to see that the mail got through. Priestley elected to go back with the Virginia Rangers, to use his political influence to help make sure people believed the truth.

We had carefully hauled ourselves down on our anchor lines and banked the fires, and that had taken the better part of an hour in its own right; now Sheridan and I stood on the catwalk and waved good-bye to the forces we'd fought beside. There was a long moment of a kind of salute, as the assembled Rangers waved back; then we cast off our lines, the stokers began to pile coal into the gas-making vessel beneath the ship, and we were off into the night sky again, climbing after the now-sinking Moon. It would be daylight soon. It had been a very long night, and though it hadn't gone as planned, it was going pretty well.

When we returned to the pilothouse, Captain Pearson was muttering under his breath and appeared angry. "What on Earth is the matter?" Sheridan asked.

"Oh, it's just the vessel we're to meet," Pearson said, glaring around him. "That man irritates me. He's annoyed me since the day I met him, and so of course it *would* be to his ship—well, his *boat*, really—that I'm transferring our King. I understand Howe's thinking perfectly, and I wouldn't dream of arguing. But how annoying, how absolutely annoying—"

"What's the vessel?" I asked, hoping to divert his attention.

"HMS *Nautilus*, also known as Bushnell's Folly," Pearson said, "the only ship on Earth where men above a certain height are not welcome, which is why the best-qualified man in the fleet is that annoying, scrappy, quarrelsome, bowlegged *little* Welshman—"

At that moment there was a shout from the forward lookout. I ran out onto the catwalk and looked where the lookout was pointing.

All around me people were muttering in wonderment, not knowing what that could be or what it could mean. But though I didn't move, it wasn't because I didn't know what it was. Quite the contrary.

I didn't move because for a few long moments I was frozen in shock. What was coming at us was one of those Closer flying machines like the one that had attacked Chrysamen ja N'wook and me not that long ago (subjective time, anyway) in the Himalayas. It was a little smaller, but it had a cabin that stood on legs that rested on four spinning disks, and it was closing in rapidly.

I pulled the Closer weapon onto my forearm and took several shots at the oncoming craft. Nothing at all happened. I had just time enough to figure out what that might mean before the weapon in my hands began to make whooping noises, and I hurriedly pitched it over the side. It vanished into the night, and the airship lurched upward several feet; Pearson was going to be mad at me for dumping weight without warning.

Down below the calm sea lit up as the device flared into brilliant light; long moments later a deep boom came up to us. But I had no eyes or ears for that—I had grabbed my Colt .45 Model 1911A1 and was standing on the catwalk in the standard police academy firing position. The first time I shot down one of these things, it had been on sheer dumb luck; I hoped the luck of the Strangs was continuing.

Or, considering who was almost certainly at the controls of that gadget, I hoped the luck of *one* of the Strangs was continuing. And I hoped it was the right one.

The craft whirred closer, and I could see that it had just one person aboard. I leveled my pistol, calmed myself, and waited.

15

The thought of Chrys wouldn't leave me alone in that long few seconds, and then I realized why. There was something she always did that I always forgot. My hand leaped into my pocket for a moment, and I turned on the help button. If this wasn't Closers turning up with a major technical advantage, I didn't know what was. And if nothing else, maybe an ATN team could get the King off this airship before we all demonstrated that you can cook anything better with gas.

The enemy ship was very close now, closing to within pistol range, and I realized the craft itself must be unarmed, or we would already be on fire and dying. It veered to the side, and I saw the other Strang—it had to be him, of course—pull down a window and draw his own pistol.

We shot at each other several times on that pass. As soon as I fired I became his chief target. But his aircraft was so little—that cabin was smaller than a Volkswagen Bug and the whole assembly not much larger than a big pickup truck—and bouncing around the sky like a crazed bat, and I don't think I came close to a hit.

If he'd had tracers in that pistol, he'd have finished us for sure—all he needed to do was to set one gas cell on fire, and we were all dead—but he didn't. The bullets were the special hollow point that deforms into a star shape that rips flesh into hamburger—I should know, it was my gun and ammo he was using—but nothing in their path was even giving them enough resistance to make them do that; his shots cut through the thick canvas into the inside, but even when they pierced a gasbag, all they did was make a tiny hole. And at the low pressures this thing operated at, it would take a long time for the gas to leak out.

After his first pass, I had considerable help on the rail; there were a half dozen Royal Marines on board the *Great George*, and they took up posts with rifles, plus of course there were the ship's machine guns. His first try had told me he was desperate, but "given the outfit he's working for, that only means he's afraid of what they'll think of him. He's more afraid of his bosses than he is of us. So there could be thousands of them on the way, but he may need to shoot us down single-handed to avoid death by torture, or worse," I shouted, explaining it to Sheridan. "How far does Pearson say we are from the rendezvous?"

"He's started our descent!" the younger man shouted back. "If we can only—here he comes again—"

This time we were ready, and I think his .45 jammed on him after the second shot—given all the abuse the thing had been through, I was surprised it had held out this long. One of the machine guns managed to rake the disks on which his strange, spidery vehicle sat, and abruptly one of those shattered and stopped.

The effect was dramatic. At once the craft fell sideways toward the stopped and broken disk, and then it began to turn slowly in a circle and rise gently upward. Two of its windows shattered as our ship's Marines found the range, and abruptly it climbed up and away from us.

There were a couple of premature cheers, but I wasn't about to believe he'd given up.

Sure enough, in a moment we heard that high-pitched whir, almost a whistle, that the strange little flying machine made, and it came back, flying not quite level and not quite straight, zigging and zagging as it approached, until abruptly it darted between our propeller towers. We fired at it as it came in and as it went out, the red blazes of our machine guns and rifles lighting up the silvery sides of *Great George*.

But the airship had been designed to bombard things below it or to fight other airships that moved as slowly and clumsily as it did. There had never really been any provision for firing much above our own heads, and in any case we didn't want to hit our own propellers. By coming in high and climbing on his getaway, he avoided most of our fire, though if a stray round had gotten one of those disks as he was coming in, we'd all have died together—I suppose that didn't matter as much to him as it did to us, and that was one advantage he had.

In the wash of his passage, two of the propeller towers twisted and bucked, and the whole ship shuddered, but they righted themselves—for now.

"He's coming in again," Sheridan said, drawing one of his useless little dueling pistols.

He'd figured it out now, and this time his dive was steep and directly over our bow, where only two machine guns could be brought to bear. Moreover, it's very hard anyway to aim accurately at a diving aircraft from underneath it, and it's harder the faster it comes at you, so our forward speed worked to his advantage. In moments the strange disked flyer hurtled down upon us out of the starry sky, grew huge, slammed through barely off our upper deck, and climbed away swiftly, futile rifle shots chasing after, as its great wake of air shook and battered our propeller towers.

With a shuddering scream, we lost the forward port prop, the structure that held it twisting just a little too far, and the big pieces of wood crashed and fell across the upper deck and dug into the surface of the *Great George*. The bulk of it slid over the back, taking one cannon with it as it shattered part of a catwalk, and fell away in a tumbling array of junk that would eventually crash into the flat black sea so far below us.

The big gas-heated Sterling engine at the base of the tower, suddenly relieved of its load, thundered as if to tear itself free of its moorings, but the tenders jumped on it and shut it down; it merely shook the whole ship for a few long, frightening moments, and then coughed and died as they turned off the gas flame that supplied its heat.

Far out there, the black dot that was the other Mark Strang in that weird craft was coming around again. If you didn't know where to look, you could easily lose him until he crossed a star—or until the instant the dark shape flashed across the Moon.

Then he was above us, climbing, getting ready for another pass.

Pearson came out onto the catwalk, briefly, megaphone in hand, and shouted word to all of us—if there were more damage, we'd find it hard to make our rendezvous; as we were going lower, we were losing our maneuvering room.

There was nothing much, really, to do about it except to try to get him again. He came in at a different angle this time, across our bow so that he zoomed across the top of the ship diagonally; the three Marines crouching up there with rifles fired at him as he tore through the space.

He surprised us that time by diving farther *after* he passed the ship; in the long moment it took to depress the guns, he got out of range.

The towers were shuddering and twisting violently, and with a horrible crack, the two propeller towers amidships got close enough to each other to bring their props into contact. There was an instant spray of splinters everywhere and a wobbling, thudding noise as the prop that had lost one blade yanked its tower around like a drunken sailor with a greased walking stick. The other tower recoiled and went over the side; chunks of debris hit the starboard amidships machine-gun crew from behind in a deadly hail of chunks of wood bigger than ball bats; then a piece of the truss, as big as a small car, carried off the catwalk on which they stood. They fell away into the darkness.

Was it only my imagination that I heard one of them screaming on his way down? We were still almost a mile above the sea, though Captain Pearson was bringing her down rapidly.

Then I heard a whoop from a ship's Marine, and turned to see him point; someone had gotten a hit on one of the three remaining disks, for the distant flyer was now shedding bits of it. As we watched, squinting at the distance, the little ship abruptly flipped over, so that it now hung from the disks like a helicopter; it dropped precipitately toward the water, then bounced back upward a little and seemed to stabilize, still hanging upside down from its two whirling disks.

The *Great George* was bucking and rolling like a whale that was slowly deciding it didn't like what was riding on its back. The three remaining engines, overloaded and not arranged symmetrically, could not keep the ship in trim or on a steady course.

Pearson bellowed more bad news through the megaphone. "We've got bad leaks in three gas cells. We'll be sinking toward the water. All crew not fighting or running the ship, get to stations for the lifeboats. And no one is to fire any weapon near any rent or hole in the ship! It could blow us all to kingdom come!"

The dying airship sank slowly toward the water, and all around I could hear the bustle of men readying the life rafts, shutting down the inessential services; there was a rattle of telegraph keys from the radio room in the pilothouse as they called in a last position, hoping to help rescue crews find them in time.

We drew lower; there was nothing for me to do in the evacuation, so I decided I was one of those people who was fighting.

The engines above were backing down to half and lower, trying to find a mix of speeds and positions where they would stabilize us instead of making matters worse, and perhaps just as importantly getting some of the producer gas burned so that it wasn't around to fuel an explosion.

The only thing you could say for that was that we were only yawing slowly back and forth, and we had been in some danger of actually spinning.

The water wasn't more than four hundred feet away when my counterpart came back at us one more time. I'd have to give him some kind of credit for his performance under the circumstances—he was flying upside down, and I don't think he'd had very much training as a pilot—but it was still a sloppy, messy approach, for whatever reason.

Maybe at that moment he just didn't want to live, figuring that the Closers were not particularly sentimental, and if he failed on this mission, whether he lived or died, they'd probably kill the version of his family that the other Strang had sacrificed everything to preserve. At least if he died in action, they were less likely to "make an example" by torturing them or selling them off as one of the lower kinds of slaves.

He lurched through our three remaining propeller

towers, the cabin of the little ship mere feet above our top deck. Sheridan managed to empty his brace of three pistols at the cabin, breaking a window, and I gave him the rest of the magazine in the .45, but veering around as he was, and protected to some extent by the cabin, he seemed unhurt.

Then the little craft plunged wildly out of control—maybe one of us had gotten him after all—and swept through the port aft propeller tower and engine housing, carrying all of it away in one big sweep, slapping off the shack that covered the engine and the wooden tower in one blow and hurling the whole wrecked mass to the water below.

The shock to the body of the airship made it turn and pitch, and a great convulsion ran through it as if it were alive; structurally, after all, it was built like a big spring, and so much weight being removed and so much force applied at the end made the whole thing slam and jump like a coil bedspring hit into the air with a tennis racket. Sheridan and I were thrown to the catwalk, and the walk itself tore partway away from the *Great George*.

Suddenly we were hanging by a twisting, turning, smooth-surfaced rope ladder, a thousand feet off the water, as the *George* rolled back and forth. Sheridan clawed for a grip on the line next to me; I reached for him, got him by the collar, and wrenched him over toward the line.

He got his grip, and we began to climb upward in parallel. The line above swayed alarmingly, dancing and wriggling like a poisoned snake, and it was all you could do to work your way forward a handhold at a time. Below us, rungs were dropping from the catwalk, and then whole sections of plank. Twice, we heard the bellow of a man falling from the airship.

Each time something fell, the ship lurched upward and rolled again. Even though it was losing gas quickly and sinking because of that, an airship is always in a delicate balance—after all, what keeps it in place and holds it up is that the air density at the top is just that much less than the air density at the bottom, and the difference is just enough so that the buoyant craft cannot rise into the thinner air above or sink into the thicker air below. The difference is no more than three or four stories of an ordinary building, or the height of a moderate sledding hill—you never notice a pressure differential across that short distance, but it's real, and it's there.

Change the mass of the dirigible by even a few pounds, and that alters the density; alter the density and the equilibrium height—the altitude at which the dirigible is stable—will change.

So as things fell from the airship, even with gas spilling out as well, the equilibrium height rose rapidly, and the airship, single-mindedly chasing that abstraction, wobbled and lurched its way upward, shaking the ladders, catwalks, decks, and everything else to which most of the crew was frantically clinging. Moreover, when weight falls from one side of the ship, the ship rolls to get the heaviest part downward; thus as it shook off pieces of itself like a dog shaking off water, it spun now this way, now that, on its axis.

Far below, the craft and tower had made a huge splash, big enough to throw water up against us even as the *Great George,* unburdened by the weight, swung up into the sky. I don't recall thinking at that moment that it was the end of my counterpart; I know that I stopped worrying about him and concentrated on staying alive.

It had been a long climb up the twenty-five feet or so of the broken catwalk, and Sheridan and I were almost at the top. It was a good thing we were both fairly young, fairly athletic, and not at all overweight, because this had been tough, but we had only about five feet to go.

Then a line parted, and my side of the catwalk and his were abruptly separated. Sheridan suddenly swung clear out to the side, just as the ship rolled. I was swung, too, but not far and not hard, and I just brushed against the heavy canvas side of the main body.

Sheridan swung out almost to horizontal, still just five feet or so away—I was reaching for his hand, but he was holding on with both—and then the piece of catwalk he was on snapped like a whip, and his hands began to slip just as the airship itself surged sideways. He slammed into the side, right where one of those hard pine ribs pressed out against the outer wall, and his head snapped sideways; he might have only been dazed for an instant, though I hope he was knocked unconscious.

I grabbed at his coat, but I got only the tails. He was limp inside it, and so, with a horrible yank, his arms withdrew through the sleeves the way a kindergartner's do when he takes his coat off over his head, and I was left holding Sheridan's coat, still warm from his body, still strong with the smell of his sweat, by its tail as he fell into the blackness below.

The airship again lurched upward, though as it died it was lurching with less vigor at every loss of mass.

For a long moment I clung to the coat as if he might somehow come back for it; then I let it fall, and it whirled away into the night, sleeves flapping.

This timeline would never have its own *School for Scandal*.

Sick at heart, I climbed the last few feet in seconds, and then scuttled along, always holding on, toward the bow and the pilothouse.

Pearson was still keeping some semblance of order, and the ship was going down fairly gently. His biggest worries were keeping the King from jumping in to help in dangerous situations, and the danger that the coal-gas generator, which was still burning—there was no way to put it out quickly— might ignite a gas cell and cause the whole airship to blow. "And Jones should be here any moment," he said. "He's irritating, but he'll manage. We only have to get to where . . . "

There was another hard slam, but this time we began to sink rapidly; a crew had finally succeeded in cutting the two most-damaged gas cells free, and they had broken through the surface of the dirigible and climbed high into the sky.

The ship was slowly spiraling downward, its keel now almost level, spinning end for end just a little faster than it would have to make perfect circles, because the propellers that were giving us headway and letting us make some use of the rudders were a bit off-center.

"The main gondola is designed to float," Pearson said, "and it has the lifeboats. The sea is dead calm. I think our best chance, almost surely, is to get it set down on the water, to begin to release as much gas as we can, and then to cut first the gas generator and then the bag free. The generator will go right to the bottom, where it can hardly do any harm, and if we get the gas cells deflated far enough, then the weight of the gondola alone should be enough to keep her down; at that point we can cut ourselves free, let the body float up and away from us, and then get into the lifeboats."

I hate feeling useless, so I volunteered for grunt duty on the crew cutting the gas generator free; there were five of us, and the job was simple enough—severing every other line holding it on. It was a little frightening because even though the generator had been sealed for more than an hour, since we got into trouble, it was still radiating tremendous heat at us, and though we were now on a mostly even keel, we were still settling rapidly enough to warp the frame up above us, and thus things bucked and swung unpredictably.

Thus, as we cut it more and more free, there was the constant danger of having it swing and brush against one of us, giving us massive burns immediately. "It's worse than that, sir," one sailor commented to me as we swung in close again. "We'll be closest to it if it goes."

"If it does what?" I asked.

"If it goes, sir. The water in there is enough to

keep the coal burning, don't ask me how, I ain't a scientist, without no more air getting in. That's why it's still hot. And when coal burns in steam it makes gas, sir, and that's what it's doing. But with all the vents shut up in it, the pressure just keeps building and building—and the gas in there is so hot we don't dare vent it, for it would go off as soon as air got to it. So you leave that thing to itself, sir, and it will go off like the biggest bomb you ever seen, sooner or later. I do suppose the old man could have ordered it vented and run the risk of starting a fire from that, but I rather fancy he's gambling all or nothing—if we get this away and into the sea before anything happens, we win it all, and if we don't— well, sir, where we're hanging, there's suddenly going to be a lot of nothing, and I don't imagine even those in the gondola will feel much."

Ever been in a lightning storm when someone points out to you that if you get hit, you'll be the person who *never* knows it happened? It doesn't help much. I kept climbing around, and we kept cutting lines—we were down to just a few, and after that we would have to wait until the generator was actually sinking into the water.

Sailors at the time weren't noted for their long life spans to begin with, and the conversion of the Royal Navy to steam—many decades before it would normally have occurred—had cost even more lives. The survivors were a little too . . . well, let's say philosophic for my tastes. During the ten minutes as the great dirigible finally sank to the calm surface of the Channel south of Kent, my coworkers developed a set of bets about whether or not dunking the hot vessel in cold salt water would distort it enough to make it rupture (and thus blow us all halfway to the Moon, I added mentally), whether when it sank it would blow up near enough to capsize lifeboats, and whether the dirigible would hold together long enough, under the strains of settling onto the waves, for us to get back to the gondola and lifeboats.

I didn't ask anyone how they intended to collect if they won; they were all betting fractions of their life insurance. I did notice that no one seemed to be betting that it would all go just as Pearson said it would, but when I ventured that opinion they all shook their heads.

"The Old Man's as good a skipper as you could wish, and he knows the *Great George* as well as any man, and if she could do what he wanted her to do, she would, but she can't. Not possibly," the sailor beside me explained.

By now the sun was coming up, and we could see that the water was flatter and calmer than one would expect at this time of year, though of course it was no warmer. In the morning light we could see just how much wreckage hung from the sides of the *Great George,* and the many rents in her fabric where things had pulled away or fallen over.

"She's been a fine vessel for all that she flew rather than sailed," one of them said, "and I hope the King—now that we got the right King—will build more like her, for she's a majestic thing."

We were now just seventy feet or so over the water, and the tail—the end we were at—was sinking just a little more quickly than the nose. The airship came back into trim a minute or two later, but now we were down to forty feet . . . and the ship continued to sink toward the water. "You men there, hold off with your axes," Pearson bellowed through the megaphone, "till we know there's enough gas out of her. We don't want you sailing off on what's left."

"Aye aye, sir," the chief of the crew answered. "We don't want that much ourselves."

Pearson nodded and turned back to his preparations. We were barely ten feet off the water, and now he was shouting to the crews aloft, "Bleed her port forward . . . now hold, port forward . . . starboard forward, bleed her . . . now hold—"

We were working our way down a foot or so at a time, the engines stopped, just drifting ever so slowly on the bare breath of breeze.

The gas generator touched first, in a great hiss of steam; the ship bounced up just a little, for the buoyancy of the water took up some of the load, but then settled steadily. Steam bubbled and curled around us in a thick, warm fog. "You're going to have to pay up," one of the sailors beside me said.

"You wait till we cut her free. She might take some time before she blows," one said, and another added, "Hush, listen."

There were creaking and thudding noises, and the moan of metal doing more than it should, as the gas generator settled into the sea. It was the kind of sound you heard in sixth grade when they did the old demonstration of heating up a gasoline can and then capping it and letting it cool, but amplified hundreds of times, and it occurred to me that the metal I was hearing buckle and warp was almost two inches thick.

People on the gondola were whooping and cheering, but the fog from the rising steam was so thick, and the noise from the distorting gas generator so loud, that we couldn't make out why.

Then a little whiff of a breeze carried off enough steam so that we could see what they saw—and we cheered, too.

Floating just two hundred yards from us, the Union Jack waving proudly from her conning tower, was the first submarine in His Majesty's Navy, HMS *Nautilus*, and there on her deck was a small man bellowing back and forth with Pearson about arrangements for taking off, first the King, and then all of us. "Captain Jones," the sailor beside me said. "Him and Pearson don't like each other much, never had, but they're the two best captains His Majesty has, and I hope he sees that."

"Jones?" I asked.

"Captain John Paul Jones, that's him. The man who fought for ten years to get submarine boats built; that one in front of you, the *Nautilus*, has been to America twice, and once ran a hundred miles without coming up, though I understand half the crew was blacked out by the time they did come up. It's said he ain't going to be happy till we have a war that lets him take that gadget out and fight; he's only half a man till then in his own eyes. But that half is more than most folks' wholes, sir."

Whatever Pearson and Jones were yelling at each other about, after a short while Pearson turned to us and said, "The gasbag crew says we're low enough, now, so they'll be coming down off her. Then you cut your lines and *run* here along that catwalk."

"Aye aye, sir!"

A long couple of minutes went by; Jones stood on his tower, arms folded, watching patiently.

Then the crew from aloft emerged from the main tunnel through the body, and one by one climbed onto the gondola. There were eleven of them, and I noted that Pearson counted twice before he gave the order. "Cut the gas generator free!"

We jumped onto the job with all the energy we had, hacking one line after another. The big piece of metal was still not entirely submerged, and baking heat was still coming off the top surface. For that matter it was still groaning and thundering, and the sailor who had a bet down that the contractions would rupture it wasn't giving up yet.

I cut the last line on my side, and the corner of the gas generator under me sank into the water. The chief reached to cut the last line, opposite me, when it parted on its own; the generator floated for an instant, and then the top burst with a boom, spewing flame and glowing metal up into the bag. The chief died instantly as something from the explosion hit him, and he fell onto the top of the sinking generator. The man who had bet it would rupture was thrown into the water; I didn't see what happened to him after that.

The airship bounced above us, yanking the catwalks to which we clung this way and that, but Pearson had figured correctly, and it was not enough to lift the gondola. Instead, it swung and twisted as the gas caught fire. Producer gas doesn't blow up easily at atmospheric pressures, and though the gas pouring out of the cells was blazing, and the airship above us had flames licking through dozens of holes within seconds, it didn't go off with an explosion.

We scrambled along the catwalks as Pearson yelled for us to hurry; I was on the port-side catwalk, which had a hole in it, so I was a bit behind the others as I had to jump that hole.

Then several people were pointing and yelling, and others were shouting for me to hurry. Ten more steps and I would be there—the crews were already cutting through the last of the cables, and the blazing structure, filled with flammable gas, was bouncing on its last couple of cables, eager to float free into the bright morning sky. Eight more steps—why were people pointing and shouting—and I would be—

Something caught my ankle. I fell headlong on the catwalk, my only thought to get those last twenty feet covered before the lines parted, the rescue sub was *right there*, I could see the expressions on everyone's face in the gondola—

And I heard the deep boom of the last lines giving way. I tried to get to my feet so that I could run and dive to safety, but something still held my ankle, something that would not let go, and when I turned to get rid of it—

The face could hardly have been more familiar. It was the other Mark Strang, and he was gripping my ankle tightly with both hands, probably getting ready to twist my foot. He must have jumped from his aircraft and been hanging around in the rigging ever since—it wouldn't have been hard with everyone so busy.

"Oh, there you are," he said sarcastically, when

he saw me see him. "Well, it looks like this is where we're going to settle the whole matter."

I looked over the side of the broken, swaying catwalk; the sea was now at least two hundred feet below, and the dirigible was still rising. Blue-and-yellow flames were playing everywhere on the framework above us.

He applied pressure to the foot, just the way he, and I, had learned in the dojo so many years ago. My ankle stabbed with pain, and before I could control the impulse I had flipped right over the side of the gangplank.

16

My hands caught the side rope, and I twisted my upper body hard, getting some slack in the ankle, letting myself swing out into space over the water, counting on his not being willing to follow me into the void.

I was right as far as it went; the trouble now was that I was hanging from the catwalk rail with hundreds of feet of absolutely nothing between my boots and the deep blue sea. Furthermore, with the fire raging through it, so many lines cut, and the whole thing rolling because most of the weight had been lost from the bottom, the remains of the *Great George* were coming apart and tumbling down to the sea rapidly. If I could live through the next ten minutes somehow, the dirigible would probably be returning to the ocean surface . . . though how fast or in how many pieces was up for grabs.

His hands were groping for my fingers, and I had

no desire to have him start breaking them one by one—and no doubt that he would do that if he could. I grabbed a line running under the catwalk, yanked it hard to make sure that it at least sort of held, and let myself swing out into space.

It was smarter than I knew. Though I looped out alarmingly into space, and there was a sickening lurch in my stomach, I had in fact gotten on the line used for a quick release on the walks, a little trick Pearson had dreamed up for the event of being boarded.

It was a great trick; the far end of the catwalk came free, and suddenly the other Strang, too, was dangling and swinging, in huge, dangerous, whip-like snaps, from the still-rising airship.

Each of us hung perhaps fifteen feet below the body, which actually was no refuge but at least had more things to grab on to in the event that what we were holding on to gave way. I shinnied up that dancing, whipping rope a lot more eagerly than I'd ever done at COTA, or in gym class for that matter, and over to the side of me I could see the other Strang just as eagerly climbing the broken catwalk.

My rope and both catwalks hooked to a long, thin truss on the bottom of the gasbag itself; it was probably a safe bet that whoever got to the other guy's anchor point first would be able to cut the line and send the other guy to his death in the ocean far below.

I was climbing as hard as I could, and so was he; we both knew the stakes. I had a slight edge for just two reasons—I had known that I was going to be swinging out into nothingness and he had been surprised by it, and also a rope tied solidly to a truss is much easier to climb than a slick catwalk that was intended to carry a few sailors, walking very cautiously, on its surface.

I got to the top first and began to swing along the truss like a kid on the monkey bars, being careful not to look down because we had been rising all this time, and I knew perfectly well that every dizzying swoop was now high above the cold sea. In just a few swings I was at the top, where his catwalk hung, ready to cut the line—when I realized that I was not wearing preprepared Crux Op gear. I reached and found neither knife pocket nor knife. Moreover, the pistol in my shoulder holster had been emptied at this clown's aircraft, and I had no more ammunition.

I tried hanging by one hand and pistol-whipping him as he approached, but though I could make him keep his distance, I couldn't deliver any kind of an effective blow with the pistol. And the moorings of the broken catwalk he hung from were unfortunately quite solid on this end.

Just to be annoying, I suppose, he was grabbing at my feet and legs, and trying to slam one of my knees with *his* .45, which told me it was as useless as mine. Meanwhile the vaguely sulfurous stench of burning gas—there was all kinds of contamination in the producer gas here—was getting thicker, and my arms were getting tired.

I went to switch hands, tucking the pistol into my holster before I did so, and just then he swung at me; I lost my .45 (or his, depending on how strict you are about property rights) as it tumbled from the holster. I fought back with my feet and reached behind me to take a big swing back; the combined motion must have been what sent the Colt out of its holster and down to the sea below.

I was gratified that it smacked his shoulder on the way; it wasn't a terribly hard blow, but it was solid, set him back a second, and made him grab on to that catwalk and cling to it with both hands again, at least briefly.

That instant gave me a chance to at least try the butterfly nut on the little gadget the catwalk attached to; it didn't turn easily, but I got it half a turn loose before I had to kick at my counterpart again. The trouble with fighting a man who is below you when you're both swinging free is that there's so much "give" in both of you that very few blows, even hard stomps to the face, land with any force.

On the one hand, if he climbed up higher, he might be able to get hold of my foot or leg and stop me from kicking him; on the other, the higher he climbed, the harder I could kick him.

At that moment, he came up with something—he threw his automatic straight up between my legs. It was a good toss—it hit right where he intended—but there wasn't much force in it, for the same reason neither of us had been able to land much of a blow. Still, it hurt like hell and made me double up and gasp.

Unfortunately for him, throwing the automatic had upset his balance, and it took him a moment to grab back on to the ladder. When he did, he grabbed one rung higher, putting his fingers in range, and I got my foot down on top of his hand and began to grind his fingers with my heel. He didn't have enough grip to let go with the other hand and grab at my foot, so I was able to keep working at his hand for quite a while, feeling the hard little knuckle-bones rolling around under my bootheel.

But again, in that position, there was only so much I could do. The force I could apply was excruciating, I'm sure, and I was wearing off skin, so that it must have stung like crazy, too, but the fact was that I couldn't actually break the hand unless I stomped on it, and to stomp it I would have to pick up my foot—at which point he would get away from me.

Far below, the broken end of the catwalk whipped around; I saw planks breaking loose, saw them flung out end over end into the bright spring-morning sunlight, and watched them tumble down toward the Channel below. We were higher, now, maybe at four hundred feet, but I did not think we would rise farther—

Until I realized we were rolling. The dirigible was rotating on its long axis; the loss of the last half of the catwalk must have just tipped it far enough so that the top was now heavier than the bottom. As I hung there from the truss, the starboard side came around and began to press against me, harder and harder, until it scooped me up, tilted me over, began to lift me. Gingerly, I put my feet on the surface.

Scant feet away, the other Mark Strang was doing the same thing. Behind him, I saw a curtain of blue-and-yellow flame rise, as the rising gas flowed through new vents, and new fires caught. The surface shuddered underneath us with great ripples, as, twice, pockets of gas blew up in low-velocity explosions, and the pressure wave traveled the length of the ship.

"We end it together, eh, as we began it?" he said. "I just want you to know you're a fool before you die."

"All right, I'm a fool," I said. "So now try to kill me."

"You've spent your time fighting for things that won't make you happy. What everyone wants is power, power over himself, power over others, the ability to get what he wants."

"Sure, that's why you're enjoying having Marie be a slave," I said. "It must make you feel great to have her give you a thousand-yard stare and say things she'd never say naturally."

That must have struck the target, at least a little, because he came after me then, in a neat T-stance skip that I recognized because it's exactly the one I use. His foot lashed out, my thigh countered, my foot thrust, he gripped it and turned, I dropped into the Crab and thrust him backward, and he did an inside turn to bring his hands to my throat just as I brought my elbows up to rake his teeth. We spun away from each other, staggering awkwardly on the fabric-covered surface of the aluminum keel, seeing if we could lure the other onto the softer, unsupported fabric nearby.

He was a little more injured, and perhaps with his drinking habits he might be a hair slower. Neither was enough to make the difference. To use my martial arts skills on him was like using them on myself; we knew each other's tricks deeply, viscerally, and we could no more surprise each other than you can tickle yourself.

I was looking, as hard as I could, for rubble I could throw, but until seconds ago this had been the undersurface—nothing loose was available. I backed toward the main interior tunnel entrance; maybe if I could fight him down there—

"You love to pull the trigger," he said, as he pursued me a step at a time. "You kill and it makes you feel good. Or if it doesn't, it's only because somebody has shamed you into feeling differently. But the truth is that you kill, and you like to kill. Ever had a woman and then killed her while you came, Mark? You and I are the same guy, we have the same nervous system, and I'm telling you, it would make you glow—"

"I'm surprised you haven't done that to Mom yet," I said. Maybe if I could get him mad enough, it might make him miscalculate.

Or it might make him faster and stronger than I was. There had to be a difference between us I could use, a difference bigger than the little bits of skin missing from his left knuckles.

"You know," he said casually, "I'll probably do it to all of them sooner or later. You get that way when you begin to have real freedom, you know, and I'm not far from having it." He took a long side step that might have been a lead-in to a flurry of punches if he got a little closer.

I took a countervailing side step to put myself out of reach. It brought me almost to the edge of the hard keel, to where the canvas bulged. I saw more gas flare and burn behind him and noticed that we were beginning, very, very slowly, to sink downward. "Must be wonderful to have that kind of freedom," I said. "Freedom to enslave, torture, and kill people you love. Gosh, why didn't I ever think of it—"

"Because you never had a chance to learn, which is why you're a fool," he said, implacably, and closed in on me again. "You haven't found out that after all the sentimental warm fuzzy stuff, the only reason people will give you all the sweet talk and hugs— and don't misunderstand me, I know we need cuddling as much as we need sex—the only reason people give you affection is to get what they want. Romanticizing it doesn't make it any different. That's what it's for. If they cuddle you and hold you, it's because they're getting something for it, even if it's just to congratulate themselves on how well they're doing it . . . and that's why they do it. It has nothing to do with you." He took a big jump forward, and I skittered back.

This wasn't the way I'd been taught in dojo— you're supposed to always attack even when you're on the defensive—but it occurred to me that just now I had no ideas about what might work, and I wanted whatever I did to work. Meanwhile, maybe he'd make a mistake . . . like talking too much, for instance.

"You know, it's funny," I said, "You obviously want me to understand you. As if it mattered for someone to understand you and say that you're right. And yet I don't care if you understand me. I think I'm plain as day. You don't suppose you want to be understood because you know you've got a problem, do you?"

"What problem do you think I have?" He was still working his way closer; in a few moments I would be near enough to the main tunnel entrance.

Behind him, there was a great boom and a puff of flames, all gold and yellow in the clear morning air. It was almost beautiful, even the flickering and dancing fires above the torn fabric and the sudden shine of the exposed aluminum keel.

Just a few more steps, and I could jump down a hole and see if he would come and get me . . . but for right now I did not dare to turn my back on him.

"Well," I said, temporizing, "you know you and I are not judgmental people. We weren't raised that way. But I'd say we are what we make ourselves, wouldn't you?"

Three steps more, just three steps more . . . the flames behind him were dwindling, probably meaning that one gas cell had blown but not all of them. We were definitely drifting downward fast now . . .

"You see we do agree," he said, and now he had seen the mouth of the main tunnel and was trying to prevent me from reaching it, moving to cover me more. He couldn't quite block it, and I couldn't quite get to it, and neither of us was a gambler by nature. The flames died down behind him, but he never looked; I have no idea what might have been going on behind me, because I never looked either. "We are what we make ourselves," he said, repeating me, "and thus the important thing is to have the freedom to work, is it not?"

"If you say so," I said. "I was just hoping to ask why I chose to make myself a fairly ordinary guy with a peculiar job, and you chose to make yourself a vicious, lying, psychopathic bastard."

His face twitched, but I got no answer from him then. The corner of my eye noticed a rain of fabric pieces and bits of wood off to one side, and before I had time to think, I had taken a hard dive for the entrance to that tunnel. He didn't quite catch me, but that wasn't only because I'd distracted him with an insult.

It was because suddenly the sinking wreckage of the *Great George* began to roll over again, and just as suddenly it lurched back upward into the sky, this time tilting up at a crazy angle.

My gut reactions had realized before I had that the rain of debris was coming from something, and then that the something was very likely that fire had burned through or into one of the propeller towers and engine shacks, allowing the huge, heavy engine, its bunker of coal, the massive propeller, and the whole wooden tower to tear loose from the pine ribs of the ship and fall to the ocean.

With such a heavy weight removed from that side, the burning hulk was able, very briefly, to climb again and to right herself, so she was rolling 180 degrees, tilting up toward where the propeller and engine had ripped off, and slowly climbing.

I hit the ladder going head down, caught myself on my hands just barely, and scrambled along it as it rapidly became, first level, and then vertical, swinging back and forth in that dark, dizzy space with only the light at each end of the tunnel—

And suddenly my head began to pound, and I

was having trouble breathing—a lot of trouble. I gasped for more air, but it only got worse.

One of those annoying parts of the brain that is right too often pointed out to me that I had gone inside the hull, where lots of producer gas had been leaking for quite a while. Producer gas is half hydrogen, which supplies most of the lift if you use it in a balloon, and more than half the power when you burn it.

But the other half of producer gas is carbon monoxide. The stuff is deadly, and I had just climbed down into a thick cloud of it. I felt an overwhelming desire to sleep, even if I fell off the rungs of the ladder, even for just a few minutes—

I tried to climb down, the way I had come. Carbon monoxide is lighter than air, and it rises; there would be more oxygen below, and though my counterpart was probably still down there (I hadn't gotten rid of him by any trick so simple, had I?), he was only dead eventually; the carbon monoxide was going to get me right now. I climbed down farther, and while I climbed I looked around at each landing I came to and fought the urge to just stretch out on one of those landings and go to sleep. Carbon monoxide kills you by tying up your hemoglobin chemically so that it can't deliver oxygen, but there's some oxygen already in the tissues, about thirty seconds' worth of moderate effort or fifteen of all-out, that's what they told us at COTA, and if I hurried I would not black out . . . I would not black out . . . I would not black out . . .

The bottom landing revealed great gaping holes in the sides of the airship, some timbers still smoldering, a couple of gas cells not yet burst, and the twisted wreck of the keel; how this thing was holding together was a mystery. There was air enough, here, so I dragged myself onto the landing and breathed hard and deep for a few minutes to get some of the carbon monoxide out. My stomach rolled, and I leaned over to throw up—

It came down right in the face of the other Mark Strang, who had been climbing up the main tunnel after hanging on god knew how. He screamed with rage—you try having someone vomit on your upturned face if you don't see why—and started to scramble up the ladder.

I whirled, sitting down on the edge of the landing, braced my arms overhead and my back to the ladder, and kicked him in the face with both feet as hard as I could. Still blinded by the mess I had dropped onto his face, and with his hands slipping in it on the rails, he fell a few feet before he could brace himself in the chimney position in the tunnel. He was about ten feet beneath me, rubbing his face, probably still blinded by pain, tears, and vomit, probably still trying to clear his head.

It had reached a point where my decisions—even if they were completely crazy—were absolutely clear. I wanted to get rid of the other Mark Strang much more than I wanted to live myself. After all, this overgrown gasbag could blow up at any time when a cell rocked against a burning timber, or might fall apart in midair, or might land so hard that I could not survive anyway. The chances of getting out of here were very slim, and in those circumstances you do whatever is going to accomplish the most good in the world. And getting this asshole, this so-different mirror face of me, this thing I could have become—indeed, you could say it was a thing I had become, for our pathways had merely parted in time—getting that out of the world, really, definitely, and completely, seemed like the best thing that could happen.

I jumped down the tunnel onto him, landing boots first on his chest and belly, which gave under my shoes like sandbags. It knocked the wind out of him and sent him thumping downward, so that now he hung by his hands, his body mostly out in the empty space below.

I grabbed the ladder and continued to climb down.

With a deafening crash, the *Great George* tore in half, and the other side end—weighted down by the remaining engine and the forward coal reserve—fell away into the sunlight as we climbed still higher; we might well reach two thousand feet before we finally descended for good.

The force of the motion yanked him harder; I saw his fingers slip a bit. Slowly he managed to close his hands around the rungs—

"All I wanted was not to hurt," he said. "All I wanted was the freedom to live the life I wanted."

"Well," I said, "you know the song." I stamped on his fingers and felt them giving under me; this time I wasn't hanging, and I could apply the full force of my body; a few stamps, and he would fall into nothingness. "'Freedom's just another word for nothing left to lose.' You're about to lose, which means you're going to be nothing—so enjoy your freedom."

The hard heels of my boots slammed down on his fingers again and again; blood sprayed the side of the tunnel with the force, and he moaned.

"Understand, at least!" he screamed, just at the end.

The only response I gave him was a series of hard kicks in the face, breaking his teeth and nose into a bloody pudding. His eyes were wide, first with terror, then with some sort of rictus, and finally they saw nothing, just before he let go and fell silently away. I watched the twisting, turning body, like a stuffed animal thrown from a great height, until I lost it in the sea below.

I had understood him just fine. That was why I had stamped so hard on his hands.

He was gone, for what that was worth, and now it was just a question of whether or not this thing would bring me down alive. I wondered if I could vent some gas to descend faster, and if that would really be wise. Right now all that was left was a middle section; the tail had burned off, the nose had fallen away, and now I was in a tube open at both ends. At least gas was unlikely to build up in here.

I had stopped rising; the airship was beginning its descent. This was a relief as far as it went; the way it was drifting, it might well make it to France before it touched down, and in that case I could probably come up with some way to get home. Of course it could also blow up at any moment.

I climbed down to look around some more; the Channel was narrow enough here for me to see both the British and the French coasts, so at least my odds weren't bad if there was no explosion. I was some hundreds of feet up, and descending, but I had no idea how fast, and it looked like I was probably seventeen or eighteen miles from France and a little farther from Britain—the narrowest part of the Channel, the Straits of Dover, was visible north of me.

A little searching around inside turned up some completely useless mallets and a couple of wrenches that fit things I didn't see anywhere; the gas cocks themselves turned with a key, which was hanging beside them, but I could see no special reason to descend faster until I knew something about my current descent.

I was definitely lower now than before, and somewhat closer to France, I thought. Not enough closer to give me any assurance of making it there, however.

Well, if you ignore air resistance, a body falls at sixteen feet per second squared. I had a pretty good digital stopwatch still in my pocket after all the knocking around, and finally a good reason to use it. Very carefully, I started the timer and dropped a mallet straight down the tunnel, watching it till I lost sight of it, the way you lose sight of the coyote in the Road Runner cartoons as he falls from a cliff.

And very much like that same coyote, the mallet eventually sent up some evidence of its impact—a big white splash appeared in the calm water below. It was a good thing it was a nice day.

It had taken just thirteen and a half seconds to fall. That was about 181, squared, and times sixteen feet per second squared gave me around twenty-nine hundred feet.

I timed off ten minutes, dropped the next mallet.

If the dirigible had been fully functional, it would have lurched upward—they are terribly sensitive when they're actually flying—but as this one was drifting downward, not much happened; I could neglect whatever effect losing the weight was having.

Thirteen point three seconds; that meant around 178 seconds squared, or 2850 feet. Round it all off and say I was coming down at fifty feet per ten minutes, which was three hundred feet per hour, and thus I'd be up here for . . . hmm. Probably about nine more hours.

The galley had vanished with the gondola, and there were no bunks inside the dirigible; besides, if another leak developed, I didn't want to asphyxiate while I was falling to my death. So I couldn't eat and didn't want to sleep. Instead, I took a deep breath and climbed up to the remnants of the top deck around the top of the tunnel, then sat down to think.

That other me had been half-right, which is just about the worst possible position philosophically, since it's harder to see your mistakes. I certainly knew I could enjoy suffering, knew I could enjoy destruction. Hell, I had enjoyed destroying *him*.

But I had not gone as far as he had . . .

It was only that I had never quite realized before that I could. I didn't want to . . . but I could.

I found that I didn't hate him, but I couldn't make myself sorry about his death. It seemed to me that maybe he had overlooked another possibility about himself. He and I each had no way of knowing how many times the Closers had kidnapped me and offered me their particular deal with the devil. I was descended from the timeline where it had never happened. He was descended from one where he had gone along with it. In how many had Mark Strang resisted, and died for his resistance?

It made me feel better, but not much. I had seen some potentials I really did not care for or like, and I would have to do something about it.

I reached that resolution as I sat up there on my fragment of dirigible, a body bigger than a couple of houses, and as we settled down, crossing the coast of France and drifting steadily onward. After a while I noticed that I was being followed by a regular parade—a couple of cavalry troops, plus more carriages than you could shake a stick at. *Great George* had not made a call in France during its trial phase; now of course it never would.

I wondered if the King would put up with having one called *Great George II*? He had hated his grandfather . . .

Well, it didn't matter much. As the sun was setting, I found myself descending into a freshly plowed field in northern France, and an amazing number of Frenchmen were coming out to meet me. I just wished I spoke French.

The middle part of *Great George* bumped along over the soft, wet soil, and then settled like a dying animal that had been run to death. I slid down the side, along one of the ribs, rappelling by a line tied off to the ragged upper deck. There were some noisy huzzahs, to which I responded by waving, which invited more of them, and then finally I jumped down into the muddy field.

I surveyed the crowd; they looked friendly and even enthusiastic. "Does anyone here speak English?" I asked, very loudly.

"I do," said a familiar voice, just behind me, "or near enough." Partly it was familiar because it was a voice I'd dreamed of hearing, and partly it was familiar because it had activated the chip behind my ear.

"Chrysamen," I said, just as she stepped forward and slipped her arm through mine.

"Come on," she said, "it's time for me to take you home. Way past time, in fact. But first we've got a parade to make it to in London, and that's just two days away, and in this miserable century and country we'll have to spend most of that time traveling."

17

After the relatively paved roads of England and the Sterling and steam carriages, travel in eighteenth-century France took some getting used to. The stagecoach was miserably uncomfortable—they designed the things for four people (four small French people who had their own built-in suspensions and seat cushions, apparently, since the French stage had neither) but there were six of us in there. Fortunately we were the only English speakers in the coach (though there were two English scholars and a Welsh poet among the nine people riding on the roof), so we had a lot of time to talk and to get caught up on news.

The great thing about working for an agency that uses time travel is that they can take a quick look, see how things are really going, and pick the best time to intervene. Once they knew I was going to win the fight with the other Mark Strang, and that the dirigible wasn't going to blow up, they had literally weeks to prepare a cover for Chrysamen, as a planter's daughter from the West Indies (I thought she looked terrific in the very low-cut styles of the day, a thought which made her look down at the floor in a completely captivating way when I expressed it). Then they dropped her into Paris and had her take the stage out to the little village, only about forty miles from Calais—which, with the roads of the time, amounted to just about a day's travel.

The stagecoach made an ungodly screaming rumble, and a wheel came off twice during the trip. My seat slammed into me constantly, and when I peeked out the window on one occasion I noticed we were running in ruts about two feet deep. April, of course, was a muddy month, so if anything it was worse than usual—though Chrysamen, whose translator chip understood French, assured me that most people were talking about how mild the weather had been and how much nicer mud was than dust.

There's a strange idea out there somewhere that because many of us like "traditional" cooking, the food must have been better in previous centuries, but the sad truth was that April was a lousy time for a meal—most of it would come out of the root cellar, where it had lain all winter, or it was dried or pickled, and in any case the meat tended to be what we'd think of as tough and stringy. I recognized the meal we had at about two in the afternoon, and I assured Chrysamen that we would have to go to my timeline and visit France if she wanted to know what it was supposed to taste like.

At last, after a day of kidney-battering and bun-slamming excitement, we pulled into Calais. By then Chrys had told me most of what had happened after I was out of it, so I was not quite so surprised at the reception we got there.

King George was a serious, hardworking fellow; apparently he was that way in every timeline. He wasn't particularly smart, and he wasn't necessarily the most amusing wit of the day, so he tended to be about as good a king as the advice he got.

Here, where ATN had intervened to try to create an accelerated and better world, the advice he got had been very good indeed, and the kingdom had been in good shape before the Closers moved in. One thing my counterpart had underestimated was just how strongly the difference was felt between the George III that secured himself in St. James, and the George III the Closers had specially created and trained for the job.

"Somewhere out there," Chrysamen said, "they've got a timeline where George III was mainly interested in expanding the slave trade, promoting wars, and in general running the country into the ground. But when they moved that one over here—Allah only knows what they left behind him in that timeline— he was truly in hog heaven. We've captured all kinds of documents, and four other Closer agents alive. It's the best look we've ever gotten at their plans for any-where.

"And what we found out they had in mind was to take the advanced technology we had brought in and turn it against these people. If there had been an American Revolution in this timeline, and that's what they were trying to start, there would have been literally millions of deaths—it would have looked like the Civil War of your timeline—and the development of all sorts of charming things like machine guns, barbed wire, and poison gas, plus bombing cities from aircraft, in the European phase of the war. Britain would have conquered the world and left the world bitter, bruised, and ready for more rebellions. You'd have ended up with a single absolutist British monarchy holding down a world empire by sheer bloody force . . . "

"And that's the point where the Closers would have moved in and taken over the top of the operation for themselves," I said. "Yep, that's what they always do. Well, in light of their known behavior it makes sense."

"We've gotten ten times the documents on this that we've ever had before, Mark. The intelligence people all want to kiss you."

"Hmm. Well, I could take applications, maybe—"

"Or you could abjure quantity for quality, and take me."

"Deal." It was a good deal, too, though I think we slightly annoyed the other passengers. It wasn't a very demonstrative century.

It turned out that because the two Georges had been so different—one so obviously trying to put people at their ease and make them feel appreciated, the other so clearly brutal—that the allegation, especially in the wake of the disastrous fire and the more than a hundred deaths in the protests, had sent the country up like a powder keg. Every single one of the fifty-nine lords and politicians the true King had written to had declared for him, and the Navy had gone over immediately. The invasion and civil war that they had thought they might have to fight had in fact collapsed completely as the Army, in turn, went over; before the real George III had even stepped off the boat in Dover, the false one was under arrest.

"He's got a terrible mess to clean up, but there's a huge reserve of goodwill," Chrys said. "It looks like this timeline is back on track—and in fact they think they're already getting signals when they're looking for its descendant lines, way up in the future. You've probably helped bring billions of people into freedom and prosperity."

We talked of other things as well, and most especially, though it was painful, we talked about just how tough it was going to be if I wanted to change . . . if I didn't want to end up the mirror image of the man I had killed.

I was glad Chrys was there to talk about it with.

I had said Calais wasn't a complete surprise, but it was still pretty impressive. The Royal Navy had dispatched a fast steamer to take us over to London; the next day there was to be a major parade, and then the King was going to begin the process of revealing the existence of ATN, the sources of help they had had . . . and to start the long, fast march toward full membership in our league of civilized and free timelines. They'd be there before my home timeline was ever even found; in a way I envied them that, and in another way I was glad we were spared the crosstime wars as long as we were.

The parade and ceremonies were impressive, but

our work here was done—a new special agent would be coming out to replace Rey Luc, and we were due to return to headquarters.

Captain Malecela himself was there for the debriefing; that, more than anything else, told me that what had been captured was vital.

"It's the first major link," he said, with a deep smile cutting into one corner of his face, yet at the same time with a ferocity in his eyes that I would have found frightening had I been on the other side. "It is just possible that their whole reason for hunting you, Strang, is that they had established that the series of disasters we are preparing for them began from intelligence captured due to your mission. That is one hypothesis, anyway." He sat back and sighed, opening a refrigerator door; Athenian offices are designed to be comfortable places to eat a meal rather than to work, because Athenians think of paperwork and that sort of thing as something you do at home, and the office is where you entertain guests. "If you two would care for beer, we are officially off duty; I've also got a wide range of cold meats and cheeses, and more kinds of bread than I would have imagined existed."

We made sandwiches and poured beer; then I cautiously said, "Captain, you said that that was *one* hypothesis. It sounded very much like it was one you don't believe."

"That's absolutely right," Malecela agreed. "I don't believe it at all, in fact. I think this is the first step, but your close connection with all the time-lines descended from your own that seem to be of so much importance—and that one of the few names we know for sure will be vital coming out of your home time is Porter Brunreich, who of course is your ward . . . well, my guess is that in some way we don't quite understand, you yourself are a point of temporal discontinuity, a place where history itself can change in a big way. If you like, you're a walking crux, Strang.

"We've also noted that you improvise very well, you get missions carried out, and perhaps most importantly—you seem to be *lucky*. That might just be significant in its own right. History is constantly trying to find its own channel and to move in its own way. That's why some timelines are so hard to start, and some are so easy; there is something up ahead, many centuries in the future, something that is beautiful or wonderful or terrible—but it's calling all the timelines to itself, and when it finds someone who will help it go where it wants to, he becomes *lucky*."

"What if it's on the Closers' side?" I asked. "I mean, maybe the future that is calling is calling them, not us."

"If that's the case, we might as well all lie down and die. Or just find somewhere to party until they come and kill us. Does either of you feel like that?"

Chrys and I had to grin.

"Now," Malecela said, "I have one simple issue and one complicated one. Mark Strang, by virtue of the fact that when you are out and working in the field, good things appear to happen for ATN, we are going to make you a Special Crux Operative. It's a new designation. What it means is that we'll be dropping you into much hairier, more dangerous cruxes, with a much wider latitude of action—but also with more resources available. That's the simple issue."

"I'm very honored," I said. "But really all I did was—"

Malecela grinned at me again. "Now, now, in the first place, you don't have to tell me it's an honor. I can only say I envy you the contribution you'll be able to make, and I think it's wonderful for someone at the beginning of a career to be given this. But the fact is that it was a pure engineering decision—we didn't decide that we ought to do this, the scientists looked at it and said you're a good bet. That's why it's such a simple decision—I'm not making it, I'm just informing you of it.

"Now, it happens that there's another and more complex decision. We would like to assign one other Crux Op who will work with you closely, as your personal assistant, on a permanent basis. This would also improve security around Porter Brunreich, of course, but the main purpose is to have an additional observer wherever you are. But despite the fact that we counted your first expedition retroactively, giving you several years in grade . . . well, we realize you don't know many Crux Ops. There are really only two you have ever worked with closely . . . Ariadne Lao—who by the way has said she would happily accept such an assignment, despite being ten years senior to you in the service—and Chrysamen ja N'wook. Now, there are arguments either way; a relatively new agent can more quickly become used to your way of doing things, a more experienced agent may have additional information you will find valuable . . . but I thought there was the possibility, since you may be working together for decades, that there might be some personal preference involved . . . "

"There sure as hell is," I said, and then realized Chrysamen's interpreted voice in my earpiece had said the same thing.

It took us a while to get everything together, but finally the day came when I stepped through the gateway at ATN Crux Operations Central and into the locked bathroom of an airliner bound from Denver to Pittsburgh, trading places with one of our couriers, who had gotten onto the flight. I returned to my seat and had just settled in when Chrys slid into the seat beside me.

She was thoroughly nervous, but I put my hand on her arm and said, "Now, it's the best possible start. The Fourth of July dinner is sacred to Dad and Carrie, and Porter has gotten to be just the same way. And I've missed more of them than anyone else, so now it's always regarded as a treat when I'm there. You're going to pick up a lot of points just for attending."

She squeezed my hand and whispered under her breath, "Just remember, I come from a culture with arranged marriages."

"You've always got the option of just being a working associate," I pointed out, gently. "I don't want you to feel pressured—"

"Bite your tongue. I'm nervous, that's all," she said, and moved closer to me.

Dad's a rotten driver, so Robbie drove to pick us

up at the airport; Carrie and Porter had come along. This was the scary part for me, too, I realized, and wondered why I wasn't nervous. Maybe history was letting me know it was on my side again or something.

"Dad, Carrie, Porter, Robbie, this is Chrys," I said.

They all said "Hello," except for Porter, who said, "Yeah, right. Bring in the most gorgeous woman in the universe and introduce her like she's someone you met bowling. It's good to have you home, Mark—you haven't changed a bit."

Afterword

Once again, this book comes with a deep debt of gratitude—to the inspired loons of the Alternate History discussions in the Science Fiction Round Table of the GEnie electronic network. Special thanks this time are due to:

Kevin O'Donnell, Jr., Jon Bunnell, P. "Calamity" Drye, Robert Brown, William Harris, Steve Stirling, Dana Carson, S. "Lemming" Weinberg, G. Tan, and Al Nofi.

And again as always, mistakes, errors, and anything you caught me at should be attributed entirely to me.

GOLD: The Final Science Fiction Collection
by Isaac Asimov

Isaac Asimov's marvelous later works are finally brought together in a single volume in this collection of science fiction short stories, novellas, and essays, including the 1992 Hugo Award-winning title novella.

FLUX by Stephen Baxter

One of Science Fiction's fastest-rising stars offers a thrilling story about a submicroscopic race of bio-engineered humans who are struggling to understand their origins and their destiny in a world disrupted by an unknown force.

THE TIME SHIPS
by Stephen Baxter

A stunning sequel to H. G. Well's Science Fiction classic, *The Time Machine*. The Time Traveler returns to the future to rescue his Elois friends from the Morlocks, the devolved race of future humans.

SOLIS by A. A. Attanasio

A stunning novel of cryonics in the far future as Charlie Outis discovers that he is a brain without a body in a world he can barely recognize.

INDIA' S STORY
by Kathleen S. Starbuck

A troubled young woman thinks she has forged a new life for herself, until she is sent between dimensions to seek out a new, more powerful teacher. Now India must travel through time and space while unknown forces vie for control of her destiny.

WRATH OF GOD by Robert Gleason

In this apocalyptic vision of a weakened America, only a small group is left to fight the rule of a murderous savage. Until their leader, a Los Alamos renegade, manages to rip a hole in Time and rescue three of the most powerful heroes from history.

SPACE: Above and Beyond by Peter Telep

This sensational novel captures the galactic adventure of the new futuristic TV series *SPACE* on Fox, following a team of young fighter pilots as they forge a fateful battle against alien enemies.

THE DISPOSSESSED
by Ursula K. Le Guin

This Science Fiction classic from bestselling and award-winning author Ursula K. Le Guin now has a stunning new package. A brilliant physicist must give up his family, and possibly his life, as he attempts to tear down the walls of hatred that have isolated his planet of anarchists.

A FISHERMAN OF THE INLAND SEA
by Ursula K. Le Guin

The National Book Award, Hugo, Nebula, and World Fantasy Award-winning author's first new collection in thirteen years—an astonishing assemblage of diversity and power from a major writer and mature artist at the height of her powers.

HarperPrism